PURGATORY ROAD

Bob Reiss

Simon & Schuster
New York London Toronto Sydney Tokyo Singapore

SIMON & SCHUSTER
ROCKEFELLER CENTER
1230 AVENUE OF THE AMERICAS
NEW YORK, NY 10020

COPYRIGHT © 1996 BY BOB REISS
ALL RIGHTS RESERVED,
INCLUDING THE RIGHT OF REPRODUCTION
IN WHOLE OR IN PART IN ANY FORM.

SIMON & SCHUSTER AND COLOPHON ARE REGISTERED TRADEMARKS
OF SIMON & SCHUSTER INC.

DESIGNED BY LEVAVI & LEVAVI

MANUFACTURED IN THE UNITED STATES OF AMERICA

1   3   5   7   9   10   8   6   4   2

LIBRARY OF CONGRESS CATALOGING-IN-PUBLICATION DATA
REISS, BOB.
PURGATORY ROAD/BOB REISS.
P.   CM.
1. SCIENTISTS — ANTARCTICA — FICTION
2. ANTARCTIC REGIONS — FICTION.   I.   TITLE.
PS3568.E517P87   1996
813'.54 — DC20   95-33250
ISBN 0-684-81119-7

acknowledgments

A very special thanks to Gordon Chaplin, Ted Conover, Phil Gerard, Alice Mayhew, Esther Newberg, Naomi Reiss, Tina Turner, Terry Tempest Williams, Brooke Williams, and Richard Zacks.

I also wish to thank the National Science Foundation division of Polar Programs for its generous support during a trip to U.S. Palmer Station, for *Outside* magazine. NSF leadership, staff, and scientists were at all times professional and cordial. Safety rules were stringently followed on the base, and personnel often worked up to sixteen hours a day.

The base in this novel, and the characters, are purely fictional. They bear no resemblance to anyone I have met.

As of this writing, the Antarctic remains the last place on earth unowned by any country; a continent dedicated to peace and science. Let it remain that way.

For Naomi Reiss. With love.

prologue

He could not believe it. It couldn't be true.

On a bright, cold day in late April, Dr. Jack Amirault raced down the Santa Monica Freeway, Dan Ryan Expressway, and over the Queensboro Bridge toward the radio room of U.S. Ellsworth Base in Antarctica.

The "highways" were raised wooden walkways connecting buildings. And Amirault was in a rage. He had just returned from a three-day research cruise and what he'd heard on landing had horrified him. Now he rushed to verify it was true.

"Robyn Cassidy," Captain Bryce had said on the bridge of the *Polar Queen,* "is on Purgatory Road."

He'd never met her, but who hadn't seen the famous activist on television? Watched and heard her speeches and gawked at her on the cover of *Vanity Fair,* in a designer bikini and cross-country skis. Making a laughingstock of her cause, detractors said. Winning publicity, supporters argued. But it was inconceivable to Amirault that no matter how some people mocked or hated her, she'd made it two hundred miles up the peninsula, put up SOS flags, and no one had helped.

"She's been up there two days."

Amirault, twenty-eight, was the youngest scientist at Ellsworth, a comer who'd won football and merit scholarships to Stanford, and earned his early doctorate with honors. "A genius, that's what your file says," Dr. Carl Lieber, head of the Polar Research Program, had said, sizing him up in his National Science Foundation office. "And a legend in your own work. It says you 'hear' rock."

"It's just sound waves. Based on the speed of the waves coming back, I guess what's under the ocean."

Lieber had grunted. "The Navy says you find things other people don't. They're afraid if we don't take you, some corporation will. Describe your relationship with friends."

"I'm loyal."

"Anything else?"

"People get only one chance with me."

Lieber had closed the file, looked thoughtful, and for a moment Amirault feared he was going to be turned down. He had wanted to go to Antarctica since he was a boy listening to his geologist parents talk about the beauty, the wildness. And looking over Lieber's head at actual photos of the base, blowups of the powder-blue buildings and harbor and ice cliffs, he'd yearned to be there so much he felt if he closed his eyes, he would transport himself there by will.

Lieber had tapped the file with his thumb. "There are only eighteen people on base, for months. You have no privacy. You have a roommate, always people. When you eat, work, *all the time.*

"In your room, at night, you want to relax, play Mozart on the stereo. A sonata. But your roommate likes heavy metal." He frowned. "That Axl person." Amirault had the feeling Lieber's kids listened to "that Axl person."

"Does this sound funny to you?" Lieber said. "A small thing. Maybe you think we should discuss research, not music. But after three months down there, 'small things' are not funny at all."

"I understand."

"You won't unless you get there. On base, if you get mad at someone, you can't leave. Can't get in a car and drive off and sulk about it. Can't insult people and apologize and everything will be okay. Wounds fester. Problems get magnified. You become family with people, or despise them."

"I'll be fine."

Lieber had sighed, shoved the file back. "People only get one chance with me, too. The Navy's got a lot of clout with this new treaty coming up. And we've never had a brother and sister working on the same base before. I hope you'll both be with us a long time."

Now Amirault pushed against the steel door to the Sears Tower building, and felt the dry heat hit him as he rushed into its basement lab area. The sense of the continent outside disappeared. He might have been in his lab at Stanford. Smells came to him; fish, rubber, chocolate cake. He was in a long hallway, carpeted in gray, lined by open lab doors every ten feet.

Except something was wrong. At midafternoon, he should have heard voices, pneumatic drills hammering rock, music from tape recorders, the electric hum of tissue grinders.

No one was here.

Amirault ran down the silent hallway. At a stairwell at the far end he took stairs two at a time. He burst through a swinging door into the kitchen, where an unwatched soup pot simmered — vegetable broth from the smell. He ran past gleaming industrial freezers into the dining area, long rows of folding tables half set for dinner.

But there should have been scientists in the lounge by the dining room. There was nobody reading newspapers or magazines in overstuffed easy chairs, like they did every late afternoon. Gazing out the ski-chalet picture window, past skuas on the railing, at icebergs in the harbor. Playing Trivial Pursuit or writing letters beneath the whalebone on the wall, after being at work since four a.m.

At Ellsworth, everything had nicknames, comforting reminders of home. The bay was "the Gulf of Mexico," the ice ringing it "the Palisades." The mountains visible far inland, on clear days, were "the Rockies." The glacier "Vail." The kitchen "Gourmet Garage." The hallway he ran down now, past the manager's office, was "the Pentagon." Bursts of screechy static thundered from the last room on the left, from which spilled a packed mass of people who should have been outside or downstairs.

Amirault bulled through the crowd into the radio room, which was crammed with communications equipment, its lone window looking out at the glacier and mountains. Every inch jammed with people, in jeans and souvenir tee shirts from other bases: *I ate chili in Chile . . . Honorary Citizen of Ukraine . . . Argentinean Antarctica . . .*

A voice Amirault barely recognized as Lieber's cried over the loudspeaker, half drowned by atmospheric distortion, "Don't do it! Do you hear me! *Don't go up there!*"

Voices filled Amirault in, babbling information.

"Nobody saw her arrive!"

Six months ago, Robyn Cassidy had announced her plan to walk the length of Purgatory Road, the 250-mile-long gauntlet of glaciers, avalanches, rock slides, ice fields, and mountain passes zigzagging up the center of the Antarctic Peninsula. A lifeless zone where air rescue was complicated by weather, radio signals were blocked by peaks, and storms could wipe out visibility in seconds.

Amirault envisioned Purgatory Road as it had appeared on TV, in hazy satellite shots. A meandering line of white, broken by volcanic outcrops. Cliffs or million-year-old mountains of rubble. For a lone human, hauling a Kevlar sled of supplies, passage would be brutal. There was only one place along the route where the solid wall of mountains broke away, just for half a mile, behind Ellsworth Base, where the glacier had torn through rock on its way to the sea.

"Purgatory Road is the closest thing on earth to another planet," a newsman had explained, as film clips showed Robyn training on cross-country skis, in lava beds high in the Cascade Mountains. "There are no animals. No plants. Greenland Eskimos, shown videos of Antarctica, refused to believe the place was real. 'Nothing lives there,' they said."

Then Robyn Cassidy's face had filled the screen. "I'm making this trip to show the Antarctic is in danger," the activist had said, as the base watched a three-week-old tape brought by the *Polar Queen*. "Antarctica, at the moment, is the greatest experiment in human cooperation in history. The last place on earth unowned by any country. Think of it! A piece of land the size of the U.S. and Mexico, and no military activity allowed. No mining. No drilling. No weapons testing. Just science. Researchers from twenty-six countries share projects, visit each other's bases, strive for the betterment of humankind.

"That's about to end," she'd said, pounding her small fists on the podium as Amirault watched, drawn, as always, to passion. "The diplomats will be meeting at Victoria Base next year to vote on changing the treaty, to carve the continent up. Oil! That's what they want! And fish in the sea while oceans are running out of life! Scientists have already begun working in secret on military projects there."

"I *wish* I was working on a secret project. That way I'd get a grant next year," Brian Phillips had retorted behind Amirault. They'd been best friends since Stanford. They were roommates on base. "Nobody's working on secret projects."

"If we don't realize what we're losing it'll be too late," Robyn had said. "I'm going to walk up Purgatory Road, visit those bases, and *prove* what's going on!"

"Out for herself," Brian had said as the tape switched off. He studied ozone loss over the continent, and skin cancer rise in the animals in the harbor. "Sexy. Ambitious. Ruthless. Phony. Remember when she broke up that seminar on Antarctica last year? Paraded in and said we should make the place a park. She's slept with half of Congress. Big talk but she's out for herself. Sure this place'll be carved up someday. When there's no more oil in the rest of the world, we'll need it. What's wrong with getting a piece for the U.S.?"

"Why do I love such a fascist?" Amirault's sister, Evylyn, had moaned, draped across an overstuffed chair in the lounge, as a storm raged outside. "I say she's right, keep one piece of the whole planet off limits to corporations."

"All I know is, walking up Purgatory Road," Amirault had said, "takes guts."

Now, in the radio room, someone cried, "Oh God! Look!"

Amirault turned. In the distance the whole sky beyond the glacier was a wall of purple. A dark mass like clotted blood raced and engulfed everything in its path.

The storm seemed to pulsate. Amirault saw a burst of bright

crimson glow and fade. A flash of green. The building trembled, and thunder, closer now, set his teeth on edge. The base could withstand a bad storm. It was usually fun to watch how crazy things got out there, with the snow flying and antennas whipping and ice crashing in the bay. But Amirault spotted the black dot against the snow a mile off, in the last jagged piece of sunlight shrinking before the storm.

He grabbed binoculars off the table. Her red SOS flags stretched straight out in the wind.

"You let her sit there two days?" Amirault said under his breath, but the whole group heard him.

He was aware, through their embarrassed silence, of faces turning to him. The man closest to Amirault, the base manager, was a stocky, crew-cut off-season Idaho wilderness guide named Rick Page.

"It's Lieber," he said.

"So?"

"Lieber said stay put."

"Lieber said stay put," Amirault repeated. "Lieber." He dragged out the word.

"He's right," snapped Laticia Marks, Amirault's girlfriend. "You haven't been here for three days, so save your opinions about things you don't know."

The purple mass slid over the black peaks beyond the glacier, and the squall line raced across the last bright field of snow. A collective sigh went up, as if they'd been arguing about Robyn for days, following Lieber's instructions with the greatest reluctance. But Amirault sensed something false, too. Relief. There was a dampness, a sweaty tinge over the crisp smell of wood polish and lubrication oil.

Rick said, "The ice is in bad shape. Send up four, we could lose four. We got ice bridges over crevasses. It's like walking in a minefield."

It was a peace offering. Amirault looked around the room. Twelve scientists. Six support staff. Lieber had been right. They'd become family. The pictures hung all around them. The shot of "Luau Night," when they'd dressed in Hawaiian shirts, roasted a pig the *Queen* brought in, and drunk mai tais. "The Boston Marathon," where staffers raced thirty miles in the gym on the base's two treadmills and donated money to AIDS research. "Casino Night." "Battle of the Bands." "Book Club Night." "One-Act Play Night."

Up on the glacier the air was white. A fine mist had begun blowing, like the ice was on fire. Suddenly it obscured Robyn Cassidy's tent, but cleared and Amirault saw the tent again.

Only minutes had elapsed but precious seconds were going by. The barometer by the window was dropping.

"My guess, she's dead already," said Hector Carroll, the only military man on base, a Navy doctor due to retire in a month, who led the prayer devotional on Sundays and took care of their flus and sprained ankles and did simple dentistry, working from a dog-eared manual with an electric drill.

"Why else wouldn't she have come out of the tent?" Laticia said.

"Right," Amirault said. "How come she didn't just ski down if she wanted to? Or get a snowboard or skip over the ice?"

When he lost his temper the universe seemed to draw in on itself, contract so he lost the edge of his vision. Laticia had gone blotchy with anger, bursts of crimson erupting along her neck.

"Who has a compass?" Amirault said.

He turned toward the door, telling himself, I'll need an ice ax. Candy, something for her to eat. Splints. When the storm hits, I'll be blind.

But Rick blocked his path, expression calm but eyes hard, six inches away. Lieber had said, in Washington, "On base there's one authority, and it's Rick Page. Rick says when you can take out Zodiacs. Rick says when it's safe to go on the ice. His word is my word. He is the law."

"Get out of the way," Amirault said.

"Jack," he said. "We called for a helicopter from the Argentineans. It broke down. We'll wait for the storm to let up, and try again."

"Again? When did you try the first time? And the Argentineans are a hundred miles away," Amirault said. "I have a compass in my room."

Rick grabbed his arm as he tried to move past. "Remember last year? The tourist plane that went down near Mount Erebus? The Navy rescue plane crashed too."

"She's a mile away," Amirault said. "We can see her, for God's sake. You're afraid, that's all."

He was aware, in some back corner of his mind, of the film coming over Rick's eyes, the hardening of facial lines, the transition from friend to antagonist. And not only with Rick. A sullen wall came at him from all directions. It was shame.

"Lieber'll kick you out of here," Rick called from behind as Amirault moved past. "Stop now and he won't know."

But the reason Amirault paused was, he saw a compass. A palm stretched toward him, the thin blue needle pointed north, toward the bay. The loudspeaker blasted another burst of static, as if Lieber sensed Rick's authority unraveling. Over the noise Brian's voice said, "Great. Do I have time to make a will?"

A wave of gratitude swept over Amirault. Brian, in his duck boots and lumberjack shirt, pressed the warm compass into Amirault's hand. But Brian looked more scared than confident. "She got herself into this. Do me a favor. Let's forget this and get a drink."

Amirault turned to the window. *Plot the route before the storm engulfs her.*

"For once," said Laticia's icy voice behind him, "can't you drop an idea once you get it in your head?"

Amirault responded without turning around. "I used to think I knew who you were."

Then he forgot them, lining the compass needle with Robyn's tent. They'd be walking in the dark. She's past the left side of the ski equipment shack, he thought. Past the flagpole, southwest 180 degrees. Past the weather shack and tallest satellite antenna. We rope up. Spread sideways to cover more ground. Go slow. Very slow.

Outside, the sky darkened and the window mirrored Amirault looking out. A blond man in an unzipped wolverine fur–lined parka, blue turtleneck protruding from the collar of his Irish wool sweater. Weather lines giving him a ruddy squint, eyes the color of dark tea. Pale ovals, goggle lines, encircling his Slavic cheekbones. Shoulders broadened by fifteen years of working out.

Brian's reflection joined him. "You have your pit bull look."

"Let's go."

The others, reduced to spectators, had gone silent. Over the whine of the intercom came a low *whooooo* of wind. Rick moved to block the doorway but his hands were at his sides, the fight gone out of him.

"Guys. Come on," he said.

Amirault led Brian back through the hall and kitchen, across the Dan Ryan Expressway, down onto a plowed path up a slope to the generator building. The wooden shack perched at the edge of a basalt moraine marking the end of the glacier.

Inside it was warm, and loud from the gasoline generator, an eight-foot-high behemoth that ran round the clock, providing electricity for the station. Against the wall, staffers stored their climbing boots, sleds to move supplies, ropes, skis. Amirault stripped from his parka to add layers that smelled of gasoline. Spare thermal long johns, double-strength wool socks, flannel-lined jumpsuit, balaclava pullover cap that made him look like a terrorist. He laced up heavy steel-studded boots with crampons for gripping ice as Brian strapped on a waist harness and ran a heavy perlon climbing rope through the clips. They both chose ice axes for probing the surface for weak spots.

Brian shook his head. "Independents." What he meant was, the National Science Foundation disapproved of private visitors to Antarctica, unaffiliated travelers, but since no country owned the place it was impossible to keep them out. The adventurers who arrived each year — the kayakers paddling across the Drake Passage, the dogsledders racing for the Pole, the yachtsmen sailing into harbors — kept getting into trouble. It was always dangerous to mount a rescue.

Amirault started for the door. "That's not the point."

But before they could leave, the steel door burst open and a tall, disheveled-looking woman rushed in. She had Amirault's hair and high cheekbones, and her eyes were red with fever. She also had Amirault's intensity, although in Amirault it projected outward, at work, lovers, politics. His sister Evylyn turned it into harsh self-criticism. She blamed herself for anything that went wrong. The two of them had stayed together for years, at their uncle's farm in Sonoma after their parents died, at Stanford, and on the base, although they worked on different projects.

At the moment, her flannel shirt hung over the waist of her thermal cords. The laces of her Eastern Mountain climbing boots were flopping.

Evylyn yanked a climbing harness off a hook near the snowshoes. But she began coughing and had to stop. Her nose looked wet. "It's about time," she rasped.

Brian jiggled the pick of his ice ax, making sure it was fastened tight. "I can't believe you got out of bed."

"Three people are better than two." Evylyn threw on a parka.

"You couldn't even make it to lunch two hours ago." Brian shoved his ax handle through the strap of his waist harness.

Furious, Evylyn looked fifteen years old. "I'll carry *you* down the glacier. I told you yesterday we should go. Ami Two, I knew you'd go."

Another fit of coughing seized her. She fell back against the locker, a lock of hair plastered by sweat against her forehead. She waved a hand weakly by her throat.

"I hate being sick," she said.

Amirault started toward the door as Brian said, behind him, "Even if she's still alive, Evylyn, you'll kill her with the flu. Jack, tell her she can't come."

"Me tell *her?*"

That broke the tension. Evylyn called from behind them, at the door, "Watch the ice." Outside, directly overhead, the sky was still blue. The sun warm through the wool balaclava, the harbor smell salty, fresh. On the peninsula temperatures could rise as high as 40 degrees.

With Amirault leading, the two moved northwest, through the plowed areas around the buildings, toward a rubbly ravine, piles of black basalt lava cracked and broken by freezing and thawing marking a moraine at the end of the glacier. A natural boundary between the civilized area at the edge of the sea and the wild continent just beyond it.

At any other time the view would have thrilled him. The base occupied a thin, rocky, rubbly strip wedged between the diamond-shaped harbor and the massive glacier behind. Ninety-foot-high ice cliffs ringed the harbor, the sun turning their geometric surfaces turquoise, aquamarine, indigo, as if shining out from deep in the earth. The bergs in the harbor changed shape and position daily. He glimpsed the uncoiling back of a breaching humpback whale beyond the docked *Polar Queen*.

"Welcome to the Banana Belt," read a sign painted on the fuel tank, beside an orca leaping out of a rainbow.

More rocky mounds lined the shore on their right, dotted with yellow flags which meant "prohibited." Leopard seals swam there, eight-hundred-pound predators known to attack humans. At the moment, a pair of fur seals played in the last minutes of sunlight, nudging each other's dog-shaped faces, raising themselves on their big front flippers to watch the humans go by. A lone chinstrap penguin waddled in lost circles and fell in behind them for ten feet, following any leader, before going back to its clownish loops.

The wind pushed into Amirault's face.

Boots crunching, they crossed the moraine. On the other side the glacier began, dusted with fresh snow, the first hundred yards marked by safety lines and red flags on bamboo poles indicating a crevasse-free area, where hiking and cross-country skiing were allowed.

Beyond the last flag the glacier stretched away in endless sameness, its snowdusting turning gently lilac as it absorbed the hues of the oncoming storm.

Amirault wiped his emotion away and slowed his mind to pay attention. He wrapped the leather thong of Brian's compass around his mittened wrist, to keep it from blowing away when the storm finally hit.

They spread out, and probed the ice as they walked. Each one had to be ready if the other fell in.

Amirault crunched up the slope, steel cleats digging into an ice cube a thousand miles long. After two months here he sensed the ice shifting. It was too slow to see but nothing around him was as solid as it seemed. The whole continent was moving. The glaciers were microscopically flowing rivers. In ten years, or a hundred, depending on the rate of flow, the spot where he walked would reach the sea.

Brian's voice carried, sharp and clear in the calm before the storm. "You were hard on Rick. You should have heard him pleading with Lieber."

"So he's human," Amirault said. "That doesn't mean I have to like it."

There was a last instant of sunlight; then the wall of storm towered over them and Amirault watched the dark line bridge the last few feet and hit. The world went gray, wind whipped the compass from his hand but the thongs held fast. Brian shouted something impossible to hear. The air filled with flying ice, ripping at Amirault's beard and clogging his nose. He shielded his face with a mitten, bulling forward.

They spread apart until the rope tightened. They advanced slowly, up a twenty-foot swath.

He kept his gaze low, scanning for her tent as he probed the surface for drops with his ax handle. Five thousand feet to a mile, he thought. Half a mile to Robyn. His gums stung from cold. The air in his lungs seemed to be freezing him from the inside out. Wind cut into the eyeholes of the balaclava, tearing at his cheeks. Brushed by a mitten, his skin crunched like parchment. He could feel heaviness in his eyelids, which were already coated with ice.

As he moved, Amirault groped with his free hand for the ice hammer and piton, made sure they were smoothly extractable. Everyone on base had practiced buddy rescue in safety classes, dropping to a squat, hammering in the piton, wrapping around the rope.

If you didn't move fast when a buddy went into a crevasse, you'd be pulled in too.

One thousand, Amirault counted.

Twelve hundred.

Brian was a silhouette ten feet away, coming in and out of view through waves of snow. At times, only the taut rope told Amirault he was there.

He held the compass to his face. The needle had stuck.

What if we're moving in the wrong direction?

He blew on the compass to warm it. The needle did not move.

It wasn't only a question of finding Robyn. Without the compass they could miss the base on the way back, passing safety by ten yards. He'd heard plenty of stories of people losing direction outside their own bases in storms, being found five feet from the door the next day, frozen.

Feel your way, he told himself. Use the slope to tell your position.

Maybe we shouldn't have come.

Amirault pushed the thought away and kept climbing. If he decided they'd passed her, they'd swing around and try another direction. Use each other as a fulcrum. March in circles in the storm.

Probe and step. Probe and step.

Fifteen hundred steps.

He was only paying half attention when the ax handle broke through ice. Amirault shouted, "Crevasse!" and yanked the rope, dropped, got out the piton. Waited for the sickening pull of a body dropping away. But the rope stopped — Brian had heard him or had found the drop too — and slackened slowly. Brian sidled up to him, out of the snow. They stood before the inch-wide hole where Amirault's ax handle had gone through.

The area around it looked solid.

Brian dug in as Amirault probed around the hole. The ax handle sank in, on the left side. He tried the right.

The hole might be a foot deep. Or drop as far down as the Grand Canyon.

Amirault probed again, farther away from the break.

The ax handle didn't go through.

Brian played out rope as Amirault took a light step onto the solid area.

They both knew the surface might hold against an ax handle but collapse from the weight of a man. Amirault applied more pressure. He tried both feet.

They kept going.

Rick was just trying to keep us safe, he thought.

But he remembered another scene. He was a small boy pressed

to a window, Evylyn beside him. Rain washed down the pane so hard it turned the men trudging up the front walkway into bulky inhuman forms. Big, silent roustabouts, soaked, unhappy Louisiana offshore men hunched and milling at the front door, afraid to look in his face, as one of the other oil company moms — not a friend, just a new neighbor, since they'd just moved here — stirred hot chocolate behind him. As thunder shook the house.

Did you find my parents?

Jackie . . . Evvie . . . we couldn't get the boat out. But in a couple of days . . . when the weather clears . . .

Amirault made out a shape. A tent!

"Brian!"

The wind whipped into his face. The ice slammed his knees when he dropped down, parted the flap, and crawled through the vestibule to poke his head in: he looked into the blinking blue eyes of a living skeleton. Eyes made enormous by sunken cheeks. Something twisted inside him. The forces that had ravaged the body had merely accentuated power in those blue eyes.

"Uh-oh. Caught smoking," Robyn rasped.

"It'll stunt your growth."

He took in the rest. Wool cap too big for her head, cracked lips parted for the barest trickle of condensed breath, ivory-colored teeth. Stove that had gone out. The body had thinned so much it might have been nothing more than a fold in the sleeping bag. The smell of tobacco drifted with blue smoke in the tent, swirling against white ice rime coating the nylon.

Those eyes.

The skeleton said, "This is a little embarrassing. Popped a knee back there."

Back where? She'd started over two hundred miles south. He envisioned the strength she must have needed to pull the sled this far, get her flags up. And then nobody came.

"You haven't been eating your vegetables either," he said.

Robyn coughed. Her voice, harsh and faint, retained the barest hint of the husky tone he'd heard from her on TV. "I missed the last food drop. And the Colonel Sanders was closed. This is Ellsworth, isn't it?"

"I have a Snickers in my pocket," Amirault said.

Robyn closed her eyes dreamily and shuddered and said, "Snickers." With her hollow cheeks she looked like one of Evylyn's Edvard Munch posters. "The Scream."

"I'm going to look at that leg," he said. Everyone on base knew basic splints, resuscitation, bone breakage. Those huge eyes bored into him. His knuckles brushed her chin when he touched the zipper. She was fully dressed in the bag, but the kneebone jutted up at the wrong angle. She moaned when he touched it. There was the faintest ammonia smell of urine from the bag.

"No problem," he said.

Then the rope jerked him backward, threw him off balance, and suddenly he was down, tangled and sliding on his back down the ice. *Get the piton!* But his hand was pinned beneath him.

Brian fell in, he thought, horrified.

He might have heard a scream above the wind.

For all her weakness, Robyn Cassidy moved fast, mobile at least from the waist up. She'd thrown her arms around Amirault but was too weak to hold on, and as they slid, dragging the collapsed tent, they tangled together in the red rope.

Amirault couldn't get his cleats in, couldn't reach the hammer. They slid faster toward what had to be a break in the ice.

Abruptly, the rope went slack.

It took a moment to realize he'd stopped. Dazed, Amirault lay gasping. Brian must have arrested the fall somehow.

A dull ache began where the rope had yanked at him, at his waist.

He looked down. Robyn still held his waist, her feet in her sleeping bag, behind her. She was exhausted, heaving. They were tangled in the rope.

"Brian?" Amirault called.

In her left hand, Robyn held a knife.

Amirault groaned, the realization beginning.

He hauled in the rope. It came easily, now that nothing was on the other end. The threads trailing from the sliced end were the color of blowing snow.

Robyn wheezed, "I sleep with it." The knife. "Old habit. From camping." She caught her breath.

"You would have gone in too," she said.

Amirault shook free of her touch. There was a grinding sensation in his stomach. From the throbbing in his hand, he realized that he had never replaced the mitten he'd removed. He crawled in the direction the rope had come from, reached the break, looked down.

A long, slick gullet of ice stretched away. He couldn't see the bottom. Gray-blue clouds of snow blew inside.

Amirault screamed, "Brian!"

Flakes billowed out of the hole into his face. They felt feathery against his skin.

Amirault lay on his back, face exposed to the elements. Stay here long enough and the snow will bury me, he thought.

He heard Robyn scrabbling around nearby. She was pulling herself forward with crabbing motions of her arms, pushing with one good leg. Her face was suddenly inches away. It was all lines. All bone and pupil. Angle and skull.

Robyn looked down at Amirault, their positions reversed. All she needed was striped pajamas to make the Auschwitz image complete.

Robyn repeated, at the end of her reserve strength, "You would have gone in too."

The glacier beneath him began vibrating. There was a roar from inside the earth.

Amirault felt himself tilting, starting to slide again. He reached for Robyn. A gap seemed to open in the earth, a jagged line appearing suddenly, and they were sliding into it, boulders of ice raining past, the snow making it hard to see.

The tent slid by him.

Robyn moaned, "My leg."

They stopped on an ice ledge, ten feet down. He was afraid to move, afraid if he even swiveled his head to look up, it would change the weight distribution, break the ledge off.

She began sliding again. He slammed her back into the ice wall. The muscles in his shoulder trembled from effort.

Deep in the ice, the roar receded, died.

The wind made an *ooooh*ing sound.

"We'll wait," he told her. But she was unconscious.

Two hours later he was still holding her there. The ice rumbled and settled. He watched a chunk detach itself from the wall opposite him and tumble into the hole, the sound of cracking and bouncing fading. His arm, pressing her back, keeping her from sliding forward, burned with pain.

After a while the storm eased. That was when he heard it. From below. *Tink . . . tink . . .*

Impossible. Steel on ice.

Tink . . .

Brian?

He told himself it couldn't be true. But he wanted it to be true. He thought, Please, God, let it be true.

When he tried to look over the edge Robyn started sliding again. He forced her back, but her weight, against his arm, pushed him toward the edge. He was drenched with sweat despite the cold. The snow fell more lightly. He moved his head forward a bit at a time.

Tink . . . tink . . .

Amirault glanced over the edge.

Below, he saw a spot of red color. Something coming up the side of the ice. Amirault went dizzy with exultation. Come on, he thought. You can do it. You can get up here. Reach the ledge and they'll send a rescue party, they'll have to, there are three of us.

His head was exploding. It was Brian. One arm jutting out the wrong way. One leg hanging. He wanted to scream but the ice was so fragile. The sound could break things up again. And now Brian seemed to realize Amirault was up there. Amirault saw the black balaclava begin swinging. Brian was looking up.

Impossible. He rubbed his eyes. Brian could not be there. It was a hallucination.

"Jack," Amirault thought he heard Brian say.

He saw Brian start to wave, a mistake. And then both arms out, windmilling, as the wave turned into a flail. He saw, as if in slow motion, the space widening between Brian and the ice wall.

This time, when the body fell away, Amirault started screaming.

He was screaming when the rescue party reached them, an hour after that.

one

One year later the *Polar Queen* swung into the wind and bucked and plunged through the Bellingshausen Sea, on its way to Ellsworth Base. In the pilothouse, the captain peered at his radar screen and decided a blip there was an eighty-mile-long iceberg, not an island. In the galley, the crew ate hamburgers at tables nailed to the floor. In the cabins, the scientists were sick.

Jack Amirault stood alone on the aft deck, balancing against the violent movement, hooked to earphones, scanning the floodlit frothing wake. It was ten p.m., Saturday night. The anniversary of the accident on Purgatory Road.

The only time he forgot Brian was when he worked.

Boombuhbuhbuh.

In his headphones, he heard an explosion, and sound waves shooting down from the *Queen.*

Wawawawawawawa.

The waves coming back after striking bottom.

Amirault's pulse sped up.

He'd found gold.

The ship tilted to port. Snow blew in the powerful arc lights shining down from the A-frame winch. Amirault gripped the railing. Through blue diesel clouds erupting from the fantail, he scanned four red floats trailing behind the ship. Wires ran from each float to a microphone-shaped soundgun, firing underwater every eighteen seconds.

Boombuhbuhbuhbuh.

The excitement moved into his belly. He pictured the soft buttery gold down there, trapped beneath silt and crust and blind colorless creatures who swam by feel.

This was his skill, his genius. The ability to "hear" rock. It was why the Navy had overridden Lieber's furious objections and sent him back to Antarctica. Why psychologists at Bethesda Naval Hospital had been advised to pronounce Amirault fit.

But now he frowned, hearing an odd echo inside the main note, the barest interruption in the purity. Just a hint. Like a flute smothered by crashing orchestra brass.

Something else down there too.

"Hey, Jack!"

He whirled. Dr. Carroll, in his orange float-suit, had come up behind him and looked Tweedledee-round in the glare of the lights. Normally he was a natty dresser, but now the hood gave his head a dome shape, turned him as alien as everything else in this environment. The jacket bunched out around his torso like a basketball. A black rubber flap snapped beneath his crotch, made the suit watertight, so if he fell in, he would float during the three minutes it took to freeze to death. Hector's gray eyes were watchful, clinical. Amirault took the earphones off and the doctor shouted, over the ship's roar, "Memorial service is starting in the lounge in five minutes. I'll read from Isaiah. You can still say a few words, if you want."

They were always watching him. In the dorm, labs, mess. Worried about him.

"Thanks, Hector, but I can't leave until my grid's finished. The ship won't cover this area again. Last trip."

Hector grabbed the railing as the *Queen* lurched. The syrupy concern drove Amirault crazy sometimes. "You okay out here?"

"Why not?"

"Want company or something?"

"Hector, I'm not going to crack up again."

Hector squeezed his shoulder. He was from Southern California and every once in a while a Moonie mannerism broke through the doctor veneer. "Did I say that? I didn't say that. I was just thinking you might not want to be alone today."

Amirault sighed. Bergy ice butted against the *Queen* with a sound like steel chains clanking. Larger floes hit the ship like crumpling cars.

"Hector, a year ago if we were having this conversation, you would have just said, 'Shut up, asshole.' I've been back here three months. I'm fine. You don't have to watch me all the time."

Hector looked pained. "The truth, Jack? I recommended they keep you out of here. You were screaming when we medevacked you out, that Brian was trying to climb out of that hole. But it's not just you cracking up. It's how you are when you're sane too. You're too independent. There's no room for loners here. If there's another emergency, no one knows what you'll do."

"There's only twelve days left. There won't be any emergency."

Hector hesitated. "I also wondered if you want to talk about, well, Laticia and me."

"No need. I'm glad she hooked up with you. We weren't right for each other."

The ship swung to starboard and the doctor stumbled off, swaying like a giant penguin, past the battened hatches and coiled ropes and extra fuel barrels. Amirault put the headphones on. The sound was still there. Eerie and wavy and tugging at his memory. Two sideways steps planted him in front of his video monitor, a freestanding unit bolted down, broadcasting a nonstop picture, thousands of emerald dots, each an echo, forming a jagged outline of the bottom and layers of rock beneath.

Reflected over the glowing dots, Amirault looked unkempt. His beard was thicker. His face thinner. His eyes were veined from sixteen-hour days.

What the hell was down there?

He thought, It's not uranium, gas, manganese.

I killed my best friend, Amirault thought.

He pushed away the thought with effort and closed his eyes and felt the acuteness of a blind man running his hands over an object to visualize it. With each explosion, his nerve endings seemed to fracture into sound and go out and rise back through the water to reattach themselves to his body. Bringing information. Each echo reverberating, ship to bottom, dying into silence broken by the next shot.

There's a canyon, he thought, sensing the cold, the steep rocky walls, the airlessness, the twisted albino creatures that swam in the dark and generated their own light.

Amirault took off the headphones.

I'll be damned, he thought.

God, this place was rich in minerals! Molybdenum was better than gold! It was so rare. It wasn't supposed to be in Antarctica, and if it was showing up in his earphones, this deposit was huge. It could make airplanes resistant to shock and corrosion. Increase the hardness of steels. Be melted into the thinnest coatings, to enable manned spacecraft someday to sail close to the sun without burning up.

Next week, when the Antarctic changes forever, which country will get this deposit, he thought?

Now he had only to record results. The sea had calmed. They'd entered Ellsworth Harbor. The lights of the base twinkled ahead. A few notes of errant guitar music; Elvis Costello singing "It's Too Late" came to him on the leeward wind. He checked his watch and was amazed to see it was after eleven. He'd been working since six a.m.

Amirault signaled the pilothouse to start reeling in the sound-guns.

Washington will be ecstatic over this find, he thought. It'll be worth millions.

It's none of my business who gets the stuff.

Amirault walked down the dorm hallway, empty because of the Saturday night party. The place looked like college. Cinder-block walls. Common bathroom. Only the photos reminded him of where he was. He passed a shot of British and Argentinean soldiers facing off, with tommy guns, on the peninsula in 1948. They'd actually started shooting. The current treaty had stopped that. Next came a shot of Hitler's Junkers flying over Purgatory Road, dropping red-and-black swastika flags like confetti, during World War II, claiming the continent.

Amirault passed a photo of the nearest "neighbors," twenty men in two rows, like a rugby team. The Brits, fifty miles north up Purgatory Road, at Victoria Base, where Robyn Cassidy had been heading a year ago, and where the treaty meeting was scheduled to start next week.

The dorm vibrated from rock 'n' roll exploding in from the garage/pub building next door.

Amirault thought, This could all be gone next year, if the U.S. doesn't get this part of the peninsula.

He reached his room and was surprised to see the door opening. He'd had no roommate since Brian's death. When Clyde Hudson stormed out, Amirault's surprise turned to shock.

The usually level Brit looked frantic; face blotchy, fists clenched. At twenty-two, Clyde still had the bony torso of a teenager, with the broad shoulders of the swimmer he had been at Leeds. He was on loan from the British station, finishing up Brian's ozone work. He must have come from the party, because Amirault smelled beer on his breath.

"Where's Evylyn?" Clyde said.

"Did you try under the bed?"

"I'm not joking, Jack."

"Excuse me then. Doing stomach curls hanging from the ceiling."

Clyde came closer and Amirault saw bits of iridescent glitter, purple and red sparkles — he'd been at the party, all right — in his white-blond hair. "She tells you everything . . ." Clyde backed a step, looking into Amirault's face. He was trembling. He had one of those English-boy faces, round like Paul McCartney's, that popped out and turned too red and looked comically ineffective in agitation. His youth was accentuated by the oversized British Army sweater and fatigues, standard issue to their civilian staff, draped over his lanky frame. He wore red Converse high-top sneakers.

"She's meeting me," Clyde said, as if daring Amirault to intervene. When Amirault didn't, Clyde seemed confused. "Who's she with?"

"Clyde, calm down. It's not like she could go anywhere." Amirault felt sorry for the kid. If the Brits would allow women on their bases, things wouldn't get crazy every time they visited any other place.

Clyde said, practically in tears, "You're the only guy she hasn't slept with, and that's because she's your sister."

Amirault moved without thinking. He pushed Clyde, by his sweater, against the wall. The photo of the Brits swung sideways from impact.

He said softly, "Clyde."

The kid looked clever suddenly, a sly light coming into his eyes. "You know where she is."

Amirault let go and the sick look cleared from the Englishman. Now he was just a stooped, anguished kid, who never should have been sent here in the first place. Clyde mumbled, "I looked everywhere. The *Queen*. The hot tub. I just need to know."

"Clyde, you're pathetic. Buck up! For the queen!"

The Brit didn't laugh. "Take a break," Amirault sighed. "In two weeks you'll be home and you'll never see her again."

The kid made a strangled sound. He'd been so reserved when he arrived that his lost control seemed worse. "I'm not going home straightaways . . . I mean, I'll go to Victoria for the meeting but . . . she said we'd meet in California after that . . . She didn't tell you?"

Embarrassed, Amirault said, "We stay out of each other's personal lives. Write Ann Landers. I have things to do."

Amirault walked past him and closed the door.

He leaned against it in the dark.

He thought, The consequences never stop.

His quarters might have been designed for a college dorm. Twin beds. Little desks in corners. Miniature stereo speakers on shelves, bracketing books by Conover, Gerard, Lopez, Matthiessen. There were photos of Brian and Amirault. On the Stanford football team. On climbing vacation in Canyonlands Park. At Amirault and Evylyn's summer cottage, near Redwood, California.

Brian seemed to be looking at him from the shots.

Amirault changed from his lab clothes, Levi's and gray Eastern Mountain turtleneck, into thermal waffle-iron long johns. He added Navy-issue Arctic pants, a black wool sweater, headlamp. No mitten liners tonight as the temperature was a balmy 29 degrees.

Time to go up on the glacier.

On Brian's unused bed lay Amirault's seismic reports, and letters from oil companies, more than usual this year. Notes from Gulf. Dutch Shell. Texaco. Aramco. Just wanted to see how you're doing, Jack. How about a drink in Sonoma when you get home? How about a ball game? How about a chat on what you're finding down there? Your dissertation on Greenland amazed us. All the other scientists said there was nothing there, and you found oil. We have a job opening for polar work.

Last week he'd sent British Petroleum the usual answer. "Love to talk about a job. But I'm not allowed to share Antarctic information."

He never heard from them after that.

Amirault saw no one as he left the building. Outside the air was still and calm, visibility sharp on land but thick fog drifting in the harbor so only the fo'c'sle antenna, rising from the gray mass, showed the location of the *Polar Queen*.

Turning north, Amirault saw a moonshaft above the mountains, a pure column of silver running from moon to earth. Beyond that an aurora, a pulsating elliptical serpent of emerald and coral, undulated west to east across the sky, slowly obliterating stars in its path. The constellation Hercules glowed with an intensity impossible in the world to the north. The snow coating the glacier had formed into sastrugi — a wavelike crust like a white ocean, frozen in place.

Amirault shivered. At this angle the base was gone. He felt alone in the vast continent. He crunched toward the generator building, where the skis were stored. The window must be open in the Penguin Pub. The sound track of *Sleepless in Seattle* echoed across the Bay. Jimmy Durante singing. From the hot tub against the Sears Tower, a converted fish barrel, he heard men and women laughing and the pop of a champagne cork.

A figure in a blue parka hurried toward him from the ditch behind the generator shack.

"Have you seen . . ." Rick Page called, realized it was Amirault, and finished more quietly: "Evylyn?"

"Everyone's looking for her."

Rick drew closer. Of all people on base, he was the one who could treat Amirault with outright antagonism sometimes. When the station manager was excited a healed split in his eyelid—an old carpentry wound—turned purple, and the stitch mark outlined itself. Rick had come up the hard way, laborer to carpenter's assistant to manager. "Who else?" he said.

"Cathy Quinn," Amirault lied. He had not realized Evylyn was sleeping with Rick, too.

"I saw Cathy at the dance ten minutes ago. It's that fucking Brit, isn't it?"

"Everyone's on edge with this treaty meeting coming up."

Rick pushed past Amirault but turned and said, "How's it feel never coming back?" Beneath Rick's half-zipped parka, he was dressed for the party, in a plaid western shirt with pearl buttons. He'd clipped his reddish beard, giving his chin an angular appearance, and his flattop prickly power. "After this season, that's it for you. No more Antarctic work. No more grants or university work. Between my report and Lieber's, you're through."

Amirault said, "You did a pretty good job of keeping me out of here this year, didn't you?"

Even in the night, he could see Rick's face darken. The wind went *oooooooh*. "Remember what you called me?" Rick said. "Afraid." He came closer. His condensing breath warmed Amirault's face. "Everyone else around here might treat you like a cripple but you knew what you were doing."

"Actually, I did see Evylyn," Amirault said. "I just remembered. She was in the ham radio room, talking to your wife."

Rick smiled with his mouth only. "You may not believe this, but it's not personal, Jack. You think you're smarter than everyone else. You think rules apply to everyone else. The Navy backs you, so you get away with it. But he was my friend too. If you hadn't dragged him up there, you wouldn't have to look for him now."

"I want to find his body and bring it home," Amirault said.

• • •

In the generator shack Amirault selected a climbing rope and cross-country skis. They leaned against the wall opposite the roaring generator, a skid-mounted, gas-driven behemoth the size of a mobile camper.

Where is Evylyn, anyway? he wondered.

He carried the skis across the moraine, clipped them on, and began the steady glide toward Purgatory Road, over the frozen crests.

He passed bamboo poles marking the crevasse-free part of the glacier, and sank into softer snow in the troughs.

The music faded as he drew farther from the base until all that remained was the rhythmic, low pulse of bass.

Amirault stopped. No crevasse marked the spot where Brian had fallen anymore, but he knew it by the angle and distance from the mountains. The key to finding his friend was to remember ice was water. It looked solid but was fluid, transporting anything beneath.

Amirault skied in slowly widening circles and a jagged crevasse opened ahead, black against white. He slipped off the skis, wriggled to the edge, holding his breath and listening for the groan of weakening ice. On his stomach, he looked down, switched on the headlamp. The crevasse, the color of blue candy ice, widened nine or ten feet down, breaking into a wall of pillars on one side, a frozen wave shape on the other. Cold air hissed out of the dark.

He saw a foot-wide ledge twenty feet down.

Evylyn's probably out in a Zodiac, collecting samples.

His forehead began hammering. With all the reflection and shadow, it was hard to be sure, but he thought he saw a dark form inside the ice.

Amirault got the rope and pounded in the piton. He made the rope fast between harness and ice.

The moon, in Antarctic autumn, gave the night a lemony sheen.

Amirault was a speck beneath the glorious aurora, backing, hand over hand, over the edge. When he passed below the lip of the fissure, the glacier surface disappeared.

It was colder in here, and he sensed the glacier moving, even if he could not see it. Amirault had inserted himself, between the ticks of a clock, between two advancing waves of ice. The silence had weight. His boots touched the ledge. Keeping the rope taut, he let the headlamp beam rove up the enormous curving wall of ice.

Did he see a body? Arms open? Feet dangling.

But the shadow was gone. The beam found nothing. The endless surface threw light back into Amirault's eyes.

Amid his disappointment, Robyn Cassidy's voice, in his head, said, "They left me up there two days!"

He didn't know which was worse, the memories of Brian or Robyn. Sitting on that ledge, holding her so she didn't slide over the edge. The storm lessening slowly, until blue sky appeared overhead. And then Rick's face above them. Rick yelling, "They're here! Two of them!"

Amirault began jumaring up. He saw himself strapped into a cot beside her, inside a helicopter lifting off. She was unconscious beneath an Argentinean Air Force blanket. He saw her on TV later, at a news conference, after the National Science Foundation had announced only that a "rescue party" had saved her.

"They left me up there for two days, hoping I would die!"

What is it anyway between a man and a woman? You meet a thousand women and they do nothing for you. Beautiful women who move like music. Who smell of spice and perfume and sex and bedrooms. Who desire you. Who touch you. Who send out every alluring signal and want you. And then you see a face in a tent and a slit of white flesh through the folds of a hospital robe, not even half a second's worth, smooth white, and each molecule of that vision takes root and grows and won't leave you alone. You can't stop thinking about it. That softness, the tangle of black pubic hair. The legs moving apart. The robe opening wider. You climb into bed, night after night, close your eyes, and there she is.

He couldn't stand thinking about her and he couldn't stop. He had never had this reaction to another person in his life.

Amirault snapped off the headlamp. The moon's silver light bathed the long empty drop.

"I didn't make a mistake," he said out loud.

He thought, What else could I have done?

He thought, I'm sorry. I'm sorry.

Amirault pushed through the double swinging doors of the Penguin Pub. Bedlam reigned in the bar/poolroom. The furniture had been pushed to the sides, and sweating dancers made the floor vibrate to Adam and the Ants music. About ten scientists, *Queen* crew, and support workers whooped it up. Amirault grinned. A. Y. Chen, the jazz saxophonist and biologist from Seattle, the weight lifter and ex-refugee from Hong Kong, had shaved the sides of his head like an Iroquois and was learning line dancing from Laticia. She looked terrific in a black tank top that matched her hip-length hair and showed off her muscled belly. Once she'd liked to swish that hair across Amirault's thighs.

In a far corner, he saw a half-dozen people toasting each other with beers in a circle, Clyde and Rick among them, playing the game "I Never." Someone would say something like, "I never had oral sex with anyone twice my age." Someone else would say, "I challenge." Everyone who hadn't done it would take a drink.

Amirault didn't see Evylyn.

As kids they'd made a deal to stay out of each other's personal business. Ten more minutes, he thought now. Then personal business or not, I look for her.

He passed up bowls of herb dip, Cheez Doodles, Fritos and pasta salad. He smeared seeded rye bread with hot mustard and shoved on white-meat turkey from a half-carved carcass the *Queen* had brought in. Cans of Heineken beer sweated in vats of glacier-chipped ice. Blue and white bunting was tacked from the ceiling, on folding tables, along the wood-paneled walls. The place looked like a finished basement.

Amirault ate standing up, then headed for the bar. It filled one corner, beneath a two-foot-tall blue neon penguin, a poster of Jimmy Buffet, and a plastic palm tree in Day-Glo pink.

It was a BYO bar, but the sign said "People's Liquor." As Amirault pushed toward the vodka, someone grabbed his sleeve. Evylyn's roommate, Cathy Quinn, said, "Want to dance, Jack? I love the way you dance."

She was the only one on base who treated him normally. Cathy was a mix of black Irish and Cherokee Indian, a small, sensual, doe-eyed woman with fluid movements, midlength copper hair, braided now, and an endless supply of quiet energy. Her work involved trying to isolate anticancer compounds in ice fish. Half the guys on base had hit on her during their years here, but she was absolutely loyal to her husband.

"You missing the invisible man tonight?" he said. The husband was back in North Carolina, an English professor at the University in Wilmington.

"I always miss him. But twelve days and counting. Launch control to Shuttle. We're bringing you home."

She blushed at her own joke, realizing Amirault couldn't come back here even if the United States kept the base.

"I found a job, don't worry," he said.

"You did?"

"Lieber wants me to take over the Antarctic program."

She was a fabulous dancer. He kept looking over her head for Evylyn.

"Last year I was mad at you," she said, "like the others. But if you had come back, all of you, everyone would have treated you like a hero. That's not fair, basing what you think on how things turn out. And it would help if you were friendlier to people, Jack."

"I get confused. Are you supposed to hit them, or not?"

She laughed. He said, "Leave Chuck. Marry me."

"I hope you meet someone too."

"No sweat. My heart is pure."

Everything here, the paneled walls, the CD library, had been a surprise when Amirault first came to Antarctica. He'd expected windblown Quonset huts, Navy K rations, dogsleds, kerosene lamps. He'd found cross-country skiing, French pastry desserts, the latest movies on video.

"Have you seen Evylyn?" he said.

"She was here ten minutes ago. Must have gone to the ladies' room." Amirault felt relieved. But Cathy glanced nervously at the group in the corner. "There's something you better know."

"Don't worry about me." He squeezed her arm and broke

off and headed back to the bar. The half-dozen lounge stools were occupied by Ellsworthites or *Polar Queen* crew arguing over a two-week-old *New York Post* spread open. "METS LOSE OPENER," the banner headline said.

Conversation faltered as he arrived. Gail Rivkin, the NYU depression expert, looked up, saw him, and got a fascinated expression. She was studying the effects of isolation on bases for NASA. Sometimes he caught her watching him, and within minutes, scribbling in her ubiquitous red memo pad.

"Cheers, Gail. Your favorite bug is here."

"Oh Jack!"

"I feel so . . ." he whispered, as if searching for the right word, *"depressed."*

She blushed.

"Six million dollars? No player's worth that," a machinist called Kojak told Hector. Kojak was a reedy, stooped-over mechanical genius from Minnesota who maintained the generators, Caterpillar and snowmobiles, and doubled as radio operator. He looked nothing like the old TV detective he'd been nicknamed for, but he constantly sucked on cherry sour balls, the way the cop had lollipops. "Even Mays wasn't worth that."

"Once they get the money, they lose drive, all right," Hector agreed, jabbing the paper. Hector was planning his upcoming retirement around the Mets schedule, even buying a condo in Port St. Lucie to be around spring training.

No bartender. You got your own drinks. Amirault pushed around the back of the bar and reached over the cluster of half-filled Dewar's, Jameson, schnapps, and ouzo bottles, choosing one of a half-dozen Moskovaya vodka liters a Georgian Republic seismology ship had brought in the week before. He washed a Fred Flintstone jelly glass in the sink, chipped fresh glacier ice with a pick, poured a triple measure, and dropped in some of Clyde's bitters, which gave a tart taste.

Amirault drank deeply. He was not a sipper.

The group in the corner looked at him, burst out laughing, and broke up. From the center of it, walking toward him, came Robyn Cassidy.

The air went out of the room. There was no music, no people. Amirault broke out sweating. He put down his glass.

He felt a sudden rushing in his head, and a wave of nausea. No, no, no, no, he thought. She was not here. The room had gone hot. She was fifteen thousand miles away, in the United States. He'd heard no helicopter landing. Seen no ship. The National Science Foundation would never let her come here again.

But she wasn't disappearing or turning into somebody else. Robyn Cassidy, flashing that famous smile, sauntered toward him in tight blue jeans, hiking boots, and a turtleneck that on her, as far as Amirault was concerned, could have won the Miss World competition. Those cobalt-blue eyes were locked on him. Floating toward him. Missiles, homing in.

"You have any vodka around here?"

The low, hoarse voice transported him. He felt a stab of pain in his groin, where the rope to Brian had been attached. She was petite but gave the impression of slender pliancy, of long legs. Her hair was blue-black, glossy, and cut very short. Her skin had an animal healthiness to it, accentuated by the sureness of her movements, and her attentive look made him feel clumsy.

"Behind the bar." Amirault waved a hand at the bottles behind him. The dancers were watching. He was amazed his voice sounded normal. "Ice is in the sink."

She jerked, stared into his eyes. "It's you," she said. "That voice . . . I only saw your eyes before, through the mask."

"World's full of surprises," he said.

She grinned. "You look just like I imagined."

She smelled faintly of vanilla, squeezing past, her hip brushing him. Close up she was even lovelier than all those photos in *Glamour, Rolling Stone, Outside, Sports Illustrated*. The pictures had her angles right; the fragile features, washboard body. The looseness in the way she moved. But they only hinted at the vibrancy coming off her. Even when she'd been injured, those big eyes had come at him with hunger. A blast of raw sensuality struck him now.

She stabbed expertly with the pick. A chip flew off the ice block and struck Amirault's cheek.

"I tried to call to say thank you. The National Science Foundation wouldn't give out your number. I wrote you. They said they'd forward the letters."

"They did. I just kept to myself after we got back." He saw himself in the hospital dayroom, reading the powder-blue letters in looping feminine script: Thank you for what you did. I'm sorry about your friend. I never got to eat that Snickers bar. Please write back.

"I never thought it was your fault," he said.

She blushed. It surprised him. She didn't seem like the type who got flustered. The powerful sense of linkage was back. It was as if they knew each other but were strangers at the same time. "People do everything for themselves around here," she said, changing subjects, scooping chips into her Victoria Base souvenir glass.

He thought, Except get themselves off Purgatory Road.

"Why did you come back?" he said.

"To finish what I started!" The awkwardness cleared from her face. "To go up Purgatory Road! But Rick took my skis. My equipment, sled, maps, compass. He stashed them on the *Polar Queen.*"

"Orders, I guess," Amirault said, thinking, What a laugh. Me defending Rick. "It's dangerous."

She was a leaner, bending close when she spoke. Now that they talked politics, the brashness he recognized from TV was back.

"I thought about this trip all year," she said. "Planned it, trained for it. The Greenpeace ship dropped me off and left. Now Purgatory Road is right there and all I can do is look at it. Fifty miles, that's all I have left. It's . . . it's kidnapping! I never started something I didn't finish in my life!"

What she was saying sank in.

"You mean you're going to be *here?*" he said. "Until we leave?"

"If I can't get out, yes."

Amirault drained his drink. His heart slammed in his chest. She said, "You know, an hour before you got there, I looked out the tent and saw a wall of icebergs, floating in the sky. A hundred feet up. The Cliffs of Dover. Total hallucination. Yellow and orange and I thought, Robyn, you messed up. Icebergs in the sky. Then I open my eyes and there's a man in a mask there. But when you actually spoke, I almost jumped out of the bag."

Get away from her, he thought. It didn't seem right to enjoy himself with her. But he couldn't help thinking, I like her mouth. I like her skin. I like the curve of her eyebrows. I like her smell.

"This is smooth," she said, rotating her glass, gazing at the little blue Quonset huts of Victoria Base on the side. "Silky," she said. "You should try that potato drink at the Polish base. They massacre the tripe, but brew a nice vodka. Keep it in the snow outside so it's always cold."

She looked angry suddenly. "Then they follow *orders* and plan how to kill everything in the ocean."

He recognized it as an attack on all of them, on everyone here. "Nice to live in a simple world," he said, passionate about his work as she was. "Bad scientists. Good environmentalists."

Robyn shook her head. "What is it with you people? How do you do it? Just go along with Washington. In the treaty. In everything. Don't rescue her for two days. You saw my tent. I could have died. But you didn't do anything until that storm was coming in."

Startled, Amirault realized she had never heard the whole story. There had been no one to tell her. Base personnel had been warned not to talk. Robyn had been unconscious the whole time. And the NSF had mentioned only that "rescuers" had brought her back.

But he didn't want credit now, not this way.

"I always follow orders," he said.

She eyed him sideways. "One minute. One stupid minute. If I hadn't let myself get distracted for one minute, I wouldn't have hurt my knee."

Amirault took a long drink. "World's fulla ifs."

"World's full of government drones who follow orders and are about to help destroy this place."

"I have some nuclear waste in my room," Amirault said. "Want to help me throw it in the harbor?"

She stared, burst out laughing. "Okay, I'm getting carried away," she said. "I'm pissed off at Rick. I shouldn't take it out on you. It's funny," she said. "I planned what I'd say to you if I ever saw you, but you get in front of a person and they don't do what they're supposed to, the way you saw it in your head. They're not nodding, understanding. Politics. It's easy to show people how you feel about that." She placed her hand on his forearm. "What if I told you I came here—no, *asked* the captain to put in here—because I wanted to say thank you in person."

Amirault remembered the knife as if it were in front of his face, snow slicing across the blade.

"See what I mean?" she said. "You were supposed to say, 'I want to thank you too.'"

"Me thank *you?*" Amirault said.

"You would have gone in."

Amirault snapped, "Boy, the world stops when Robyn Cassidy arrives, doesn't it?"

"I wasn't tied to that rope," she said. "You were."

Evylyn's voice said from behind them, "Isn't this a cheery reunion."

Amirault whirled. His older sister looked nothing like the cute, happy Evylyn in the group picture behind the bar. The Evylyn who'd taught him to drive, shown him how to do math homework, celebrated with him when he'd gotten into Stanford, and when they'd both been accepted to Ellsworth Base. Hair wilder tonight. Face puffy from drinking. Wrecked much of the time this year, but heart-wrenchingly worse on anniversary night.

She said, shoving her face at Robyn, "Still got your knife?"

Robyn yanked her hand off Amirault but Evylyn's gaze remained fixed at the point of contact. Amirault smelled liquor on her breath over popcorn. Sweat. Teriyaki sauce. Spice cider–colored lipstick smeared her upper lip. Amirault grew aware of another odor beneath the rest. A sour tinge of male cologne, perfume, and sweat.

"People are looking for you," Amirault said.

Evylyn pushed up to Robyn. Her face was twisted and blotchy. "You fool other people, but not me," she said.

Robyn recovered nicely, gave her a cool stare, woman against woman, knowing Evylyn had been Brian's lover, emotionless but letting Evylyn know she couldn't be intimidated. Amirault thought, "fooled people"? What's that mean?

Robyn slid off the stool. The chemicals churned inside him. He couldn't help it.

"I'll be around," she told Amirault.

She sauntered away.

"Ami Two, I believe that woman has the hots for you," Evylyn said.

"She was heading to Victoria Station," Amirault said. "The Greenpeace ship dropped her off."

He thought, sick with excitement, Why am I explaining myself?

Evylyn snickered. "Right!" She slid onto Robyn's vacated barstool and the music changed to Enya, a slow tune, lots of grabbing and grinding. A.Y. danced with Robyn. His hands worked down her turtleneck toward her pretty ass. One minute she's furious, the next she's having a party. Two minutes with her and he was a nutcase.

He said, "Rick was looking for you. And Clyde."

Evylyn pulled a tortoiseshell compact from her hip pocket. Her hands weren't steady enough to apply eyeliner properly. She left a smudge over her right eye. She looked like a drunk who'd lurched sideways on Ash Wednesday in church. "Clyde," she snorted, "is nine years old. What are you drinking? That Russian stuff? Egh. Is there any Grand Marnier left? Ami, put it on ice, please. And don't be mad at me."

"You're a little looped, Evylyn."

"Only a little? I have to try harder."

"How about a sandwich instead. If you're going to be a vegetarian for health reasons, you might as well eat some food."

She put a hand on his wrist, where Robyn's had been. "We require a drink," she said, like Queen Victoria.

When Amirault went around the bar to get it, he saw Robyn jitterbugging with Haystack, the big Minnesota carpenter. Clasping her slim waist, Haystack lifted her bodily off the floor, her legs kicking along the side of his hips. Hector shouted, "Go, Robyn." Gail, Cathy, and the others closed in a circle around the couple, clapping.

"You're mad at me," Evylyn said with a phony pout. "You wanted to be with her."

But he couldn't be mad at Evylyn. He knew he sounded like a

boring parent. "I know you hate this kind of talk, but don't you think you're going a little overboard with Rick and Clyde?"

"Give me a break," she snapped. "In two weeks we go back to the mainland. AIDS, syphilis, chlamydia, herpes. Here we're clean, Ami Two. It's like the sixties all over again, or at least what people say it was like. They tested us before we came and you never know when good times can end abruptly, know what I mean? You do know what I mean, don't you?"

He was shocked. She never brought it up. "You had the flu," Amirault said. "You couldn't come with us. You were running a fever. You could barely stand up."

She drained her Grand Marnier and held it out for more.

"No."

"Loosen up," she said. Her features hardened, made her look old. "Memorial service at four o'clock. Big blowout party at seven. Live while you can, Ami Two. If you won't fill it up, I will."

Amirault's head was throbbing. "You look like you're going to be sick."

She slammed the glass down, knocking it over. It rolled on the bar and bounced off the leather bumper. She slid on her stool, but she was just leaning closer.

"We were going to get married. We were going to surprise you. You think Jane's a nice name? Not fashionable, but names go in cycles. Heather. Tabitha. Egh. We wanted a baby."

"Jane's a good name."

"Brian didn't even want to come up with a boy's name. He was sure it would be a girl. He said the mother's personality determined the sex of the baby, and I was too feminine to have a boy. He was *such* a nut."

Her voice had gotten loud and people were looking over. Amirault said, "I miss him too."

"Oh," she said sarcastically. He had never, in all the months, seen her this bad. "You miss him. Did you see him go over?" She leaned so close he saw the pit spots in her skin, where makeup had been applied unevenly. "Did he scream? Could you see his body bouncing? Ping, ping," she said, jerking a hand back and forth like a body hitting walls of ice.

"I told you," Amirault said. "When I got there he was gone."

"But you were glad you hadn't gone in."

"That's right," Amirault said, looking into her face. "I'm still glad." He added, "What's happening here? What happened to you tonight?"

A laugh. "Isn't Brian enough?"

"No. It's something else, too."

She looked frightened suddenly.

Behind them, Hector Carroll said, "Vince Coleman wasn't worth two million. You coulda played better than him, and he was injured most of the time."

Evylyn reached across the bar, crumpled the sports section and waved it in the air. The dancing stopped.

"What do we get from being here?" Evylyn shouted. "Nothing! We're not friends! Lies!" She righted her overturned glass and put it to her mouth and sucked at it, as if she thought there was still liquor in it. She slammed it back on the bar.

"Two million dollars," she said, weaving to her feet. "Two million dollars for playing a game. And what do we get? What do they pay us? Look what we do and we get nothing. Jack finds oil. He won't say it but we know it. Secrets! And now they're firing you after this year. Clyde! Ozone! He'll save a few million people in the end from going blind! Cathy curing cancer! You don't even have tenure! Gail's work'll help space travel. Scientists get nothing! Who cares about us?"

"I'm tired of you," Cathy Quinn called from the pool table. "Every party! 'Poor pitiful me!'"

"Little stupid animals," Evylyn said. "Stupid little animals floating in the sea. Copepods. Who ever even heard of copepods?" They were the creatures she studied. "Who cares why they eat things? *I* don't even care anymore."

"I'll walk you back to your room," Amirault said.

She cried, "We could die and they don't care. Fall in a hole and nobody remembers! *She's* here! Have parties and get drunk, and *don't touch me,*" she cried when Rick tried to put his arm around her. "Mister Limp Dick."

He stepped back, mortified.

Evylyn subsided a little.

Her eyes searched the crowd.

"My head hurts," she said. "Ami Two, take me to my room."

Behind them, as he half steered, half carried her, he was aware of the music turned up. The beat of feet again. Dancing again.

"I didn't mean it," Evylyn said on the stairway, going coherent to incoherent and back again. "I'll apologize to him tomorrow. To everyone tomorrow."

"They don't mind."

"You miss him too. Robyn Cas . . ." She mumbled something he didn't catch, and then: "Locked the doors . . ."

From the ham room came a long burst of static, and a voice, a teenager with a midwestern twang, called, "Ellsworth? Rogers Park, Chicago, calling. Ham patch, guys! I have Kojak's girlfriend on the line."

She shook him off, gathered herself with effort, took on a momentary exaggerated drunken dignity, and tried to walk by herself. "Remember that vacation in New York?"

"Who could forget?"

"You made us stay for all the sets at Bradley's. You got drunk and played the piano and everybody booed."

"You wouldn't leave that condom store in Greenwich Village. Chocolate condoms. Cherry condoms."

"Remember the Chinese wedding in the restaurant on Elizabeth Street?"

"Remember when Brian tried to cook the menu? Worst thing I ever ate. General Brian's Death Pork." They both laughed. "And you blamed yourself."

"I bought the wrong ingredients."

"Evylyn, he wrote the wrong ingredients down for you to buy."

She burst out crying. "I should have known anyway."

She leaned against the wall and sobbed.

After a bit, using all her effort, she said, "I'll apologize to her tomorrow."

"It's fine . . ."

"I don't want to hurt anyone else."

She was almost sick and he got her to the bathroom. He wiped the sweat off her forehead with a damp, cool towel. In her room he got her on the bed. She fumbled with the alarm clock. He took off her shoes and put a blanket over her. She kicked it off.

"Stay with me, Ami. We'll play a game. You pick. We'll play a game."

"Sure."

"We'll play a video game. Return to Zork." A pause. "I didn't mean what I said. You're the best Ami Two in the world. Listen to me." She clutched at him. "You have to forgive yourself."

"What happened to you tonight, Evylyn?"

She nearly knocked the lamp off the night table. The photo of her and Brian, in Washington, crashed down but the glass didn't break. There was a stuffed panda Brian had given her, with a red heart pinned to its chest that said *Love*. There were games on the shelves: Pictionary, Othello, cards, Trivial Pursuit, and piles of video games. There was a mobile of brightly colored tropical fish, and a coleus plant under an ultraviolet light. "Color," Evylyn always said. "There's not enough color here."

She opened her eyes. They looked feverish.

"You find things down there," she said, gripping his wrist. "You don't even tell me. They don't let you talk about it. They made you swear, didn't they?"

He sat there until she started snoring, thirty minutes later.

Amirault turned the thermostat up, if she was going to keep kicking the blanket off. He opened the window a fraction. The digital clock read 1:00 a.m. From outside came the deep, lonely foghorn of the *Polar Queen*, leaving on a two-day research cruise. Only a handful of people remained on base.

As he closed the door she gave a little cry in her sleep, but her mouth was pressed into the mattress.

In his own dream, later, Amirault was back at Stanford, in a bar called Jolly Roger's, with his professor of seismology. The man had bet him it was impossible to determine what kind of rock lay under the ocean just from listening to sound waves. "You need the printout, and even then it's a guess," the professor had said, played tapes of different bottoms, and asked Amirault to identify them. "You lose," the professor had said when Amirault misidentified a uranium deposit as platinum — except two months later, drillers had found platinum at the spot.

The professor lifted a mug of Sam Adams in the dream. "The golden ear, Jack. You have the golden ear."

The professor started screaming.

The sound grew so loud Amirault opened his eyes.

The clock said 3:30. In the hallway outside, a woman was screaming. He yanked the door open and saw people in tee shirts and underwear staggering into the light.

"I saw it," Robyn cried over and over. "It's terrible. I saw it."

Robyn, eyes wild, terrified. Staring into Amirault's face but not seeing him.

"Evylyn's had an accident," Amirault heard Rick Page say.

two

Amirault raced toward the prohibited zone, the rocky mounds abutting the Zodiac dock. He could hardly breathe. *She's in the bay*, Robyn had said. The snow had stopped and rose-colored patches smeared the Prussian blue of the predawn sky.

He heard others coming behind him. Ahead, a warning sign read: "Leopard Seals. Keep Back."

He crested the rocks, almost slipping on a spot where someone had been sick. His heart moved into his throat; he saw a dark orange lump floating in trash six feet offshore, in the dark water. She wasn't moving.

No, no, no, no, no.

Behind him, Rick barked orders. "Get a gaff from the Zodiacs! Get the shotgun!"

But there was no time. In Antarctic waters you had three minutes before the cold reached your veins, stopped your heart forever. Amirault yanked his right boot off. He'd not tied it, not fully dressed, just thrown a parka over his flannel pajamas and grabbed gloves off a shelf near his door.

He didn't feel the shock of snow on his bare foot. But before he could get the other boot off he was seized from behind. As Amirault struggled to reach her, Rick's face loomed. The manager barked, "We don't have time to fight you, too! Look!"

Cutting the water, by the floating ball of fabric, he saw a V-shaped line zeroing in on her. Leopard seal.

Amirault stopped struggling.

The muzzle struck her parka. Amirault winced as fabric ripped. She was only six feet away but she might as well be a thousand. People screamed, "Get away!" waved their arms, tried to frighten the thing, threw rocks at it.

"Put on the fucking boot!" Rick yelled.

Then the eternity passed and Hector was there with the gaffs and the seal sank away, eight hundred pounds of predator circling down there, probably looking up. Trying to gauge the threat. Were these new creatures dangerous, or just noisy?

Amirault grabbed one gaff from Hector's hands and reached to haul Evylyn from the water. But yank too hard and the hook would cut her, or rip free of the jacket. A. Y. Chen ran up with the base shotgun and gave it to Rick. Amirault heard the loud click of shells going in.

Who dumped trash?

A crushed Tang box, a Sprite can, a ball of waxed paper smeared with tomato paste, bobbed near her arm. Laticia's voice gasped, behind him, "Why was she on the rocks?"

No one was supposed to go on the rocks. Ever. Warning signs were posted in the dining room, *Queen*, garage, dorms. "There are better views elsewhere," Lieber had lectured in Washington. "Better hikes on the glacier. Better spots for taking samples. Two years ago a leopard seal broke through the ice and tried to pull a krill researcher named Calvin Obidawa into the harbor. There is never any point to going on the rocks."

Inside he was screaming. *Not again. Not to her.* Balancing on slippery kelp, he and Hector hooked the float-suit at the same time.

"Slow, slowwww." Rick, on the rocks beside them, pressed the shotgun to his shoulder. Eyed the water. "That guy's around here somewhere. Waiting to make his move."

Amirault told himself she still lived. That the miracle had happened. All those stories about people surviving ice water. Metabolism down, drifting in a lifesaving coma, alive, asleep, in suspended animation from which they woke and told stories of seeing bright lights. Pull them out later, an hour even, and incredibly their bodies oozed back to consciousness. Their eyes fluttered open.

Be alive.

Amirault's gaff clattered on the boulders. The rocks slammed his knees as he and Hector dropped down to haul her out. Her head was tilted oddly, face turned away from him. Her weight was incredible, as if they pulled a sand-filled dummy from the sea.

"Oh my God!"

Clyde, on his knees too, helped.

In the distance came a muffled explosion; an ice field collapsing from its own weight on Purgatory Road.

Amirault turned her over and heard Cathy scream behind him. Evylyn's face looked like one of Clyde's lab samples. A lone eyeball stared out from a violent mass of meat and bone.

Suddenly the water by her feet erupted and something burst from the surface, a huge snake head lunging. Teeth slashing at Amirault. He held on tight as the shotgun roared.

The leopard seal, head boiling, sank away, leaving a gauzy red smear on the surface. It had come so close Amirault could still smell its breath on the morning air.

"Get her back!" Clyde shouted with the high pitch of a girl.

The rocks were too sharp to lay her down. They had to carry her to the snow. The crowd fell back. White stuffing wadded from the parka where the seal had bitten through. Her chest wasn't moving.

Oh God, God, the right side of her neck is torn open.

Hector was saying, "No pulse."

One of her hands was only partially attached.

Palms flat, Amirault pushed on her chest to get her breathing. Seawater spilled down her jaw. He tilted her head, lowered his mouth to hers. Hector was giving orders, something about getting oxygen, syringes, blankets.

"Breathe!" Clyde sobbed.

Her chest rose, air dribbled out of her, and Amirault exulted. But it was his own breath, coming back out. Not hers.

Light, at dawn, was a fragile coral color.

Bone bits stuck to Amirault's lip. He spat them out.

He let Hector push him back when the equipment arrived. Watched as the doctor gave her oxygen. Jolted her with electric current. Spoke to Evylyn, gentled her, filling the big hypo. "You can do it. Kick in there. Come on, Evylyn."

Cold sweat poured down Hector's face.

He injected her in the heart.

After a while, he gave up.

In the brightening light Amirault saw that the snow around her had gone orange, stained with seal shit the color of krill.

He did not have to turn to know the hope had run out of them. An inhuman wail erupted. Clyde tore at his face with his bare fingers. As if wanting to pull his eyes out, to eradicate what he saw.

I never took him seriously, that he was in love, Amirault thought.

From one of the islands nearby, in the harbor, elephant seals bellowed. They sounded like a cross between fat men snoring and power mowers starting up.

Hector's face blurred. Amirault realized he was crying.

He was alone and someone was screaming and it was him. The agony was horrible. He had lost his parents a long time ago, his best friend a year ago, and his sister now. Grief was something you never accustomed yourself to. He rocked her, as if it were possible for her to still feel comfort. He had never been so aware of being alive. He felt every muscle, every bone, living. Every breath going out of him. He was cast back into a desolate place at once familiar and alien. He knew that she could not possibly have died, that she was still alive, that the inhuman, torn thing in his hands was not his sister. He knew she was gone forever.

In the darkness Amirault wanted to let himself be swallowed into unconsciousness.

He was aware, at length, that the others had closed around him. They were in a circle around him and they were touching him. Hands on his shoulders and arms and around his neck. Snow was melting on his bare ankles. His pajamas were soaked.

He said, to no one in particular, "She was asleep."

And then the group helped him up and Rick, from far off, was saying they should go in now. Something about Hector autopsying her and people coming back to Rick's office, reporting to him, though that would be hard, so he could figure out what happened. And a group meeting later so they could all learn details.

The group broke into ones and twos. People were crying. Cathy and Amirault helped lift her, carry her to the infirmary. "I'll call you when I'm finished," Hector said, and shooed them out.

They brought Amirault to his room. In the half light of dawn he lay on the bed in his wet pajamas. He was empty. Finished. He should have stayed with her all night, not just until she was asleep. Should have . . . should have . . .

Amirault saw her on a horse in California, waving to him. He saw her as a high school senior, back from the Sonoma prom, with a corsage on her wrist. He saw her from across a table in the Stanford cafeteria, embarrassed but sassy, saying, "You'll never guess who the guy is. Don't even try. It's Brian."

Amirault saw two kids by a willow-lined pond near Napa. The water was green and chalky and cool in summer. There were bologna-and-lettuce sandwiches in Saran wrap on a blanket, and a red thermos filled with punch. He saw his older sister saying, "You and me, Ami Two. It's a pact."

Amirault closed his eyes, did not sleep, was lost in a violent emptiness. Crueler images came now. Imprinted on his retinas was what had just occurred.

At last the anger came, a small relief, and with that, clarity.

He sat up.

Someone had been out there with her.

There was a light tap at the door and the knob turned and Rick announced himself. He apologized for intruding but hoped Amirault would understand. Lieber was the kind of man who insisted on getting bad news right away. Rick had interviewed everyone else and hoped Amirault would be able to answer questions. He was gentle. The antagonism that had marked him before was gone.

It struck Amirault that Rick had probably lost his coveted job this morning. After two deaths in two years, Lieber would blame Rick.

Rick said, "Only eleven people on the base now. Everyone else left on the *Queen*. Nobody saw anything."

"Did you?" Amirault told himself he must not blurt out what he had realized. Not until he knew more.

"I was sleeping."

A ticking began in the back of Amirault's head. He watched Rick carefully. Someone was lying.

He said, "What do you want to know?"

"What she talked about when you took her to her room. And in the pub."

"Why?"

"Her mood. Things that might give a clue as to why she was there. She either fell in or . . . Do you really want to talk about this?"

"You came here."

"Lieber's going to ask if it was intentional."

Amirault said, "She wouldn't kill herself."

"I'm just saying what Lieber'll ask."

She'd said plenty, and Amirault had been going over it. She'd told Robyn, "You don't fool me," and, "Who you gonna kill this year?" She'd called Rick "Mr. Limp Dick." She'd said, "Jack, you find things down there. They make you swear not to tell." She'd said, "I don't want to hurt anyone else." She'd said everything and nothing.

Amirault needed time to think. "She didn't say anything I remember."

Rick thanked Amirault for his time.

"She wouldn't have gone on the rocks," Amirault said.

Rick looked helpless, the silence meaning, What can I say? She was there.

That was when Amirault knew that he had to take a chance and tell Rick. It was crucial to call Lieber and get a real investigator here right away. And Lieber would never believe just Amirault.

Amirault said, "Somebody was with her when she went in."

He kept his voice low and measured. He knew, after last year, that he had to appear calm.

Rick froze. "What do you mean, *when she went in?*"

Amirault felt his heart pounding. "Remember? We were running toward the rocks. I was the first one. I saw her in the water. Someone had been sick on the rocks. It was all over the place. A wave washed it away. Remember? It was there."

"So?"

"There was meat in it."

"Meat."

"She was a vegetarian."

Rick moved gingerly to Brian's bunk and sat down, and they watched each other. From outside, in the hallway, came the sound of someone's stereo, Chen's probably, since the music was Gregorian chants. Rick seemed stunned, skeptical. Had he known this already? Or was he just being careful around Amirault, to keep from upsetting him more?

"Meat."

"That's right. But there's more."

"You actually saw meat in it."

"It didn't register at first. But then I remembered. Half the staff here spend their lives cutting animal stomachs open. We see this stuff all the time."

Rick frowned. "Excuse me, Jack, but we were running. It was dark. You had fractions of seconds. And you were looking at her. Not the rocks."

"You don't believe me?"

"I didn't say that."

"Do you believe me?"

Rick said quietly, "I talked to everyone. Nobody said they were with her." But Amirault detected edginess in the voice. Rick said, "You don't think someone left her there, do you, after she fell in? You're not saying somebody hurt her?"

"I'm saying someone isn't telling the truth. Maybe they didn't hurt her. Maybe they're just afraid; they were with her, she fell, they panicked, they ran. Now they're scared to admit it. But something was wrong with her all night tonight. Something happened to her before the party."

"She told you that?"

"I felt it." Amirault paced. "I want a real investigator. Someone from the Navy. Not us. Someone who knows how to piece together things. Call Lieber."

"Even if you did see meat, how do you know it wasn't from the seal?" Rick asked. "Seals eat meat."

It stopped Amirault. It was a good question. He sent his memory back. Saw the rocks, and Evylyn beyond them, in the water; it was like moving a camera angle, back a little, up a little, magnify the rocks. He saw the lumpy meat. Phlegm. Peas.

Peas.

"It wasn't the seal."

"Okay," Rick said, surprising Amirault. The capitulation came too fast. "We'll call Lieber together after we get the autopsy results. And in case you're wondering why I'm doing this, it's because you'd contact him anyway, so I might as well be there." Which was right. "But I'm warning you. If he asks what I think, I'll tell the truth."

"Call now."

"But . . ."

"Or I will."

Rick rubbed his cheek. "Satellite line's twelve bucks a minute for anyone, when it's working. I can't stop you. He'll ask to talk to me, and I'll tell him what I think."

Amirault called Lieber, who was in his office, the time difference being only two hours this time of year; seven a.m. at Ellsworth Station, nine in D.C. At the moment, the line sounded clear. Lieber offered condolences. "We're not qualified to be looking into what happened," Amirault said.

"Meaning Rick isn't."

"Meaning any of us."

"But specifically in relationship to Rick, why is *he* not qualified?" Lieber said.

"Personal reasons," Amirault said.

Rick squeezed his eyes shut.

Lieber said harshly, "*What* personal reasons?" And when Amirault hesitated, added, "I trust Rick. If I shouldn't, you better spell it out for me."

"Rick had a relationship with her."

"You're suggesting he hurt her?"

"I just want a good look into what happened."

"You're saying he wants to clear it up fast because he's married."

"Yes."

The satellite line was clear for a change, Lieber's voice might have been coming from fifty feet away, not fifteen thousand miles. "You've had a bad shock, Dr. Amirault. I'm very, very sorry. Maybe Hector should give you something, you know, to calm you. But it's none of my business who people sleep with. It happens when you put men and women together for months. It's between you and God. I care about the base running. We've had two dozen bad accidents in the fifty years since we started the Antarctic program. We've never had an attack."

"I guess that makes one impossible," Amirault said.

"Sounds like an accident," Lieber told them. "Poor Evylyn. She was Brian's girlfriend, wasn't she? Rick, keep at it and let me know any developments. Rope the rocks off. We may reexamine the drinking policy. And for God's sake, keep Robyn Cassidy away from things. Lock the labs and offices. We'll wait for the autopsy. Unless Hector comes up with something solid, it's officially an accident. Meanwhile, Jack, why don't you leave the room a bit. I'd like to talk to Rick alone."

"Meat," Rick repeated afterward, coming out of the office, white. Lieber had chewed him out. But there was also a glimmer of triumph in his eyes. He still had his job. "That's disgusting."

Amirault said, "I was there half a minute. I know what I saw."

Rick had a brightness in his face that hadn't been there before. "Lieber suggested we keep this conversation to ourselves."

"I'm not imagining things."

"It's been bad for you, Jack. I lost my brother a couple years back, and it was terrible. We all loved Evylyn. And all Lieber's orders in the world couldn't keep me from going after someone if I really thought they harmed her. I've had my problems with you, but you've suffered enough, so listen. Lieber's not a big fan of yours. He's worried about bad publicity, especially with half the world descending on the Antarctic for the treaty. Control yourself.

Lieber suggested I remind you that we had to restrain you last year."

"Don't threaten me."

Amirault stood outside, on the rocks, by the prohibited zone. He was alone, an hour later, gathering himself. There was nothing to do until the general meeting in ten minutes. He told himself, over his mounting grief, how crucial it would be to stay calm. Rick wouldn't be on his side, and neither would Lieber. He'd have to convince the others alone.

But it was starting again. He'd seen it in Rick's face. He could imagine what Lieber had asked Rick when Amirault had left them. *Is he cracking up again?*

The snow where Evylyn had lain was flattened down by dozens of footsteps. It was impossible to know which ones had been here first.

Amirault heard a crunching and turned to see Clyde shuffling toward him, parka open to his British Army sweater. He never took it off. He probably slept in it. Showered in it. Would grow old in it.

The kid's face was streaked with tear tracks. He looked sucked in. Bonier. Adding years in seconds, like some speeded-up science fiction old man. Wind whipped his straw-colored hair and blew his baggy, Navy-issue camouflage pants against his skinny legs.

Clyde, the perfect little controlled Brit when he'd arrived here. "Pass the steak sauce, please." "Just a small whiskey, thank you." Barely able to walk now. Tottering like a human tropism toward anything that had been part of the woman he'd loved. Her friends. Her room. The water she'd died in.

"It's horrible," Clyde whispered.

"Yes."

They smelled bacon cooking against the smell of fallen snow. They heard, on the wet breeze, the rapid-fire voice of a radio announcer giving the Lee, Massachusetts, morning traffic report. The cook spent all summer back home taping the things. Eighty-five degrees today, clear and sunny, the voice said. An overturned tractor trailer is blocking northbound Route twenty near the Best of Bombay Indian Restaurant. Construction is slowing traffic on the Mass Pike overpass. Stay tuned for the ten a.m. Bob Lundangelo sports call-in show.

"Ever find her, before the party?" Amirault said. Watching.

"What?"

"Evylyn. You were looking for her in my room."

Clyde the Zombie. Voice flat and dead. "She'd been out in the Zodiac. I mean, she wasn't drinking yet then."

Amirault looked up. "Taking samples," Clyde said. "Alone out there. Working all the time. She came back with her jars full of copepods."

"She always was a hard worker."

"I was obnoxious to you in the hall. I'm sorry," said Clyde.

"Don't worry about it."

The sun, beginning its daily circular route around the Antarctic, glistened on the uncoiling black body of a humpback whale breaching in the harbor. It turned the icebergs turquoise and made the water chalky green.

"Who did she go out to meet here, Jack? Do you know?"

Amirault looked up sharply. "How do you know she was meeting someone?"

"Why else would she come?"

Amirault sighed.

"You loved her," Clyde said.

"Yeh."

"Maybe she was already gone when the seal hit. Three minutes," Clyde said. "Maybe she didn't feel it."

"Maybe."

"Tuesday night at Dino's. Crab*mania*," the radio announcer said.

Clyde rubbed his eyes with his sleeve. "She was going to drop Rick," he said. "She told me. It isn't right, sleeping with someone else when you're married." He was rambling. "I was in bed," he said. "Dreaming about her. I woke up and looked out and everyone was running."

Clyde's eyes were wet. "I've been walking. Gym. Wet lab. Ham room. Hot tubs. I know this is stupid. I keep thinking she's going to be there."

"I feel it too," Amirault said.

The kid looked grateful. There was a whooshing noise in the harbor, and now two whales were blowing out there. Big one and little one. Mother and calf.

"You want me to leave?" Clyde said.

"It doesn't make a difference."

"Go ahead. I know you're still loyal to Brian. Tell me if you want me to go."

"Clyde, you want to stay? Stay."

"It didn't even look like her," Clyde said, powerless to stop talking. "Her color. It wasn't even gray. Just . . ." he said, casting about for the right word, "nothing."

Clyde started crying again. But it was soft now, not hysterical. After a few moments he said, "Whenever she told stories, it was always her and you and Brian. She admired you. She said you were tough — what a word, like it's a good thing. That you could go through hardship and still fight. I thought, How can I measure up to you?"

"To me?"

"I know you don't like me, but I understand. I'd feel the same way if I were you."

"I like you," Amirault said, exhausted.

"I was jealous of you," Clyde said. He giggled, a high, hysterical sound. "I still am."

"Jealous."

"That she liked you so much. Even though you're her brother."

"I changed my mind. Go away," Amirault said.

Clyde took a step back. "Go away, Clyde," he echoed. Amirault had never heard bitterness in the boy before. "Go away, Clyde, your father and I have to dress for the party. Go away, Clyde, teacher has a personal life, you know. Go away, Clyde, find another girl or fly off to one of your dreamy fantasies, like Antarctica. Go back to the lab and play with your weather balloons and check for ozone damage. Spend your time with things that can't tell you to go away."

"Damn it, Hector! Say it in English," Rick snapped. "Tell them what happened so we can all understand."

Rick pounded the dining room table, sending a flurry of papers into the air. The mess seemed oddly empty with only eleven people in it, squeezed into two tables. They sat waiting for the autopsy results. Coffee mugs steamed in front of Gail and Laticia. At the smoking table, in back, Chen lit up.

"None of this medical jargon," Rick said. "Tell us everything. I want all questions out of the way now."

Hector exhaled. He exuded a tired, disheveled sadness. He had not shaved this morning; his eyes were red.

"Sorry. It's easier to give bad news this way. Makes the pain distant for the doctor. But of course, crueler for everyone else.

"Plain English. Near as I can tell, she died about three. She was alive when she went in. I found water in her lungs. And the blood she lost from seal bites flowed freely. I'd say she was also alive when it hit. Cause of death . . ." Hector glanced at Amirault. "Shock. Cold. Terror."

Amirault pictured the cold dark water, forms tumbling over each other. He remembered the seal coming at him this morning, on the rocks.

"There was a lot of alcohol in her blood. She was very drunk. I found a pattern of bruises on her right arm and temple, consistent with hitting the rocks when she slipped."

Slipped, Amirault thought.

Rick stood off to the side, arms folded. He said, "If anyone has questions, now's the time." His subdued manner gave no hint of what he might feel inside. He was a good administrator, whatever his personal faults. "It's been tough on all of us, and I don't want Hector to spend the next few days giving the same answers."

His gaze settled on Amirault, then flicked away. "Well?"

Clyde cleared his throat, at the far end of Gail Rivkin's table. From his red nose it looked as though he'd been crying all morning. "How much did it hurt?" he asked.

Hector looked pained. "We'll never know. The seal didn't pull her in, or there would have been bite marks on her ankle. So it's a question of how long she was in there before the thing hit. I'd like to think she was numb, even unconscious. Plus the alcohol would have acted as anesthesia. The seal must have been attracted by the trash."

Amirault looked up sharply. He spotted Robyn at the other table. Small and alone, wedged between Kojak and Haystack. Staring back.

"But it hurt," Clyde whispered. His shoulders started moving. Gail Rivkin massaged them.

Amirault spoke up. "What had she eaten?"

Irritated murmuring broke out around him. To them it was a pointless, offensive question, a scientific inquiry in a time of grief.

Hector replied, "She'd been sick. Her stomach was empty."

Here goes. In a loud controlled voice he announced, "Somebody was with her, on the rocks."

The room erupted. "Who?" "What do you mean?" "You mean somebody left her there?"

Rick yelled for quiet, but the room had grown tense. "Jack has a theory," he said. "Tell them what you think." Amirault did and the buzzing broke out again. Rick said, "Hector? Did you have the impression she'd been in a fight?"

"No."

Rick pulled pensively at the skin around his lower jaw. "Anyone want to tell us something? Was anyone sick out there? Robyn, you? You see an extra pair of footprints? Were you sick on the rocks?"

Nothing.

Rick nodded. "Tell you what," he announced to all of them. "Anyone wants to come to me privately, tell me something, I'll keep it quiet. That's a promise." But Amirault knew he was only saying it for his benefit. "Meanwhile, Jack, let's drop this for a while."

"What do you mean, drop it?"

He saw the trapped feeling in their faces. Gail watched him, fascinated. Laticia shook her head: *You'll never learn.* Hector looked concerned; Chen stared emotionlessly, eyes huge in those bottleneck glasses. Cathy Quinn's lower lip was out, like a five-year-old. She said, "Oh Jack, you loved her so much."

"I'm not imagining this."

He felt Cathy's hand slide along his neck, begin rubbing him.

As if by unspoken agreement the meeting began breaking up. "I'm not kidding," he said as they rose, pushed back chairs. "What are you going to do, just walk out of here?"

He knew he was blowing it. Losing his temper.

"I say we make Lieber call the Navy, get an investigator!"

"We went through this," Rick said kindly, as if Amirault had forgotten it, and hadn't the brain capacity to remember simple things. Was there a hint of victory there too? "She was drinking," Rick said. "She went out there. She was upset. She slipped."

Amirault said, "She wouldn't go on the rocks, no matter how drunk she was. Give me some credit for knowing my sister better than you."

He scanned the sullen, fearful faces, looking for a glance, a hunched back, a quick exit, anything suspicious.

He pled with them. "If Lieber won't send someone, let's find out what happened ourselves!"

"We did find out," Cathy said softly. "We've been in with Rick all morning. Come on. You want to take a walk or something?"

"I don't need a *walk!*"

Laticia voiced what he knew they were all thinking, her voice laced with phony pity. "Of course you think there's more to it than just an accident. After what happened last year."

They were gone then and the depression that he had been battling clamped down on him. He sat, aching for her. Knowing he would never depend on his sister's faith in him again, only a memory of it. He heard a squeak and looked up to see Robyn Cassidy in the doorway, regarding him with an unreadable expression. All he felt was surprise that another person was still here.

"I'm really sorry."

"Yeah."

"It . . . it was the worst thing I ever saw. Maybe I just didn't see those things you did."

He heard Evylyn saying to Robyn, *You fool everyone else, but you don't fool me.*

The silence spread out. She'd changed since this morning into clothes that gave her a fresh, softer appearance. White cashmere sweater which outlined her small breasts. Silver necklace with pendant of breaching whale. Stonewashed jeans and soft leather hiking boots; she had small feet. Some people are at home instantly, anywhere.

Amirault said, "Aren't you scared to be here alone with me?"

"I've been there before."

"What were you doing, anyway, out there at three-thirty?"

A defensive flush suffused her face but she suppressed whatever she was going to say, whether from secrecy or consideration, he did not know. "Nothing. Thinking. I was looking at the harbor. It felt good to be off the ship."

"Thinking," Amirault repeated. "Walking around, at three-thirty a.m., thinking."

Robyn smiled. "Do you think on a schedule? With me, it comes any old time." She shrugged. "And let's face it. I know I'm not supposed to be on the property unescorted. So it was better to do my walking when everyone else was asleep."

He saw Evylyn, in his head, fumbling for her alarm clock. If she'd set the clock, and hadn't had an experiment scheduled, that would prove she'd met someone out there.

If the alarm went off why didn't it wake Cathy?

"What did you tell Rick you saw?" Amirault asked.

"I saw garbage in the water. It made me mad. It must have been dumped from the *Queen*. There's no need to dump it. And there's leakage from your fuel tanks. The bottom's corroded." She frowned. "If you have money for parties, you should be able to fix your stupid tank."

Her two minutes of sympathy were up and she was back on her pet subject. Amirault said, "You were walking around checking the station. Finding things to expose to the press."

She sat down at the far end of the table. "Of course I was. There's only nine days left to stop that treaty." She stopped, reining in the politics. But Amirault wanted to keep her talking. "No," he said. "Tell me."

"I'll show you. But do you really want to do this now?"

Maybe it'll have something to do with Evylyn, he thought.

They got parkas. Outside the sun was up. Laticia was walking around near the Dan Ryan Expressway, bending over occasionally and probing in the snow. White, puffy clouds moved so quickly across the blue sky they seemed propelled by a force greater than wind.

"You want help?" Robyn asked as they walked toward the dock. "Checking them out? You're going to do it, aren't you?"

"Maybe."

"How? Make a list? Find out what they were doing? One by one?"

Amirault's throat was dry. "Why would you help?"

"Well," Robyn considered, gazing out at the harbor. "You might say I owe you one. You might say I have a slightly different view of what you did last year than they do. That I trust the way you see things more."

"And I might say you want something in return."

"Help me get my equipment back so I can go up Purgatory Road."

Laticia came up to them. "Jack, remember those little bear earrings? The silver ones. One must have fallen off last night. If either of you see it, it's mine."

Sensitivity had never been her strong point.

"Fallen off *when* last night?" Amirault said.

"Don't start," Laticia said, and moved off.

Amirault watched Robyn's face, trying to figure out what he saw there. He couldn't tell.

"When I was sixteen," she said, walking, calm, feminine, "I used to go out on the Pacific by myself. I'd take a boat and go out off Southern California, way out, and dive. I learned to dive early. If you don't want to hear this . . . if you're too upset . . ."

"Tell me."

"One day I was down there and the most beautiful thing happened. I was surrounded by a school of enormous fish. Silver. Flashing all around me. Magnified in the water. Hanging there, like we were in the air."

They reached the empty dock. No one would work today. She held out a hand for his help, balancing, while she climbed down into a Zodiac boat. There did not seem to be any seals around.

Even through the two mittens, the pressure of her small fingers sent a jolt of energy into Amirault. She looked up at him, face open. She said, "After a few minutes, the fish began to speed up.

"Suddenly they were crashing into each other, and into me. I was terrified. They almost knocked my air tank off. Something hit me in the back. And then I was being pulled into that mass of fish. Get in."

Amirault climbed down into the Zodiac with her. The boat rocked a little. At this angle, the high bank blocked the base off from view. He experienced a brief sense of freedom.

"I was in a tuna net," she said. "I was hauled out of the water. Those fish were crushing me, cutting me. Their spines. I couldn't breathe. A real holistic experience," she said bitterly. "Air animal and sea animal, running out of oxygen at the same time.

"Then the net spilled us out and I lay on the deck of a boat. And all these men ran to me, while everything else was dying around me. But me, the human, the creature like them, that was the only important thing to them. The death on that boat. The blood on that boat." She shuddered.

Already, in just five minutes, the sky had gone whiter. The counterclockwise coastal winds of Antarctica altered weather faster than anywhere else in the world, Lieber had said.

She said, "I was on that boat a week. Till their holds bulged with tuna and dolphin. When I got back, I went to the newspaper in Santa Barbara. No one wanted to write what I'd seen. They thought I made it up. Same with radio and TV. I handed out brochures in a supermarket. The guard chased me away. I posted notices on telephone poles. Finally I put on a bikini and stood on the dock with a sign that said 'Killers.' Everyone showed up then, cameras, reporters. Put on the bikini, they didn't care about facts anymore."

"Meaning do anything to get what you want, say anything, try anything."

"Yes."

"What did you want to show me?" he said.

"That," she said, pointing at the pristine harbor. "And that." She craned to see the man-made base. "You people here — you said it was okay to talk about this — you're the ones who are going to wreck it. You're the ones giving out information. Making governments hungry for this place."

Amirault scraped ice off the side of the Zodiac, and bunched it in his fist. "It's ice," he said. "It's dead. It was never alive in the first place. It's ice."

"Oh, you know better than that," she said.

He had a terrified feeling suddenly. There was something in her face, her tone, in the way she looked at him that pulled his secrets toward the light. Not the easy secrets, the work secrets. Not the promises he'd made to the three captains in the windowless room in Washington. But the secrets he wasn't sure he knew himself.

Amirault didn't understand if this was the rare thing in her he'd detected from the beginning. He didn't know if it was a talent or an accident of chemistry. He didn't know if he trusted her, and when he turned the feeling over in his logical mind, he found he didn't trust her at all.

It reminded him of something Evylyn had once told him, after she'd been to a political rally, met their senator, talked to him as they ate barbecue.

"I know it's bullshit," Evylyn had said. "But during those three minutes he talked to me, he really made me feel like the only person in the world. And I know he forgot me right after."

Robyn said, "If we can show people what really goes on here, on this base, the secrets, maybe there's still a chance to stop that new treaty."

"But secret things don't go on here," Amirault said.

She grinned up at him. "You know better than that."

He was weary of the politics. "This talk isn't going to have anything to do with Evylyn, is it?"

"I thought you knew that." She hesitated, but drove on. "With the right information maybe we can break up the minerals meeting."

Despite the events of the morning, Amirault broke out laughing. "We," he said. "All that talk and you don't have any facts at all. And even if there was something to find, you think it would change anyone's mind? Those diplomats don't care about us. The treaty's going through."

He was surprised to find himself disappointed. He'd liked it better thinking she'd come to see him.

"Amirault, who do you think will ultimately use the information you gather on the sea bottom? High school students? No, men with oil drills. That's who."

"I work for the Navy. They use my maps for navigation. Submarines."

She laughed. "Since when do submarines need to know what's under the ground?"

"You know a lot about what I do."

"People call us up at Greenpeace and tell us things. People who work for the government, even. They like to stay anonymous. But they have concerns."

"Concerns about Evylyn?"

She hesitated. He had a feeling she was deciding whether or not to tell the truth. "Concerns about you."

Amirault watched her eyes, tried to analyze them. That peculiar sense of linkage he felt with her grew stronger when she called him by his last name. But it was a lie.

"Did you talk to her last night? On the rocks?" he said.

"No."

Evylyn's voice, in his head, said, *Robyn Cassidy . . . Something wrong . . .*

"You didn't come back here to say thanks to me," Amirault said. "You're here to steal things."

"You can't steal what you paid for yourself," Robyn said. "I pay taxes."

Amirault flashed to Evylyn suddenly, in bed, saying, *They tell you not to say things.*

Robyn got out of the Zodiac. "There's something else you should remember," she said. "If someone really hurt her, you just announced that you know about it."

"Good."

"They'll be watching you, too, now."

"Good!"

"Good?" She kept smiling. It seemed to amuse her. "Good?"

The room was dark except for a Tensor lamp which cast a bright cone of light on a steel desk, the edge of a blotter, a computer keyboard, a pencil holder that used to be a can for Green Giant peas. The figure locked the door and moved swiftly to the computer. It was an hour after Amirault's conversation with Robyn, and from outside came the growl of the snowplow.

The lab area was deserted. Fingers moved into the light and turned on the computer.

Worked swiftly.

E-MAIL. The blue glowing letters swam up on screen.

The fingers typed, HE'S FIGURING IT OUT. Then pressed the send key.

Drummed, waiting for an answer. Two minutes later the screen blinked. YOU HAVE MAIL.

THEN STOP HIM, the message read.

three

The lights burned down on Amirault and he hoped the officers wouldn't take his grant away. The Pentagon room was small, bare, and windowless, with all the personality of a cardboard box. Three Navy captains scowled at him from behind a conference table, the women occupying the left and center seats, the man on the right.

"I hope you didn't tell anyone we called," said the captain in the middle.

"No."

It was a week before Amirault's first trip to the Antarctic. He'd come to Washington for introductory seminars at the NSF; Nothing about Pentagon meetings. But then his phone had rung in the Georgetown University guest center at eleven-thirty last night.

"Eight a.m. Be prompt," the crisp voice had ordered.

Behind the officers were color photos of the smiling President and a frowning admiral with silver hair. Amirault's back hurt. He was thirsty. But no one offered him a drink from the water pitcher on the table. He racked his brain to think what he could have done wrong.

"Thanks for coming in for this little chat," the captain in the center said. She was a black woman in a pressed uniform, and she spoke with a pronounced southern drawl. "We've had a leak, Dr. Amirault."

"Leak?" He envisioned a faucet. Then he went weak.

"A small leak," she said, but they looked too concerned for this to be something minor. "Details of a project we would have rather kept in-house. Did you read the *Post* today?"

"I haven't talked to journalists," said Amirault, who'd not read the papers. Denials made you sound guilty. He remembered Nixon, in old news footage, saying, "I am not a crook."

The man, older than the other two, wrote steadily in a leather notebook. The woman on the left leaned toward Amirault on her elbows as if to get a better view.

The speaker wore more decorations and was small and pretty in a sinewy way beneath her Navy blues.

"We called you in," she said stiffly, "to remind you of our agreement. The Navy owns your research. Don't share results with anyone. Not best friends, lovers, co-workers. Even your sister, who we understand will be on your base."

"You know she'll be there too?"

The captain smiled, liking the power that came from knowing things that made other people squirm.

But this only irritated Amirault, who saw the warning as ridiculous. "But we've already spent the last three days giving presentations to each other on our work. And anyone can learn it, at least the subjects, by reading the NSF catalog. If you're worried about leaks, why let that go on?"

Government, he thought. If you're going to kick me out, just do it.

But the speaker nodded wryly. Amirault was surprised to see she shared his view. "You're right, but we sometimes work at cross-purposes," she said. "Congress wants disclosure. We prefer things circumspect. The subject of your work is public. Results are not."

The woman to her left was taller, pale-skinned and blond, wearing small pieces of jewelry: tiny pearl earrings, thin wedding band, gold-banded watch. She seemed less severe than the others, more academic. But Amirault had no illusions.

"Scientists in Antarctica are in a . . ." She paused, needing a word, which the man provided: "Gray area."

"Yes. Your work isn't top-secret but it's valuable. And remember, people on Antarctic bases don't need top security clearance to get there."

"What are you saying? *Spies?*"

"Scientists. Visitors. Ship crews. Spies," she said, "is a strong word. Let's not talk about spies, but how things work." She poured herself a glass of water. Ice in the pitcher tinkled against glass.

"North Korea. How do you think a scientist gets out of North Korea? Do you think critics get visas? Who gets visas? Japan. Close ties exist between government and industry in Japan." The other captains nodded. "And in other countries."

"Then why allow them on our bases?"

"Because the treaty says so. Dr. Amirault, the composition of the sea bottom is strategic information. You have a special talent. You find things other people don't. Your maps allow submarines safe passage. Believe me, a lot of people would be very happy to learn what you know." She held up her hands, changing tactics, becoming friendly, conspiratorial, an ally. Or were they just trying to get him to relax and trip himself up?

"We're not accusing anyone of *spying*. If we really thought that, we'd bar them, okay? But our job is to make sure it stays that way. We called you in to remind you, as long as we fund you, you will observe safeguards. Don't publicize results. In fact, we'd appreciate it if you don't mention our little chat today."

Amirault thought, Fuck the little chat. You called me in to scare me. He said, goading them, "Isn't withholding research against the spirit of the treaty?"

The captain on the right stopped writing and looked up sharply. Amirault wondered if they divided up roles, or if they came naturally. The inquisitor. The recorder. The explainer, who said, "The treaty says *governments* share results with each other. It doesn't give timetables. We pay for your work. *We* get results first. We'll share them in the end."

Amirault bit back, "When? In twenty years?"

The inquisitor said, in a low, pinched tone, "Dr. Amirault, you've gotten two hundred thousand dollars from us, over four hundred applicants. Didn't you ever ask yourself why? You scientists are funny. You don't like to think about practical applications. You like basic questions. But all science has practical applications in the end. More and more the Navy has to justify projects to Congress. If you want our money, it isn't enough to study the life cycle of the doohickey anymore."

"If you have to know answers before you start studying, there's a lot of valuable stuff you'll never learn," Amirault said.

Amirault had a vision of the other Ellsworthites called in here, crammed into the little chair, under hot lights, a parade of intimidated researchers. The panel doing its tough guy/nice guy routine. The explainer said, "Humor me."

She sipped water. Amirault's kidneys burned. "Imagine Antarctica. A hostile environment. Twenty-six countries set up bases there. We're all friends at the moment, unprecedented cooperation, blueprint for the future, wonderful wonderful, just like Robyn Cassidy says, peaceful blah blah blah. But we're also aware one day that might change. We might decide to carve it up. Slice off one coast for Britain. Next for the Ukraine. We're all running out of resources at home and Antarctica has them."

She sipped water. Amirault sensed they enjoyed making him wait for their verdict. "Keeping these eventualities in mind," she said, "we all act like friends — no, really are friends. We help each other, work with each other. We honor the letter of the treaty. No major top-secret work going on, like the environmentalists claim."

The man, who Amirault decided was old for his rank, said, "They're paranoid nuts."

Are you going to let me go or not? Amirault thought.

"But," she said, "that doesn't mean things aren't proprietary. We hold a little back. Everyone does. Believe me, the Italian Antarctic Survey people have bottom maps. So do the French, Japan, all of us. Of course you'll like to talk about your work, up to a point. We understand it's even part of socializing down there. Giving periodic presentations to keep the others up on what you do. We're not saying don't do it. We're just asking you, since we're paying for your research, not to share results prematurely. Not to go out of your way to broadcast them. If you have trouble with that we'd like to know now."

"No."

"Good. By the way, we know you weren't the leaker. The leaker was on a different base. The leaker is gone."

"Politics isn't my department," Amirault said. He felt them already getting interested in the next case, the next victim. He wondered if there had been any leak. Maybe it had all been a scare tactic. But he was relieved.

I still get to go, he thought.

"What the hell are you doing?" Amirault said.

It was the next morning. Rick jerked up and whirled and stepped back quickly from Evylyn's desk. The top drawer hung open. He'd been rifling the contents. Papers were strewn on the blotter, a notebook was open, a lower drawer had not been closed. The books on her shelf, usually lined straight, looked ragged.

Rick stood, turning crimson, in the narrow aisle separating Cathy's neatly made bed from Evylyn's rumpled one. As if Amirault's sister had gone to the bathroom and might momentarily return.

Amirault glanced at her night table, where she'd fumbled with her alarm clock last night. He'd come here to see what time she'd set it for. It wasn't there.

His gaze traveled down Rick's arm to two watermelon-colored envelopes in his hand.

"Are those hers?" Amirault demanded.

"Sorry, I have to keep everyone out of her room," Rick said.

"*Personal letters?*"

"You'll have to leave."

But Rick made no move to resist when Amirault snatched away the envelopes, both addressed in Evylyn's neat, looped hand. The first to his aunt and uncle in Sonoma, stamped with the base logo —a grinning penguin wearing a ski hat, standing on the Antarctic Peninsula, webbed feet on Purgatory Road.

"I need those to wrap up my report," Rick said defensively.

"You said the investigation was over."

"*You* said you wanted it to go on."

"Since when do you do anything I want?"

A dazzling column of sunlight slanted in through the window, infusing drifting motes of dust between them with a golden glow. The left side of Rick's face had a halo. It made it hard to see his left eye. On the right side, the cheekbone seemed blunter, the muscles slack, a dead look in the brown eye.

Amirault said, "Her things."

"I need those back. They might give us some idea why she was upset."

From the corridor outside, Amirault heard a radio. An announcer saying, "I'm standing on the Antarctic Peninsula. At Britain's Victoria Base, where dozens of prefab houses have been erected to hold diplomats from forty-two nations, twenty-six voting members, sixteen consultants already arriving for a historical minerals meeting scheduled to begin four days from now. . . ."

Rick took half a step toward him, immersing his whole face in the sunshaft. "You have to trust me, Jack."

Amirault laughed. As he tore open the first envelope and unfolded the letter, Rick came closer but stopped, unsure what to do.

Amirault scanned the letter.

"Dear Aunt Celia," it read. "I'm having an okay time this year. Work's good. I miss Brian. I'm happy Jack's here, and, in the long run, glad Laticia left him. She's SUCH a bitch . . ."

He couldn't speak, suddenly. It was like hearing her talk, with lots of exclamation marks and dots between sentences, breathless little rushes of enthusiasm.

Then the pain came crashing in.

He regarded Rick over the top of the stationery. There was a faint whiff of Obsession from it; Evylyn's perfume.

"You don't give a damn about what happened to her," Amirault said. "You just want to see if there's anything in here about you."

"That isn't true." But Rick looked frightened.

Amirault forced the emotion from his face. He let his eyes drift down to the stationery. "And I can see why," he lied, to see what Rick would do.

Rick grabbed for the letter but Amirault whipped it away, folded it, and shoved it in his pocket. For a second, there was a look of desperation on Rick's face. A palpable air of violence hung between them in the room.

Then Rick said, miserably, "What are you going to do with those?"

Amirault said nothing, not wanting to make a mistake, wanting Rick to think that something he feared was in the letter. He scanned Rick's pockets, looking for bulges, hints that he'd taken anything else. Amirault saw no evidence of it. And the clock was too big to fit in a pocket.

But he'd read nothing useful. She missed Brian terribly. She dreaded the upcoming anniversary. She was "seeing" a couple of guys on base. She was looking forward to chatting with their aunt on the ham radio next Tuesday night.

At that moment, Amirault felt another presence in the room. A sense of malevolence, a residue of hatred as clear and undeniable as when he listened to sounds on his tapes. It was so tangible it was almost a smell.

He knew he should push away his anger and try to think clearly. Rick's invasion here might be nothing more than the act of a frightened but innocent man.

The radio announcer said, "The harbor is filled with ships of many nations, and private boats belonging to industrialists and oil companies. All of them converging on one of the most isolated spots on earth . . ."

"I want to see your report to Lieber," Amirault said.

"You know I can't do that."

"I don't 'know' anything. You're not a policeman. There's no crime, you say. I'm her brother. You can do whatever you want." He envisioned the file cabinets in Rick's office, filled with person-nel information, profiles, medical records, performance notations. And every interview Rick had done.

"Don't be so paranoid," Rick said. Amirault, trying to read his expression, thought how a face was nothing more than moldable epidermis. Ruled by hidden muscles working beneath.

He froze. He thought he'd detected a movement from the hall-way outside the door. He cocked his head and listened, but heard nothing more.

"I'll trade you. Her letters for your files," Amirault said, thinking, After I read them first . . .

Sweat popped out on Rick's forehead. "I can't." But he was weakening. Amirault sat on Evylyn's bed, crossed his legs, and waited while the manager's face went from fear to craftiness to surrender.

"You're right. I wanted to know if there's something about me in there," Rick said. "I love my wife."

Amirault shrugged.

"I met a woman three years ago. My wife caught me." Rick's jaw muscles knotted. "I promised her I'd never . . . do it again."

The radio said, ". . . with me is Wu Kai Nung, a former Washington-based diplomat for the People's Republic of China, now the Antarctic treaty representative from that country. Any change to the existing treaty must be by unanimous vote, isn't that right, Mr. Wu?"

The room seemed to have shrunk and grown warmer. Amirault welcomed the confession but felt sordid hearing it. It made their quarrel useless, and wouldn't bring Evylyn back to life. He wanted to get her back to Sonoma, away from this probing. From Rick, Lieber, all of them.

"Mr. Wu," the announcer said, "I wonder if you'd also comment on reports that some countries may already have violated the existing treaty by withholding information about valuable mineral deposits, so they can claim those areas for themselves . . ."

Rick looked exhausted. "I started out as a carpenter's apprentice," he said. "I worked for dog shit wages. I couldn't get in the union. We lived in a trailer." His color began returning. "We had kids. And then I found out from a friend about jobs in Antarctica. Double wages, good benefits, you could even have the money paid directly into a fund. It took me two years to get here, and two more to be a full carpenter. I worked my ass off to become manager. This job is my kids' future. It's a house for us. I feel terrible about Evylyn. I do. I know you think I'm being callous. *But this is the best job I ever had.*"

"Congratulations."

Rick was sweating freely. *"No one saw anything out there.* They're observant people. They observe for a living. They loved her too. You're making things worse."

But the accusation amused Amirault. "You going straight home when we're finished, Rick? After we get to Punta Arenas? Flying straight to Idaho? Or meeting your wife somewhere first, little romantic interlude. Champagne, hot shower, daiquiris. Get to know each other again before going home to kids, bills, busted washing machine."

"You're out of line," Rick said.

Amirault said, "What'll you tell her? You have one of those honest marriages? 'Honey, I was screwing one of the scientists, but you're the one I love'? 'I did it to pass the time. It was nothing meaningful'?"

Rick stood up.

Amirault said, "I want to see the report. A brother has the right. We're *not* the same. The best I can say about you, the *best*, is that you want to close it up and keep yourself out of it. Or is it more than that? She was 'upset'? Isn't that the way you put it? You including her sex life in your report?"

"What happened between us doesn't affect anything."

"It did if you're speculating on her mental state."

". . . and what about charges that once the minerals accord is dismantled, several small countries plan to push for nuclear testing in Antarctica?" the radio announcer said.

The sound of elephant seals bellowing came faintly over the radio.

Rick had gone purple. "All right. I was looking for her when I saw you last night, but I never found her. She was in the Zodiac, collecting samples . . ."

Clyde had told Amirault this much already.

"And after that she was with Clyde."

Amirault straightened. "How do you know?"

Rick's fists were clenched. For an instant it was the memory infuriating him, not Amirault. "He was waiting at the dock for her. They went to his room. I followed them." Rick's face looked distorted, vindictive. "I heard them in there, laughing. Fucking and opening wine and playing Mario Brothers."

"You were listening at her door?" Amirault said.

Rick looked mortified. "Laughing at me," he whispered. "I wanted to kill them both."

He stood up stiffly and went to the desk and scrawled something on a piece of paper.

"My wife's phone number. Go fuck yourself, Jack. But I'm not giving you any files."

He slammed the door going out.

Amirault's stomach seemed to have shrunk to a small, hard ball.

I'm Evylyn, he thought. It's three a.m. The alarm clock goes off. I'm drunk and I've only slept an hour. I'm groggy and dressing, bumping into things. I put on a float-suit instead of a parka, because I know I'm going near the water. I've been upset all night. *Something special happened.* It's not just Brian. It's something else.

I bump into Cathy's bed.

How come she didn't wake up? How come the alarm didn't wake her?

Where *is* the alarm clock?

It wasn't on the shelves and desktops, or behind the night table. Other than a wire from the lamp, going into the socket, he saw nothing on the floor.

"The only country still holding out against voting for the change is New Zealand," the diplomat Wu was saying in perfect English. "More developed countries will need the minerals here to maintain their place in the world for the next hundred years, as supplies run out elsewhere. Otherwise they will be blackmailed more and more; for oil, gas, steel. Less developed countries deserve a stake too. New Zealand must be convinced to go along."

"I don't know anything about her clock. But I'm glad you're here. I have to talk to you."

Amirault advanced into Cathy's lab, where she'd been working to a soft, crooning blues tape. A male vocalist sang, "Love me, love me, please love me, please love me." Cathy wore a white frock in her lab, with pens in the pockets. Her hair was up, and her oversized, peach-framed glasses gave her a shiny, excited look.

"This could be it, Jack," she whispered. "After eight years. Oh God. This might really do it!"

"You found a cure?"

"We'll know in ten minutes, but there was activity yesterday. I covered the dish or I'd keep looking at it every five minutes. I'm not going to check until the forty-eight hours are up. Wait with me. I want someone to be with me. A friend. You."

The room was standard: a clutter of sinks and tissue grinders, books, science journals, binocular microscope, slides, flasks, culture dishes, vials, notebooks, dissection kit.

There was a refrigerator in a corner marked with the bright red and white three-ringed *Biohazard* sticker. Inside would be racks filled with live cancers.

"Enough to kill everyone in New York," Cathy said.

He looked into her eager, open face and wondered again how she could have slept through all the commotion from Evylyn. He joined her peering into a containment box, a glass, vacuum-sealed compartment the size of a file cabinet drawer, where she experimented on the viruses with compounds she created from the tissue of dead ice fish.

Two petri dishes sat in the box. A piece of green plastic, folded like a tent, covered a third.

It was funny, he thought, that cancer could be innocent. But there was something purer, less bitter and deceitful, in Cathy's fight. The antagonist was obvious. You knew what it was.

"What kind of cancer?"

"Breast."

"*Love me, love me, oh please love me,*" the man on the tape sang.

"Is that why you wanted to talk to me?" Amirault said. "To show me this?"

"No. I've been thinking about what you said upstairs. I want to help."

A ticking began in the back of his head. Between Cathy and Robyn, that made two offers in two hours.

"Why?"

"You look suspicious! Because the worst thing for you is to feel alone, and that's what's happened, isn't it? You're angry and hurt and you feel like the whole world is against you. I'll tell you right out, I don't believe anyone hurt her. But I'm not afraid to look into it, and besides," she said, touching her upper lip with the tip of her tongue, showing a hint of nervousness, "there's Kronsky."

At the mention of the Russian name, Amirault remembered Lieber's awful warning speech in Washington. The sobering reminder, amid happy travel arrangements, of what the continent could do.

He was transported back, sitting in the dark auditorium, lights of slides playing across his face. He saw a Quonset hut on fire. Black smoke against white. Timbers smoldering. Soldiers running with burn victims on stretchers to helicopters.

He saw a row of tilting crosses, in the snow, with the gutted wreckage behind.

"To his friends and co-workers, Kronsky seemed normal," Lieber had said. "None of them sensed the terrible forces ripping him apart."

"I dismissed what you said before but then I thought," Cathy said, "isn't this exactly the kind of situation Lieber warned us about? Kronsky, an engineer, an Antarctic veteran, a man everyone likes. A man with a secret problem. A wife cheating on him at home, writing him letters about it. A man who blames his job."

Amirault remembered the story as she recounted it. "At first little things go wrong on the base. A radio breaks. Some toilets stop flushing. Then the lights on one side of their runway go out when the supply plane comes in. Finally a cook goes downstairs to get borscht one night and finds Kronsky setting fire to the galley. He's piled his clothing on the floor and soaked it with kerosene. It's too late to stop him. Three men die."

"Let's face it," Cathy said. "We laughed at those stories, but Kronsky happened because people ignored warning signs. If someone really hurt her, if we have some crazy here, I don't want to be the one standing out in a storm watching my base burn down."

"Five more minutes," Amirault said, looking into the box, "to the Nobel Prize."

They were both aware of the red second hand on her World Wildlife Fund wall clock creeping in an arc between the one and the two.

Cathy seated herself in front of the box. Her slender fingers trembled as she operated brass levers to lift up, by robot hand, one of the dishes. It was shaped like a cassette tape, lined by three rows of glass wells with cottony pink fuzz growing inside.

"Lymph cancer in the first row. Prostate in the second. Hodgkins has that bluish tinge. Buy a little human tissue. Sprinkle the viruses in the wells, like seeds. Two weeks, they're coming up like corn in July. Tell me what you're thinking about Evylyn."

He seated himself on a stool beside her. Cathy emitted a faint lemony smell mixed with the less pleasant aroma of formaldehyde.

"I keep going back to the rocks. She either met someone there, or walked there with them. She knew she was going beforehand, because she wore a float-suit, not a parka. Why the rocks?"

She gave him a listening, trusting look. It was nice to be able to talk about it.

"To look at something?" she said.

"Like what?"

"I don't know. The trash? She was pissed off somebody dumped garbage from the ship?"

Cathy got off the stool, glanced at the clock, opened the refrigerator. She removed a stoppered tube containing a substance resembling dried oregano, and held it up like a wine expert examining a cabernet. She was trying to pay attention to him but the pull of her work was too strong at this moment. She'd put years into this project, and risked the cruelest disappointment by allowing herself to believe a crucial experiment would work.

"This is my pal, *Chaenocephalus aceratus,* or what's left of his liver," she said. "The rest of him's in there, liquefied, killing that cancer, I hope. Been swimming around isolated, for twenty million years. One of the oldest fish on the planet, and after all that time, we have no idea how he ticks. Brain the size of a bread crumb, blood contains natural antifreeze. A miracle of adaptation to cold. If Laticia ever figures out a way to combine the DNA from this guy with, say, Frank Perdue's chickens, we'll have poultry farms in Greenland. Alaskan reds. Good old *aceratus.* It's even dumber than a bonefish, but it never gets cancer. My dad died of cancer. Screaming in pain."

"I didn't know that."

"It was the year I met Chuck. Thank God for him. Like God

was keeping some kind of cosmic balance. Why do you think she went on the rocks?"

Amirault said slowly, "Why would you want to go to a place that's prohibited. Maybe *because* it's prohibited."

She frowned. He said, "To have privacy. Everywhere else on base, people are all over the place. Watching. Did you ever have a fight with someone here? The whole place knows about it in five minutes."

"Why not go in a dorm room and close the door?"

"Because the second you raise your voices, anyone on the other side of the wall hears. And with Evylyn, between Rick and Clyde, half the time this year someone was listening at her door. How much time now?"

"Ninety seconds. Oh God. My hands are sweating."

"Sixty seconds."

"Why don't we make a list and eliminate people," Cathy said. "You and me." She pressed her face near the glass like a nine-year-old staring at a Christmas sock, waiting to rip it off the mantel. "I can't breathe. This is stupid. I shouldn't get so hopeful."

Amirault said, "We'll divide up the names, see where everyone was last night. Eleven people should be easy."

"And it's not really eleven. It's nine. We can cross off you and me right now."

The ticking in his head started again.

"Time's up," she said. But she sat there, doing nothing. "I can't look. Do you think this is what it was like when they found vincristine?"

She meant a miracle drug from a plant in Madagascar, that helped cure Hodgkins disease. Researchers impressed with its reputation as a folk cure had tested it against many cancers before they found the ones it worked against.

Almost reluctantly, she maneuvered the steel pincer fingers toward the plastic cover and lifted. The petri dish slid slowly into view.

"Damn," she said.

The pink growths completely covered the inside of the wells.

"I'm sorry." Amirault felt terrible for her.

"I thought I had it."

"You will."

She slumped, her lab coat suddenly looking too big on her. "I'll never get it."

He put his arm around her. "You will. Tomorrow. Next week. Think how it must have been after the sixth try with vincristine."

Cathy collected herself and went back to the refrigerator. She stood, back to Amirault; then her shoulders straightened. She opened the refrigerator and held up the next prospect.

"Lung cancer. And I'll try bone. And ovarian."

"That's the spirit." Amirault nodded. "Why didn't the alarm clock wake you when Evylyn got up?"

Her head jerked. Without the experiment distracting her, she had a frightened, vulnerable look. The glasses made her eyes look bigger. A flush of color rose on her neck.

"I knew you'd get around to this."

For an instant he didn't quite get what she was saying.

Then, dumbfounded, he said, "You mean you weren't there?"

"I wasn't *doing* anything," she said. "It wasn't like I was doing anything. I was listening to music, that's all."

"With who?"

"A.Y."

"In his room?"

"I knew you'd take it this way," she said. "He's great on the electric saxophone. I wear the earphones. Do you know he was number three in the Big Ten competition? *He* wanted to do more. But I said no."

"I'm not judging you."

"You are."

"I'm just surprised, that's all." But he would check it with A.Y. Everybody around here has secrets, he thought.

"Christ, I feel like I'm talking to my father," she said. "Even if I did do something, it would be none of your business."

"I know."

"But I didn't."

"I *know*."

"How could I know something was going to happen to her?" she burst out.

She stared at him. "Oh God, Jack. Stop looking at me like that. You can't think I'd hurt her. Jack? Don't be paranoid."

It was the word Rick had used.

From the hallway, outside, he thought he caught a flicker of movement.

"Did you hear something?"

"No."

He didn't know what to say. His head was reeling. She was right about A.Y. being her business. But why had she let him think she was in the room with Evylyn all this time?

He said, "What about the alarm clock? Did you take it? Did someone borrow it?"

She didn't know. She looked white. Shaken. Miserable.

"I feel bad about the way I yelled at her at the party," she said. He remembered her shouting at Evylyn, *Poor pitiful me!*

Cathy stared down at the floor. "I didn't have to tell you," she said. "I didn't tell Rick. I could have said I was sleeping."

"Yeah. Sure," he said, disgusted with Rick's skill at asking questions. "Good luck with the new batch tomorrow."

Amirault's head swung up. He was listening.

She laughed harshly. "You know what the Italians say," Cathy said. "Revenge is a dish best tasted cold."

Amirault barely heard her as he darted for the door. He heard running footsteps out there, but when he got to the hallway it was empty and the door at the far end was swinging shut.

Her voice, behind him, cried, "What are you *doing?*" He raced down the hall, took the steps two at a time.

Amirault sped into the lounge level, smashing the door open, racing through it.

He stopped.

Nobody there.

He heard himself breathing. The sliding glass door of the picture window was open.

Gail Rivkin stepped in from the balcony. Her eyes grew wide when she saw him.

"Were you just downstairs?" Amirault demanded.

"No."

"Did someone come up here?"

She looked scared. "I didn't see anyone. I . . . I lost a pair of sunglasses. I thought they were out here."

"Someone just ran up the stairs!"

Gail glanced around nervously. So fucking timid.

She took a step back. "Jack," she said. "You don't look good."

"Were you down there? Listening."

"Stop, Jack."

She backed out of the picture window onto the balcony, the ski-chalet-style deck normally used for bay watching, stargazing, picnicking. "It was you," he said, coming toward her. A blast of cold air hit him in the face, knifed through his clothing. In the harbor below, a big skua was swooping up from the water, a fish in its beak. Her eyes were enormous. She kept backing. Her back hit the railing. He moved toward her, feeling everything unraveling. He said, harshly, "Tell me the truth!"

four

"Okay! It was me!"

Amirault halted, stunned by the admission. He'd known Gail had been outside Cathy's lab, but to hear it froze him in place. They were alone on the balcony and she extended her palms, as if that would block him. Had she had time to slide the glass door shut, Amirault would have run past.

"Why, Gail?"

Around them were Adirondack chairs, a bleached whale bone, scattered fossil souvenirs from cliffs above Purgatory Road. Impressions of ferns, fig trees, sequoias in rock. A curved section of Lystrosaurus spine, dead 200 million years ago, when Antarctica was a swamp.

Gail's voice went high and wavery. "Think about what you're doing!"

As if there were something wrong with *him*.

Her breathing condensed into quick, small puffs. In her terror every mousy aspect was accentuated. Her hair, cautiously mid-length, stopped thinly above her shoulders. Her green velvet beret was askew. Her features—button nose, high forehead, good lips, and diamond-shaped beauty mark—had never coalesced into memorableness. She seemed bony rather than lean, timid rather than shy, washed out rather than pale, and her eyes, gray-green at the moment, absorbed hues around her instead of the other way around.

Behind her a twelve-foot drop led to the plowed road between the Sears Tower and the empty dock.

"Calm down, Jack. We'll talk it out, okay?"

"You were following me."

"No! I saw you go in there. I was curious, that's all."

His eyes went to the black hardback notebook clasped to her Irish sweater like body armor. Gail's permanent appendage. Tendons to fingertips to pen to book. She probably slept with it.

"Curious," he repeated in a flat, dead tone. He turned the word over in his mind. All winter she'd been watching him, jotting notes, studying him, fascinated.

"NASA E-mailed me to report on you."

He could almost hear her professor advising her, as if people could be taught compassion in class: Soothe the subject, befriend the subject. Instead, she looked trapped. Over the massed, high-pitched cries of penguins across the water, he heard a new sound, a mechanical droning. Small plane, he thought. It was a speck to the west, above the dark peaks, a Twin Otter, heading toward Victoria Base and the minerals meeting. Coming from the Russian or Ukrainian or Palmer bases to the south. Looking dwarfed and puny, leaving a thin, wavery trail dissipating in the bruised purplish sky.

Gail's words tumbled out. "Because of Evylyn. Don't get mad. *For NASA it's an opportunity.* Stress! What kind of researcher would I be if I didn't study it?"

"Human." But it was hard to stay angry at someone who looked so frightened.

Gail actually seemed hurt. "That's not fair and you know it. You think it's easy to ignore my feelings?" She glanced at the sky, envisioning the astronauts her studies might help one day. "What if one of them dies up there? How will the others react?

Should NASA send married couples? Siblings? Parents and kids? Pets?"

"I don't give a damn." The pressure bloomed in his head. "Let me get this straight. NASA E-mailed you to follow me? To listen in doorways?"

"They didn't suggest a method. I told you. And I wasn't following you. I saw you go into Cathy's lab and I hung around outside."

"And Evylyn's room, too?"

"I don't know what you're talking about."

He searched for a hint of deception, a blink, twitch, anything, but there was none.

Then again, he thought, screaming with frustration inside, What do I know?

"I'm not a guinea pig, Gail! She was my sister!"

Beyond the railing the harbor was always changing. A fog bank rolling in was actually a new iceberg. Another berg off the generator building, shaped like the Rock of Gibraltar yesterday, had split in two overnight. A pair of Weddell seals sunned on the wreckage. Growlers, small chunks of prewinter ice, floated by the dock. Within a month they would mass and clog off the bay, isolating it.

He snapped, "If you want to know something why not just ask, instead of creeping around?"

"You make me nervous."

"For Christ's sake!"

"Your behavior's erratic," she said, starting to shiver. "You've made wild accusations. You go on the glacier every night."

"Yeah. Charles Manson."

"You seem so para—" She caught herself.

"Paranoid?" He felt the heat all over his body. He'd never noticed the asymmetry in her face before, the slacker muscles around the left eye. "Go ahead. Rick said it, so did Cathy. Purse your lips. P."

Running footsteps came from behind them, from the lounge.

"See? You're getting angry."

"Who the hell wouldn't?" Clyde and Laticia ran out onto the balcony. Amirault knew he was raging but couldn't stop. "What'd you learn from studying me? Let's hear your suggestions for astronauts! You gonna ask them to watch out for leopard seals in space?"

"Very funny."

"How about a 'grief chart'? To quantify stress. You know. Give numbers." His voice dripped with sarcasm. "Five's moderate grief. The astronaut can handle it. Eight's bad. Twelve's 'paranoid,' when he blames other people for his sister's death."

Clyde said, "We heard shouting."

"Gail, are you all right?" Laticia asked.

Amirault turned on them. "What did you think I was doing to her? Lose your temper around here and everybody acts like you're going off the deep end."

"Who said anything about that? Did I say that?" Laticia said. She draped her arm around Gail's shoulder and glared at Amirault. Like Gail was some invalid.

"A grief chart?" Gail said. "Charts are valuable. But I understand how they would seem insensitive to you."

The exhaustion closed in on him. He had not slept more than two hours in two days. Under the combined weight of their scrutiny he wondered, for an instant, if anyone had ever been outside Evylyn's room at all. He spent his life hooked to earphones, studying sounds, not people. I'm doing everything wrong, he thought, driving them away. Maybe Brian never tried to get out of that crevasse last year. Maybe Evylyn just fell in.

The pain in his temples flattened out, spread down his spine as a quick, regular throbbing. The breeze off the water carried a diesel smell. He wondered when the *Polar Queen* would be coming home. It was out there beyond the ice cliffs somewhere, pushing aside bergy ice as orcas raced across the bow.

"Why don't we go inside and have coffee," Clyde said. Like it was morphine or Prozac and it would make everything better. Like they'd all go home friends.

As they made their way in, the base seemed to shrink. A knot of onlookers had gathered at the far end of the mess. Rick. A.Y. Hector. He felt people everywhere: in the dorm rooms, showers, galley, radio room, generator room, ship, Zodiacs, mess. In the gym. Eleven sets of emotion building toward spontaneous combustion. They all felt it. It was thick in the air. The only difference was that the others expected it to arrive from a different direction.

Cathy emerged from the stairwell.

"Are you all right, Jack? I couldn't leave the experiment. You ran out so fast."

"I'm fine." He should print up flash cards. "I'm terrific." "Don't worry about me." "Fresh as a daisy." "I'm in control." And then he felt something else. The malevolence again, palpable, close. Like a hiss in his earphones.

Maybe NASA never E-mailed Gail at all.

Find out what she's got in that book.

"Gail," he said quietly, "interview me, I'll cooperate." They seemed surprised by it. Laticia and Clyde exchanged glances. Cathy looked worried. Gail looked shocked. Amirault continued smoothly, "Here's your chance. I want to clear up your misconceptions." He didn't add, Then maybe you'll clear up mine.

Gail looked doubtful. "A whole interview?"

"A to Z."

A greedy look came into her face. She even relaxed, but maybe just felt safer with others around. At NASA this would be a coup. "It's funny," she said. "After what happened, I guess this place can get to you. Maybe I overreacted."

"I did too," Amirault said.

She laughed uneasily. "I'd like to get out of here sometimes, even for a half hour. Pressure builds up. You don't realize till it blows."

They all nodded, agreeing, watching.

"Then let's get out now," Clyde said. "I wish, after what happened, that I didn't have to work. But I have one last experiment. On Aruba. Weather's fine for Zodiacs. Why not come?"

"Aruba" was a rocky island a quarter-mile across the harbor. It was low and hilly, a million-year-old lava bed where everything except irregular columns of basalt was covered with a half-foot of snow. Two-ton elephant seals lay in rows on shore, leaking yellow snot and rolling in their own excrement. A thousand chinstrap penguins waddled around like Charlie Chaplins, from the rookery to shore to Amirault and Gail, tilting their heads like drunks in tuxedos, as if trying to remember if they'd met.

Between the ammonia stink of guano and the elephant seals, Aruba was the worst-smelling place Amirault had ever been.

She said, "Have you slept since Evylyn died?"

"No."

"Eaten?"

"No."

"Alcoholic intake?"

Amirault sighed. "I haven't had a drink, Gail."

"Details," Gail said, writing. "Nothing is inappropriate. Let your mind wander. Tell me how you feel."

"Bad."

They were alone at the moment, but Clyde was a hundred yards to port, bending over a penguin he'd anesthetized. He was tagging it. Which meant it was blind, as ozone damage here grew worse. Rick and Cathy had disappeared behind an outcrop. Laticia and Hector were off with cameras, to photograph seals for Hector's nature collection, they said. But they weren't taking pictures. People were in shock after last night.

Everyone stayed in pairs and carried snowballs against fur seals. They weren't as dangerous as leopard seals. But if they massed and got bold they could attack.

Gail wrote in shorthand, in quick strokes with a cold-proof pen. "Do you feel guilty? Angry? Can you define 'bad' for me?"

"Do they train you to ask questions this way? Give you sensitivity seminars?"

"You said you'd cooperate. Come on."

The wind shifted, grew cooler and damper. She played with the zipper on her coat. He could not see her lowered eyes. Here it comes, Amirault thought. She said, "When did you decide someone had been with her?"

Now, he thought.

He said casually, "When's the last time you interviewed Evylyn?"

"Oh, no!" Her face closed up. She lowered the pen. "So that's why you made the offer. Her answers are doctor-patient privilege."

"Doctor?" Amirault said. "You're not a doctor, and Evylyn wasn't a patient."

"I still have a responsibility. You wouldn't want me sharing *your* answers." She thought about it. She brightened. "Then again, you don't answer. See? I can make a joke."

A hundred yards away Clyde finished collaring his penguin and stood. Released, the creature waddled in frantic circles. Often the tagged birds were eaten by leopard seals, and their radio signals dropped off into the void. Amirault and Gail strolled into a small depression, out of view of the others. Atop a rise to the left, he caught sight of two fur seals following their progress with lateral movements of their dog shaped heads. The larger one lowered itself to the snow, and pressed its flippers to its sleek black body. Amirault gripped his snowball and changed course. Fur seals liked to slide down hills after you. You could never be sure if it was a game or an attack.

"Why are they scared of snowballs?" Gail said.

"Because they don't know what they are."

"Do you think," she said, looking out at the vista, the bergs and ice cliffs, "in a couple years there will be hotels here? Ski chalets?"

"The Trump."

"Oh God."

"The Sheraton Ellsworth."

She shook her head. "I never really thought it would happen. But once they sign that treaty, I have a feeling there'll be a big land rush."

The seals fell behind. He said, walking, "Don't say no until I finish. I'll answer every question, I promise, really answer to your satisfaction. But I want something back. A trade."

"I will not tell you Evylyn's answers."

"It's up to you. But it seems to me you're ignoring an opportunity. Even if there used to be a doctor-patient privilege, I'm next of kin. Her medical records come to me."

Saying it hurt. A fist clenched around his heart. "And NASA would appreciate a little creative researching," he said. "Don't look at it as betraying a trust. Think of it as flexibility. Don't you think NASA wants researchers who can innovate?"

She pursed her lips, but said nothing. Her condensed breath came out long and easy. She was considering it.

"Question for question," Amirault said. "Stop anytime. Don't tell me anything till you're satisfied with my answers."

Amirault spotted Laticia and Hector, fifty feet away, behind an outcrop. Hector aimed a camera at him. The sun flashed on the lens.

He said, "I'll answer first. I won't make jokes. I'll be completely truthful. Come on. One question."

He felt a surge of triumph when she clicked the pen open. "Tell me about you and Evylyn after your parents died," she said. "And the Amirault Club."

Amirault was rocked. It was a question he'd never expected. Nobody here knew about the Amirault Club. How the hell had Gail found out? He saw Evylyn, twelve years old, in her room in Sonoma. A girl with braids and jeans and bare feet. Looking down from her bed at Amirault, sprawled, age ten, on the rug.

She'd said, "It'll be between us, Ami Two. A private place, where we can say anything. No one else'll ever find out unless we agree to let them. That is, if you want to form the club."

Not that there'd been anything to hide, but he'd loved those Thursday afternoon sessions, door closed, secret handshake, attendance required, nothing — not best friends, ball games, homework — ever superseding the Amirault Club. Total freedom. They hadn't convened it in years, but had kept it secret until three years ago. Until just before Antarctica, when they'd agreed to tell National Science Foundation psychiatrists anything they asked about their parents' death. Those interviews were supposed to be private.

"They let you see my file! You saw our files! I don't believe it."

She seemed proud of it. "It would be pretty stupid to authorize a psychological study and deny me information about subjects. I'm not allowed to keep the files. They're locked in Rick's office. I'm waiting. The club."

He told her.

"One time," he said, "she told me about these boys stopping her on the way to school. Making cracks about our parents being dead. Laughing, saying 'You killed them.' Ugly stuff. I'd known something was wrong with her because usually she was happy, but that week she'd been picking on me, yelling about nothing."

Like yesterday, he thought, chilled.

"Evylyn was so private, even when someone bothered her she

tried to take care of it herself. She was tough on the outside, but inside, torn up. And if someone told her off, she'd brood about it for hours before deciding they were wrong."

"What did you do?"

"I got a shovel from the garage and went down the block to the leader's, a kid named Larry. All three of them were there. I broke his collarbone. The other two ran away."

Gail stopped writing. Amirault said, "They were going to ship me to some juvenile detention facility. But when they heard the story they gave me another chance."

"You used violence."

"I protected my sister," Amirault said. "I've been talking ten minutes. My turn. Evylyn was particularly upset last night. I had a feeling it was something besides Brian. Do you have any idea what happened?"

Gail considered, wanting to honor the deal but not reveal too much. "I think things were coming to a head," she said. "Brian, Rick. She blamed herself for what happened last year. She thought she should have gone up with you. She blamed herself for you being kicked out. Her feelings were intensifying with people scheduled to start leaving this week."

Hector was still aiming the camera at them. Amirault heard the whir of the shutter. He wondered if they could hear Gail. He turned the two of them in the other direction.

"What happened yesterday?" he said.

"I don't know. I hadn't interviewed her since Tuesday. She told me about a dream. She was on the fantail of the *Queen*, at night, and Brian left behind onshore getting smaller." Gail seemed upset remembering it. "My turn. Do *you* dream about Brian?"

"Yes."

"What do you dream?"

"That's two questions. If you saw our files you know more. She was in rough shape after last year. Lieber's always so careful, I was surprised he let her come back."

She almost didn't answer. But then she said, "I didn't see her whole file. Just parts relating to my study. You're right. The psychiatrist considered her risky, not for life in general but for an isolated

base. I got the impression she had pretty heavy backing, that someone was pushing for her to be here."

Amirault started. "Who?"

"I don't know."

His head began to hurt. "What exactly did the file say?"

"It was just an impression."

He envisioned the little creatures Evylyn studied. The copepods
the size of poppy seeds that floated in the harbor outside. What
"powerful backers" could be interested in that?

"She never told me anything about backing." But he remembered her in her bed, saying to him, *They don't let you talk about
it . . .*

Gail shrugged. "For me it's NASA. For you, the Navy. Do you
tell us what you're really working on? We're all useful to someone
or we wouldn't be here. We're like the court musicians at the
palace of the Medicis. The people in power want a presence. What
do you dream about Brian?"

"That he's falling. That he's screaming for help. I can't help
him but I try. Sometimes he's so far away he's a speck."

She looked startled. "You do blame yourself."

Amirault saw sympathy there. "He made his own choice," he
said, sidestepping. "My turn. Was she sleeping with anyone besides
Clyde and Rick?"

After all the jibes he'd thrown at her, he was surprised to see this
was what upset her. Her face flooded with color, her breathing
grew ragged.

She slept with Evylyn?

Impossible.

I know my sister.

"Why are you asking this?" she demanded. "You sound like a
policeman. Why do you care who she slept with?"

"Because someone was with her on the rocks."

"Rick," she said, voice dripping. He'd never seen this level of
emotion in her. Like he'd pressed a trigger in her.

"Rick is a pig. He goes after everybody. Do you know he even
goes to that whorehouse in Punta Arenas? He does. He tells me
about it. He brags about it. He's such a pig."

Amirault thought, Rick and Gail?

Her pen trembled, and for the first time — maybe sharing stories had done it — he felt a connection with her. Friendship would be too strong for it. A momentary intimacy closed them in.

"To mention them in the same breath, Clyde and Rick — they're different," she said, shaking her head. "Clyde is serious. People think if you're serious it's something to make fun of. But he cares for things. Look at his project. Saving animals."

"He's pretty special," Amirault agreed, wanting to see what else she would say. Knowing now why Gail had come here in the Zodiac. Because Clyde had suggested it.

"He is. You see that, don't you? He's going to be a great scientist. He's sensitive. Look what those British did to him. They're crazy. Putting boys year after year on a base. It's not natural. Did you ever talk to Victoria Base on a Saturday, while we're having parties? We're dancing, men and women, having a good time, and fifty miles away they're putting each other in stocks and throwing food in each other's faces. Medieval Nights, they call it. Twenty-year-old boys. And then Clyde gets here, his body's going crazy. No wonder he couldn't help himself when she reeled him in. But she didn't even care."

"You and Clyde," Amirault said, dumbfounded. "You're jealous."

"Me and nobody," she said bitterly. "She couldn't keep her hands off him. But I had to listen to it, every week." Her voice went hard, and her eyes were black marbles. "He'd say, 'She's so beautiful, Gail. Do you think she really likes me? Do you know what she likes me to do?' "

She stood up and the book dropped and her hands had hooked into claws.

"NASA wants it all, everything people say. The more I get, the better they like it. So I'm listening to his sex talk. I don't care if she was your sister. He says whatever he thinks." She mimicked Clyde. "She likes my tongue, Gail. Oh Gail, I'm happy to have someone to tell this to. I can't stand that I'm going to be away from her when they send me back to Victoria Base. Do you think she and I could really work out?"

Gail froze. Her hands dropped to her sides, and slowly her

fingers straightened. Her breathing steadied. She picked up the book. They watched each other. Small flakes had begun falling, and the wind moaned like a person in pain.

She said calmly, "Thank you very much, Dr. Amirault. I appreciate your being candid with me. Next Sunday at three. You and I have one last session. Remember those dreams. Dreams are windows. NASA likes dreams."

Amirault heard a shout from the right. Clyde was waving for everyone to come back. The sky was turning black. Amirault had not noticed the clouds roiling in. The only words carrying over the wind were "hurry" and "Zodiac."

"Please keep my secret about Clyde," Gail said.

The *Polar Queen* radioed it was delayed coming back to base. It had engine trouble and had anchored farther down the Peninsula. "Looks like it's just us here for three more days," Laticia said.

"I'll come with you," she said when they got back to base and Amirault went off to the "Library of Congress." All project descriptions were there, and after what Gail had said, he needed to read about Evylyn's. The "library" was a converted storage closet adjacent to the ham radio room, lined with floor-to-ceiling shelves. One wall for paperbacks, one for recent magazines, newspapers, and nonfiction. Two filled with literature on Antarctica, National Science Foundation handouts. "Survival in Antarctica." "Sea Life off Antarctica." "Minerals in Antarctica." "Ozone Hole over the South Pole." In one corner was a small table with a computer Nexus line on it.

"We have to talk, Jack."

From the foldable card table in the center of the room, where they sat, he heard Rick's wife shouting over static, through the ham patch, on the other side of the wall, *"I ran into your brother today at the mall. Over."*

"I'm telling you this for your own good. You're wrecking your chances to get a job," Laticia said.

Her left shoulder touched his right. She was warm beneath her black cashmere sweater. It seemed like twenty years since he'd met her at the first Antarctic seminar.

Amirault said, "When you say the word 'you,' you mean 'me.'"

On the table, the thick eight-by-eleven paperback annual *U.S. Research on the Ice* was open. It listed bases, projects, budgets, and was dispensed to Congress, job applicants, journalists, high school students. Designed for the public, it was utterly honest in intentionally misleading ways. Basic research is our mission, read the italicized quote under Lieber's beaming face.

Laticia issued a thin, unamused laugh.

"Jack, Hector's brother-in-law is a VP at Exxon. I think he can pull strings for you. I think he can convince them to overlook one incident. But not two."

"Don't worry, Laticia. No one will think less of you because you used to go out with me."

"That's not fair," she said, pressing closer. "I still care about you."

Despite himself, he felt himself stir. "Money," he said, "is what you care about."

"What's wrong with that? What's wrong with wanting to be rewarded for what you do? If I ever get my DNA work done I'll patent it and make a million dollars. You could do the same, you know. Hold back some of your work from the government. Just a little. Sell it to a company. Insure your future. Get a good job."

"Like with Exxon?"

"Jack," she said, "do you ever miss us?"

Her thigh pressed his under the table.

"Parts of us," he said.

"Hector's sleeping."

"Is this what you used to do when you were with me?"

She recoiled. Her thin, pretty brows plunged toward her nose. Her mouth formed an ugly inverted crescent. She said, "You'll never get a job."

"I'll do fine."

"You have nothing," she snapped. "You don't have a job. You don't have friends. You don't have money. You don't have me."

"See? Every cloud has a silver lining."

He flashed to Evylyn last night. *I don't want to hurt anyone else,* she'd cried.

He flipped pages and found his own project. "Dr. Amirault will study the composition of the sea bottom." Which was true as far as it went.

"Jack," she said, still there, "I hate to see you like this. People are getting scared of you."

His throat went dry as he found Evylyn's project. "Dr. Amirault will study the diet of the copepod, a little-known plankton. Its habits and habitat." Which is what he already knew.

"I want to help you," Laticia said.

From the other side of the wall, Rick's wife said, "I miss you, sweetie," her voice oscillating from atmospheric distortion. Grist for voyeuristic listeners hooked to earphones from Lagos to New York.

"Jack, you're not listening to me," she said, reading over his shoulder. "Why are you so stubborn?"

His eyes dropped to the bottom of the column, where funding agencies were listed, mandated by law.

"University of California . . . Ford Foundation . . ."

His index finger stopped beneath the final listing. Laticia gasped. He felt his skin start to heat.

"What do *they* want with her?" Laticia said. "I mean, she never even talked about this."

Because they order you not to, he thought. Because none of us ever read this thing. Because she knew the questions that would start if she mentioned her new backers. She was always better at keeping secrets than me.

"U.S. Navy."

For an instant he was back in that little room at the Pentagon, with the three captains, sweating as they warned him, played word games with him.

Laticia said, "Looks like she picked up a new sponsor this year."

Amirault had momentarily forgotten she was there. "What you said before, is that what you do with your work, Laticia? Hold results back to sell to a company?"

"Oh, pul-lease!," she said, slamming the door behind her when she stormed out.

• • •

"It's time for the Creature Feature," Evylyn cried.

Amirault felt sick watching her smiling on the video screen. The Penguin Pub was still a mess from the party last night. The pool table was covered with planks. The furniture was scattered. In one corner, A.Y. had fallen asleep and snored softly. He'd been on the floor looking under a couch when Amirault arrived. "I lost my watch. Did you see a watch?" he'd said.

Applause and laughter rocked the TV set.

He had not been here since last night. Papier mâché covered the punch table. Red, white, and blue bunting looped from the ceiling, dangled to the floor. Popcorn kernels sat soggily in a Pyrex bowl beside half a dozen warm cans of Heineken.

"Elvira of the Dark couldn't make it," Evylyn said. "So I will host this afternoon's presentation — *The Copepod That Ate Ells-worth Station!*"

She looked so alive, so vibrant. She'd be warm if he touched the set. His vision blurred. He wiped his eyes. This had been filmed three days ago while he was on the *Queen,* and clearly she'd been in a good mood then. He couldn't see the audience in the video but they'd be sprawled on the chairs, pool table, carpet. Lectures had high attendance rates. Every distraction did. Out of the dark, in the video, came the voice of the assistant cook. She hooted, as if at a monster movie, "Aaaaaaah."

Evylyn's hair was washed, shiny. Long silver earrings flashed when she tossed her head. They'd been a present from Brian.

"Oh God," Hector said, strolling in. He seated himself on the far end of Amirault's couch but seemed to watch Amirault, not the set.

Evylyn said, "*Plankton* is the Greek word for 'wander.' Plankton live in all water, swept by the current . . ."

"I want to talk to you, Jack," Hector said.

"You and everybody else."

"Here's the copepod," Evylyn said, "a plankton, a carnivore, swimming in the water. Last year we learned how it had sex, in my film classic, *I Am Curious, Copepod.*"

Hoots and whistles erupted from the audience.

"This year I'm concentrating on how it finds prey." Evylyn's voice grew crafty. She said, doing a bad Peter Lorre, "It's hoongry. Ve-ry hoooongry."

"Now. As a doctor," Hector said.

Amirault waved for Hector to wait. On-screen, the copepod drifted into view, magnified under a binocular microscope. It looked enormous, dangerous, streamlined for attack. Amirault stared at it, fascinated even though Evylyn had been talking about it for years.

It floated there, quivering from water movement. Lobster-shaped, it had a wild beauty; pearly and translucent in the center, delicate cooked-shrimp color at the side. Two sharp pincers protruded from the "chest" like *Tyrannosaurus rex* hands.

But the most memorable feature was an antenna shaped like a Salvador Dalí mustache, running at right angles to the "head," a sharp terminal point.

"In its miniature world it's a killer," Evylyn said. "As unaware of us as we are of it."

Small rods jutted from the antenna.

The screen was bright from light shining down in the microscope. Amirault saw wavy lines — current — washing around the animal.

"It has no eyes," Evylyn said. "It's a cannibal."

In the background, people in the audience hummed the theme from *Jaws*. The cook squealed, in the high-pitched voice of *Saturday Night Live*'s Mr. Bill, "Oh nooooooooo."

Hector said, "Jack?"

"Wait a minute."

Whoever had been videotaping the speech swung the camera to give Amirault a view of the rapt front row. Rick was there. Cathy. Laticia. Clyde. A.Y. He saw two of the Minnesota boys, big, bearded carpenters who wore Hawaiian shirts in winter and looked like a cross between mountain men and ZZ Top.

"My question is, if copepods can't see, how do they find prey?" Amirault's belly began to hurt.

A smaller creature drifted into the left side of the slide. It had a blobby, vulnerable look. Cilia, tiny black hairs, washed back and forth around its body. This animal was about to die.

"Watch," Evylyn breathed.

The smaller creature washed closer to the copepod. Suddenly the black hairs began moving frantically, but too late. The pincers began to open. Evylyn said dreamily, "Don't you ever look at the world and wonder why things turn out that way? Why one life becomes a lion and another an elephant? Why one is a killer and one is prey?"

He hadn't heard Laticia come in, but her voice floated out of the darkness, behind him. "Figure out what this has to do with the Navy?"

Hector whirled and stared at her. Amirault heard Hector's sharp intake of breath. On-screen, the copepod lunged left. The two animals locked together. Amirault imagined the small one screaming, its primitive nerve endings exploding in pain.

The copepod began absorbing its prey.

Laticia shuddered. "It was cute three days ago. Today it's awful."

Hector said, looking concerned suddenly, "What *about* the Navy?"

Evylyn's face filled the screen.

"See the rods sticking out of the antenna," she said. "My theory is they're sensors, picking up vibrations. I've almost figured out how they work."

Amirault had the same clenched feeling that came when he was trolling with soundguns.

The audience shouted joke questions at Evylyn: "How can I get a copepod to bring home for Christmas?"

"Daddy, daddy! I want a pony and a copepod!"

Amirault flashed to her in this room last night, at the height of the party, shouting, "Stupid copepods. Who cares about them!"

"Dat's all, folks," Evylyn said.

The screen went blank. There was a whirring from the video monitor. Amirault rewound the tape. *Vibrations*, he thought.

Hector, half turned on the couch, seemed anxious about something, Amirault thought. No. More. Hector had become frightened.

"The Navy was funding her?" Hector said. "So our last pure basic researcher bites the dust," he said. "Submarines."

Or planes. Or torpedoes, Amirault thought, aching. Whatever she'd been working on had potential applications to those, too. Subs needed greater ability to sense things underwater. Airplanes treated the atmosphere like a fluid, and the same rules of physics applied.

If I hadn't been so preoccupied with Brian this year, if I'd talked to her more, maybe I would have seen it.

But had she found anything?

And then there was Hector, on the couch a few feet off, composing himself back into the base doctor. Looking at the pleasant, attentive face, Amirault thought, You did the autopsy. You announced how she died.

"I was wrong to get mad at you in the dining room before," Hector said.

What did Amirault know about Hector, anyway? He'd never spent time with the doctor and would love to get a look at those files in Rick's office. Maybe there would be secrets about the others there too. He ran over facts. Hector had grown up in California, San Diego, he thought, or Los Angeles. He was divorced. He had two kids in college. He'd been stationed on an aircraft carrier off Iraq during the Gulf War. He led prayers. He was due for retirement. Facts were useless. Amirault knew nothing of what went on inside.

"Apology accepted." It was funny, Amirault thought, looking over the crisply pressed oxblood shirt, the pleated Italian cords and shiny loafers, that the only official Navy representative on base was the only person who dressed like a civilian. Hector always seemed the same, laid back yet competent. Surfer meets medical school. At forty-nine, he still had thick blond hair falling over his forehead, but it was salted with gray. He was the oldest person on base and that, plus being a doctor, gave him a parental role. People came to him with problems. He'd close the door of the infirmary. They'd talk things out.

"And on the boat before. I was abrupt with you," Hector said. "Everyone handles grief in different ways. I shouldn't have snapped."

Get to her lab. See if she found something.

"I'll walk with you," Hector said when Amirault stood up.

Amirault wondered if they'd agreed to babysit him. Decided to keep someone with him all the time. The two men headed outside and across the pedestrian walkway. Hector, now that he had Amirault's attention, seemed in no hurry. Or maybe Hector and Laticia had worked out a dual approach.

Hector said, "Do you really believe what you said in the dining room?"

Amirault stopped and rested his hands on the railing. He pretended he was going nowhere in particular. It was warm on the walkway; the stars were clear.

"What difference does it make to you?"

"That someone lured her out there," Hector said. "Tricked her?"

"Why is it so important to everyone to keep me from asking questions?"

Hector blew out air and said, as if Amirault had not spoken, "Let's forget our differences for a second. You had a shock last night. You're facing an uncertain future. I know I'm not a psychiatrist, but it doesn't take one to imagine you feeling some weight here. Responsibility."

"Which gives me delusions."

"Delusions," Hector said delicately, "is a pretty strong word." He laughed. "I'm just suggesting you have all that pressure, and nowhere to put it. Are we getting angry here? I hoped you wouldn't."

"I'm not getting angry. I already am."

Hector squeezed Amirault's shoulder in one of those maddening Southern Californianisms, sending good vibes through the cosmos. He said, "You have over a week left here. I'm leaving in three days for Victoria, which means no doctor here, and I'm not comfortable with that. Especially now."

"Don't worry about it."

"But I do. What if I gave you something to help you sleep? Gail said you haven't slept. Your eyes are red. It's over-the-counter stuff. Nothing heavy. No side effects. Sleep like a baby. Twelve, thirteen hours. Next day, if things aren't better, we can talk again."

"You mean, next day she'll be alive?"

"You talk as if Evylyn didn't matter to the rest of us. You know that's not true."

Amirault slumped. "I do."

Hector smiled as if he was getting somewhere. "I had a patient, an officer in Iraq," he said. "A lieutenant. He lost men. It wasn't his fault. He knew he'd done his best, but inside," he said, putting an index finger to his heart, "he *did* think it was his fault."

"And you gave him a sleeping pill and the next day everything was better."

"Gail," Hector continued, "mentioned that she thought you were feeling strained."

"Is that a big white rabbit on your shoulder?" Amirault said. "Or a chicken? I thought Gail keeps everything confidential. And by the way," he said, sick of the probing, "where were you at three a.m. last night?"

Hector kept smiling but there was less professionalism in it. "Cathy's better than you at asking questions," he said. "She goes right up to people, talks about research, works around to it. I gather you two are making a list."

"If she's so clever, how come you know what she's doing?"

"Because we live in a space the size of a house, and everybody knows everything. And nobody, none of us, thinks Evylyn was pushed. Even Cathy. You have to know she's humoring you. Going along with you to give support."

Hector's hand came out of his pocket with a small foil packet, a transparent plastic shield containing two blue pills.

"I don't like to let things fester," Hector said. "Every year, at the end, I ask myself if there's some loose end I want to tie up. To be a good Christian. It's bad to leave things hanging. Take the medicine. Try it for one night."

"Where were you?"

Hector withdrew the hand but did not put the pills away. He looked sad. He said, "With Laticia, like I am every night."

"Asleep?"

"As in, did I get up while she was sleeping, meet Evylyn, and sneak back to bed?"

"Maybe Laticia did it."

Hector didn't laugh.

Amirault said, "Do a lot of autopsies in Iraq, Hector?"

Hector stiffened. But he kept his tone soft. "One would have been too many. But yes. We were on the *Jefferson*, twenty miles out. The Hueys would bring in casualties. Two, three times a day. Not just our guys. Egyptians. French. Italians."

His voice fell. "I felt more like a butcher than a doctor. Filling out death reports. It's why I asked for transfer to Antarctica. Quiet. Clean. Everybody friendly. And private," he said, which struck Amirault as odd. "I thought when I got here, the autopsy part would be through."

"I guess we all had some nasty surprises."

Amirault let him drop the packet in his pocket. "If you don't want to take them, don't," Hector said. "You want to talk, come to me. As long as I'm here."

Amirault felt the hard edge of the foil packet digging into his thigh, through his pocket. Would it hurt to take them? A little sleep? Maybe tonight, he would swallow them down. Maybe the pills would clear his head.

Hector walked off, finally leaving Amirault alone. Which took care of the babysitting theory. He was torn for an instant over whether to go to Evylyn's lab now, or up on Purgatory Road. But with little time left here, he knew his trips were limited. If the weather turned bad, tonight could be his last chance to find Brian.

Besides, if he waited till later, when the others were asleep, he'd have privacy in her lab.

The lab would wait.

He suited up in hiking gear in his room. In the generator building, as the big machine roared, he ran his eyes over the skis against the walls, searching out his powder-blue Karhus. He spotted the polar-bear-head logo, but only one matching ski was there. The drumming noise from the generator made his headache worse.

Someone must have borrowed his skis and not put them back properly. Slobs pissed Amirault off.

Secrets, Robyn Cassidy had said.

He moved along the wall, clenching his teeth against the pain in his forehead. There was always an oily smell in here and a bulb had blown out in back, leaving a pool of inky black around the spare parts shelves.

Where the hell was that ski?

Amirault massaged his hammering temples.

When the wind blew the door shut he felt the sharp metallic bang in his joints.

Amirault spotted the polar-bear-head logo on his other ski. But now there was an odd sluggishness in his feet. And when he touched the ski, he couldn't feel the edge. He heard himself panting. He felt like he'd run miles.

I must be getting sick.

A wave of dizziness swept over him, and his vision blurred.

Carbon monoxide, he thought.

Through the dizziness Amirault knew he had only moments to get out of there. He stumbled toward the door, which was going in and out of focus. A valve must have come loose on the generator. The door was at the end of a long tunnel, small and distant. Amirault flailed, tripping but staying up. The oil smell was tremendous. A gigantic hammering noise filled his brain.

He reached the door, watched his hands, groping.

Turning the knob.

I made it, he thought, coughing. But the door didn't move. The knob turned, all right, but the door wasn't opening. Through his failing senses he realized it was locked from the outside. He was trapped.

five

Amirault crashed to the floor, dying. He heard his head strike concrete but thought, dreamily, I don't feel a thing. His body felt like it was wrapped in gauze, in great masses of cotton. The peripheries were shutting down; the blood flow to his brain slowed. The roaring generator looked far away and the air vibrated against him in pleasant waves.

Fresher air by the floor revived him, slightly. He remembered a safety drill story—Admiral Byrd saving himself during a carbon monoxide leak by sucking air near the ground.

But Amirault's muscles refused to work when he tried to roll over. Who cares anyway? he thought, drifting off again. The taste of old tuna fish filled his mouth, putrid and pungent along the edge of his tongue. I should get to the door, he thought, but he couldn't remember why.

Amirault lay on his back, listening to his breathing quicken. The steel latticework on the ceiling zigzagged, leaving bright trails of light. They reminded him of the meteor showers that swarmed over the base in February. Pretty, he thought, blacking out. Very pretty.

• • •

The reverend finished the eulogy, the mourners stepped back, and gravediggers shoveled dirt onto the empty coffin in the rain. Brian's parents and friends stood watching. Evylyn sobbed softly. Cathy and Gail held hands. Amirault watched from under an oak tree as Brian's dad walked up.

"Arna and I are proud you went up after Robyn," he said.

"Thanks."

"We're worried about you. Evylyn says you stay in that cabin. You don't talk to anyone. Come home with us, as long as you like."

"I have a report to write at home," Amirault said. Then the edges of the scene wavered and he was looking at a glass medical cabinet, at a reflection of a man lying on a steel bed. A baby-blue blanket covered the man. That's me, he thought in wonder. I didn't die.

Beyond the image were rows of medical instruments: forceps, scalpels, beakers marked *Cotton*. A cardboard box that said *Q-Tips*. A hypodermic needle in a clear plastic wrap. Amirault's reflection raised its hand to the bandage on its forehead. It felt thick and lumpy and when his fingers reached his face, little pinprick pains stabbed his cheeks, and maybe it was a trick of light, but the furrows down the sides seemed deeper than a day ago.

Amirault saw someone else in the reflection, behind him, against the wall.

He turned. Robyn Cassidy looked back from a steel chair beneath Hector's eye chart.

Even as he watched, her face changed from frightened — not an expression he'd previously associated with her — into the unreadable lovely mask. She was scared I wouldn't wake up, he thought. Then he thought, Or was she scared I would?

"Do you know where you are?" she said.

His throat burned. "Timmy's Big Boy Burger Den?"

"You got it."

"No onions on mine," Amirault said.

"How about the biggie fries?"

"Water," Amirault croaked.

She rose quickly and Amirault noticed the crumpled blanket on the floor beside her. The tray with a half-eaten sandwich and

Ellsworth penguin logo coffee mug. Her hair was mussed on one side, as if she'd fallen asleep against the wall.

"How long have I been out?"

"Three days." She ran water at the tap.

"Three *days?*" The ammonia smell of the room was overpowering; the fishy taste in his mouth brought the scene in the ski shack back. The thundering machinery. The locked door.

Someone tried to kill me.

His skull hurt. She brought the glass toward him, past Hector's skeleton chart, a naked man dissected in half, sliced up the middle. The right side vulnerable pink skin, hair, half a penis, one eyebrow, half a mouth. Left side peeled away like Evylyn after the seal attack. Reduced to components. Muscle. Tendon. Bone.

He drank greedily.

Robyn said, "We've been taking turns watching you. A couple more minutes in there and you would have been dead."

He was parched. His insides had turned to dust. But with each cold swallow came more painful sensation. His throat felt so raw an image came to him, a scalpel sliding down his esophagus, scraping flesh. He was clammy with a greasy chemical coating that seemed more than sweat.

She said, "You look cold. Want another blanket?"

Robyn reached and ran her index finger down his face. They had not touched except for the time in her tent, a year ago, when he'd felt her forehead for fever. The two of them seemed to require injury to make contact. He wanted to pull her down and put his mouth on hers and make it black-and-blue. He wanted to feel her skin, ears, breasts, belly against his teeth and lips. He knew if he did that, he would be lost, and he needed to keep thinking.

"Gail and Clyde pulled you out. They were on the railing, they saw the light from the ski shack. You left the door open. They went to close it. I better get Hector," she said. "You're gray. Do you want more water?"

He drew back from her touch. "The door was open?"

No, no, no, he thought. She's lying. It couldn't have been open. He remembered his frantic struggle to get out.

From outside came the deep, low foghorn of the *Polar Queen*.

Two blasts meant loading. He'd slept away precious time. The boat was readying to sail north to the treaty meeting. *Taking whoever tried to kill me away.*

But even that wasn't right. There was no way to know who had locked him in. Don't tell her anything, he thought. Don't tell anyone anything. You can't trust any of them.

"More water," he said, running over suspects. Rick and Clyde had been sleeping with Evylyn. Gail had resented her because of Clyde. Cathy had lied about her whereabouts. Hector asked questions about Evylyn and the Navy. Laticia had tried to buy him off with a job offer.

And Robyn, a foot away, had come back the night all the trouble started.

Amirault understood then. Whoever had locked him in the shack had returned to unlatch the door, to open it so people would see light spilling out.

You wanted them to think it was an accident. But you came back too soon.

"You look funny," Robyn said.

"The carbon monoxide leak. How'd it start?"

"The manifold on the generator. Screws worked themselves loose."

"Just worked themselves loose," Amirault said.

"Well," she said, "Rick figured the vibrations must have dislodged them."

She jerked when Amirault seized her wrist, but didn't try to pull away. Water sloshed over the glass onto his blanket.

"I told you," he hissed. "I won't help you. I won't work with you."

"Cathy told me what really happened last year," Robyn said. "How you disobeyed orders to save me."

Amirault fell back on the pillow. Robyn said, "In the mess, during dinner. They were all talking about you, the accident, and she blurted it out. She was furious at the others. She said, 'I don't care if we're not supposed to tell.' She's a good friend to you. Why didn't you tell me? At the party, I was saying those horrible things to you about following orders."

"What difference does it make?"

"It makes a difference to me," she said fiercely. "You risked everything to get me down, and you don't even believe in what I do."

"That's for sure."

She seemed small suddenly. "I had this view of you . . . that you were just a government drone and . . . Cathy said Brian only went up there because of you. No wonder you said the things you did. I'm sorry. I mean, I'm just sorry."

Amirault didn't want pity. "Now you'll have something to announce when you get back," he said. "How the government tried to kill you." He turned away, toward the cabinet. Her reflection didn't move.

"I don't know what to make of you," she said. "The way you go after things. You don't stop and you don't care what anybody thinks. You just keep pushing, like me."

"Peas in a pod," Amirault said. "The supreme compliment."

He fell back. She put the glass on the end table and stood gazing down at him, rubbing her wrist. She seemed to be considering saying something, but drank his water instead. If it were the sea bottom, he thought, I'd take a chance, challenge the mystery, shoot the sound waves at the target, wait for a response. But it wasn't science. Science was easy.

As if she sensed an opportunity, eagerness came into her. She sat on the bed, her tight haunches on his mattress. The vanilla smell of her mixed with the toxin he'd absorbed. Her face had gone shiny. He knew the look by now. It was like every time emotion rose in her, it triggered a switch and diverted her into politics. He thought, amazed, She's going to talk about the treaty. All that compassion was phony, a means to an end.

Fanatics. There were synapses missing. Map out their sensory system and there would be gaps when it came to human emotions. All the passion diverted, pirated by duller, colder parts of the brain. He thought, Everyone uses everyone. He thought, She's here to use me. He thought, Then why am I disappointed?

She said, "It's a last ditch. We have to try anything." We, Amirault thought, laughing inside. You and me.

"You know what's going on at Victoria Base?" she said, her words coming faster, as if he actually cared. "Right now at this second? The biggest sham of history. Forty-two countries pretending they've stopped acting like human beings."

Amirault, weary, gazed back at a machine that looked human. "No more fighting," the machine was saying. He had a vision of a worn tape running inside her face, beneath her muscles. "They're saying, Give us this place and we'll treat it well. We'll be benevolent. We won't hurt things. And to prove their good intentions they trot out the record. See, they say? Forty years of honesty. No commercial activity. No mining or military research. But they're lying, desperate, their economies are crumbling, they need to plunder this place. The second the ink dries on the new agreement, they will."

"You disgust me," Amirault said.

"Hate and love," she said, almost touching thumb to index finger, "are close."

"Someone killed her."

She squeezed his wrist. "I know."

"You *know*? Say anything to get what you want, do anything, try anything. Isn't that what you said before?"

She tossed her head. "You've been imagining what I think since I got here," she retorted. "Maybe you can be surprised too."

"Surprise me."

"You find dead rock, so you think you know living tissue."

Amirault said, "It's not a person. It's ice. Not alive. It melts when you touch it. What's so important to you about it?"

She was breathing hard. "If we can show the lie . . . the rotten part under the surface, prove people are killing each other over this place, over military secrets, you'd burst the illusion. Maybe it would help stop the treaty. I know it's a long shot. But we have to try everything. Shake 'em up. Keep shaking. You never know what can come of it. I mean, everyone's saying she worked for the Navy."

"Use my sister, you mean."

"It's not using her. She would have wanted it. She's the one who wrote Greenpeace about this base."

"You're lying!"

Robyn leaned so close, for an instant he thought she would kiss him. He was clenching his fists so hard his tendons hurt.

"You know I'm not lying. How well did you know your own sister? Let's work together," she said.

"Well!" boomed another voice as Hector advanced into the room, grinning like the doctor after a successful operation. His orange parka was half unzipped, grimy from physical labor. He'd been helping load the ship. He brought the cold with him. His rubber boots made sloppy sounds on the floor and left a trail of melting glaze. He said, "He's up. He's talking. I was afraid you'd be asleep when we pulled out of here."

Amirault's throat hurt. "Sure you were."

"We're heading out in a few hours. Quite a party up there, Jack. All the bases are sending scientists, representatives. TV all over. History, Jack. I'm excited."

Hector turned more professional. "And you'll be flying to Punta Arenas soon as the Chileans get a Twin Otter ambulance flight in here."

Amirault glanced at Robyn. All the force had cleared from her face, leaving that model beauty he saw in magazines. Lips shiny. Nose turned up. Beauty mark in the low left quadrant like a planned imperfection. No wonder she loved ice. She shifted beside Hector so their hips brushed; the doctor's glance flickered sideways and back to Amirault. Hector suddenly looked more greedy and vulnerable. Great actress, Amirault thought. But who's the audience? Him? Or me?

Hector got a stethoscope and pulled a stool to the bed. "Let's hear what Mr. Heart has to say," he said. He fastened the rubber tips into his ears. Amirault felt exhausted just from being conscious. The rancid taste in his mouth would not go away. "Deep breath," Hector said. "Again. Cough." Robyn, over Hector's left shoulder, winked. It was not a feminine gesture. Hector said chattily, "It'll be a few days before the poison works out of your system. You're going to be tired. Just brushing your teeth will be an effort. But you were a lucky guy."

The doctor worked smoothly, tapping, listening. He used the reflex hammer. He joked, "Let's see if there's more brain damage than usual. Read row three of the eye chart, please. Good. Tell me your mother's maiden name?"

"Rockefeller."

"Bad jokes intact."

"Robyn said I've been out three days."

Hector grinned with his mouth only. He pressed his index finger lightly into a black-and-blue mark on Amirault's knee. "I helped you along, Jack. Shot you up with a little sleep aid."

"That the stuff you wanted me to take in the lounge?"

Hector hesitated. "Better," he said.

"Where are my clothes?"

Hector shook his head. "Not recommended."

Robyn brushed against Hector again. Everything looks suspicious to me, Amirault thought. The doctor wagged his finger. "You'll hurt yourself. Robyn," he added pleasantly, keeping his eyes on Amirault, "would you mind finding Rick and bringing him here? Robyn?"

Amirault tried to rise but the pain exploded in his head and he had no strength anyway, not enough to fight Hector, who pushed him down. Robyn walked out with an unreadable backward glance. Amirault was out of breath just from his half-minute effort. "I want my clothes."

"Uh-uh." They were alone now. "Jack," Hector said nonchalantly, "what were you doing in the ski shack?"

"Renting a movie."

Hector nodded. *"The Great Escape,"* he said, "was always my favorite." More delicately, he said, "The reason I asked is, I know you go up there every night and get your skis, but that just takes a minute. You would have had to be in there longer than that for the CO to knock you out, especially with the door open."

"Especially," Amirault said.

"Robyn must have told you some bolts on the exhaust manifold got loose somehow. Instead of being vented outside, CO was pouring into the shack."

"Somehow," Amirault repeated, staring into Hector's face. *"Somehow.* As in, did I loosen the bolts myself?"

Hector turned away and slid open a steel drawer. Amirault

couldn't see what he was doing. "What the hell," Hector said. "I thought I had a dozen bottles here. There are only ten now."

Amirault said, "You think I was trying to kill myself? Or somebody else?"

"I'm asking a question, that's all."

They looked at each other. Hector slumped. "What am I saying?" he said. "Yeah, I *was* wondering that. What's happening to us?" He shook his head. "It's good I'm getting out of here."

Amirault dragged back the covers. His hands felt weighted and his knees looked gray. He swung his legs over the side. Hector, holding a syringe up five feet away, didn't make a move to stop him this time. There was no need to. Amirault gagged and fell back, gasping. Hector held the syringe up to a bottle, pulling the stopper. "One more minute and you would have been gone," he said.

"No shots," Amirault said.

"Who's the doctor? You or me?"

Hector held the syringe up to the light. The liquid inside had a delicate rose color. "A rest will do you good in Punta Arenas. There'll be no one here to take care of you. And the infirmary's not equipped if something major goes wrong."

Amirault fought to get up.

"Right arm or left?" Hector said.

"I need to go to Evylyn's lab. To see something."

"I'll do it for you. What is it you want to see?"

"Get away from me," Amirault said as Robyn hurried back into the room followed by Rick, A.Y., and Haystack, clutching a hammer.

"We got a little resistance here," Hector said over his shoulder, not taking his eyes off Amirault. "Come on, Jack. Coupla days," he said as the others closed in on him, "of sleep."

Amirault tried to fight them. The ring of faces bent close. "Keep his head steady," Hector said, pushing the sleeve of Amirault's gown up, swabbing his arm.

"The door was locked!" Amirault cried. "You have to believe me!"

"They never should have let him come back," one of them was saying. It might have been Rick, but Amirault couldn't be sure.

• • •

Amirault awoke later and his head was clear, which made the pain sharper. His joints felt raw. His lungs burned with each breath. Surprised, he saw he was still in the infirmary. The Twin Otter had not come. It didn't make sense until he heard the storm outside and saw the glass cabinet vibrating.

Amirault craned to see the clock. *Thursday.* He'd been out twenty-four hours.

He tried to rise but felt a swift cutting pain in his wrists and ankles. He looked down. Brown leather straps bound him to the bed.

He stared for a moment, then launched himself against the straps. The leather dug into his skin. He ignored the pain and pushed harder.

Amirault fell back, heaving. Blinking the sweat away.

"Hey!" he yelled.

There were no windows in the infirmary. He had no idea if it was day or night. But now he grew aware of country music playing, faintly, down the hall and Ry Cooder singing "He'll Have to Go."

"Hey!"

A.Y. stood in the doorway, in a blood-spattered lab coat, holding a scalpel in his gloved hand. Through his bottleneck glasses, his brown eyes blinked, enormous.

"You're up," A.Y. said.

The blade glittered, the edge an ocher color. The big biologist came across the room toward him, stopped, seemed to realize he held the scalpel. "Sorry." His gaze was on the wrist straps. Amirault remembered him dozing in the video lounge during Evylyn's show.

"Hector buckled you down for protection," A.Y. said. "You were tossing around."

"Where is Hector?" Amirault hid his relief.

"Gone."

A.Y. put the scalpel on the cabinet and started undoing the straps.

Amirault was careful not to say anything until they were off. He sat, legs over the side of the bed, rubbing his wrists and ankles. His skin burned where welts marred it, but he felt better, more alert, than the last time he'd come awake. Hector had been right about sleeping, although the doctor's motivation was something else.

A.Y. said, "Everyone is outside. Big storm. Bad storm. The storm ripped off the garage door in the Sears Tower. I had to finish up my last experiment."

"The *Queen* left?"

A.Y. nodded. "Before the weather got bad. Hector. Clyde. Most of the work crew." A.Y. seemed nervous talking about it, and Amirault noticed that with each roar of wind the wall directly across from him seemed to undulate in and out. It was built to give in high wind, but he'd never seen it move before.

"It's crazy in the harbor," A.Y. said. "All the animals left. Ice flying all over. Rick called a repair alert."

"That gives you plenty of time to play the saxophone for Cathy," he said, checking her story.

A.Y. stared at him. "I'd like to try a duet with her. If I convince her to take out her flute."

Amirault stood up. A wave of dizziness hit him but passed. He took a step. His coordination seemed adequate. Repair alert meant semi-emergency. Scientists had gathered in the lounge, had been assigned to work crews. "In a worst-case scenario," Lieber had lectured in Washington, "one building could be abandoned and the other shored up."

Amirault found his clothes in the closet. The putrid taste surged into his mouth as he pulled on his shirt, and he heard A.Y., on the phone, saying, "I loosened the straps, Rick." A.Y. sounded defensive. "No one told me not to."

Amirault hurried up. He was pulling on his second boot when Rick arrived with Haystack and Kojak, looking tense and exhausted. Clumps of snow covered their shoulders. Their hair was soaked, plastered down. A diamond-shaped cut oozed above the corner of Rick's lip. The threat was in his eyes: One accusation, one comment, one *paranoid* comment, and you'll be strapped to the bed again because I have no time to deal with you. The others reflected the mood of the overseer. They would do what Rick told them.

Amirault held up his hands wearily. "I'm fine. I'm fine. I just want to go to my room and sleep."

The laborers looked at Rick for guidance. Between Evylyn, the generator "accident," and the storm, tensions were at a breaking point.

If you killed her, Amirault thought, you'll never let me go.

Rick said, "Do you remember what you were saying before?"

Amirault rolled his eyes. "Yeah, yeah, being locked in. Somebody locked me in. I remember."

They were all watching him. He poured contrition into his voice. "I'm sorry. I thought the door was locked but obviously it wasn't. I know you have work to do." He went back to lacing his boot.

He didn't like the silence. He looked up, needing to take control here. "Can I help outside?"

That tipped the balance. "Maybe later," Rick said. "Go rest."

"Come get me if you need me."

A long howl of wind faded into a cracking sound inside the wall. They watched the metal slowly relax back into shape.

"Storm can't last much longer," Kojak said, but his voice lacked conviction.

Amirault assured them he could reach his room without help, watched them leave, and waited five minutes. The hallway was deserted, Evylyn's lab only twenty paces away.

It was locked.

Not only that, but he noticed the other lab doors were closed too. Cathy's lab was locked. And Clyde's. Even Amirault's was locked.

Because of Robyn, he realized. Rick had sealed everything for as long as she's here.

Amirault cursed. He had to get into Evylyn's lab before anyone came back, had to know not just her exact experiments but *whether she'd achieved results*. He needed to see her notes, her computer. But the master key would be on that big silver chain dangling from Rick's hip.

He could try to break in; there were tools in the office. *But if they find the doorjamb splintered, they'll know it was me.*

Amirault thought of another option. Hurrying, wobbly, he made his way to the dorm. Lights were flickering in the long, deserted hallway. The wind seemed louder up here. Somewhere a window shattered. In Evylyn and Cathy's room, Amirault rifled his sister's desk, closet, suitcases.

Finally he found her spare keys in her duffel bag. Back at the lab, he tried the serrated brass model. It didn't work. He tried the round-headed Medeco and the oval copper-colored Jet. Someone's coming, he thought, but it was a cracking sound from Clyde's lab, as if wooden shutters had blown in. The whole building was making an *aaah*ing noise. The Arrow key slid in smoothly. Tumblers lined up.

Swinging the door open, Amirault felt his heart pounding. The shutters were open but the daylight was blocked by raging snow outside. It was cold. He groped for the light switch and stood blinking, surrounded by her possessions. He knew he should hurry but her presence was so tangible he couldn't bear to break the spell. She was in here. All her hope and brashness was around him, permeating the lab. The marble-topped table and binocular microscope. The half-filled beakers. The stoppered sample bottles. The dog-eared looseleaf notebook. Her government-issue desk was adorned with Gary Larson stickers. On the blotter was a silver-framed photo of Amirault and Evylyn in Washington, at the group dinner on the last night. Brother and sister side by side, in an Ethiopian restaurant on Columbia Avenue, holding beers to the camera in a toast. He recognized Brian's hand in the left corner, clutching a Michelob, from the Phi Beta Kappa ring.

Hurry. But go too fast and he'd miss something. Amirault flipped through the looseleaf. He wished he knew exactly what he was looking for. His emotions swung wildly. Confronted with the scientific compilation of numbers, the columns of figures and notations, his suspicions suddenly seemed ridiculous. He saw himself the way others did, wild with grief, imagining things.

There was a series of pencil sketches of lobster-shaped copepods, and she'd jotted numbers, measurements, beside each head and pincers. Nothing.

Amirault abandoned the book and seated himself before her Sharp laptop computer. They'd bought machines together in New York, talked the salesman on Thirty-second Street into giving them a two-unit price. He was an expert at operating it, but oddly, feared turning it on. What would he do if there was nothing here, either?

The machine's humming was almost drowned out by the wind. Amirault whirled at a shattering noise; the window had blown in. The temperature plummeted and snow blew through the smashed pane in a funnel shape, churning into a widening circle as it reached farther into the room. It began piling up on the synthetic carpet. During the two years he'd been here, no storm had been this bad.

A flake oozed into glaze across blue letters on-screen. With fingers stiff from toxin, he punched up her list of files: TAXES. COPEPODS. JOBS. THINGS TO DO TODAY. NEURAL. GRANT PROPOSALS.

A.Y.'s voice called, out in the hallway. "Jack! You down here?"

Shit.

"Jack?"

The knob turned but he'd locked the door. Amirault held his breath, listening for a key.

COPEPODS, he typed. A graph swam up on-screen, its columns labeled date, diet, size, age. Same as the notebook.

He tried GRANT PROPOSALS and read a pitch to the National Science Foundation: "I am interested in how copepods propel themselves through water."

THINGS TO DO TODAY included NN, Arlington, Mexican recipes.

Amirault leaned forward, trying to will information from the machine. Arlington? The Pentagon was in Arlington. Who or what was NN?

He jerked as a loose glass shard tumbled from the sill and lodged, edge up, in the miniature drift below it.

NEURAL, he tried. The computer hummed, taking its sweet time.

Uh-uh, Evylyn, the screen read. *Ze passvord, pliss.*

A sharp pain started up between Amirault's eyes.

The cursor pulsated. Evylyn, at nine, had loved to give him riddles and then torture him if he didn't know the answer, by saying over and over, "Well? Well? *Well?*"

From the hallway outside, voices again. "The window's busted in Cathy's lab!"

And Rick's voice: "You left the shutters open?"

"I thought *you* closed them!"

"Get my keys! They're in the garage!"

Sweat grew cold on Amirault's forehead. They'd be coming into all the labs. There was a crackling sound as the remaining glass blew into the room, hit the screen, scattered on the keyboard. His wrist was cut. A ruby-colored dot welled by the bone joint.

Password, he thought. He punched in BRIAN. He tried their parents' names, her birthday. Their aunt. I'll never get it. The goddamn password. He heard a door slam in the lab on the other side of the wall. "These are the wrong keys!" Rick was shouting in the hall.

Think.

What's special to her? More special than anything in the world.

No, he thought. Not that.

But he keyed in AMI TWO.

The screen hummed and went blank and his heart was breaking. But he looked at a blueprint now, topped by the words NEURAL NETWORK. For an instant he didn't understand. Then he did. NN, he exulted! Astounded, he realized he was looking at something he did not know could exist — a computer re-creation of the sensory system of a living creature. The lines, twisting, pairing and splitting up, joining and rejoining in looping, tangled, crisscrossing masses, represented nerve endings, synapses, pathways where the animal processed information about prey it tracked.

The snow blew in and he was seized by love and admiration for his sister.

Neural networks had only been theory until now. He'd known her work would have applications to undersea warfare but this diagram was beyond anything he'd anticipated.

He heard her voice in his head: "Once I duplicate it, it's simple to program the same blueprint into a machine, Ami Two."

"Like a submarine," he told her.

"Or a torpedo." It was the obvious next step. "Torpedoes use sonar to home in on targets," she said, voicing his thoughts. "They can be fooled by soundmakers. But if they sense water displacement around the target, like my copepods, you can't fool them anymore.

"It's worth billions."

Amirault told her, "That's why you were shouting about money, in the bar."

"Every navy will want it," Evylyn breathed.

I'm Evylyn, Amirault thought, transported. I've had a horrible year. I've invented a weapon. I'm sworn to secrecy. It's tearing me up. People could die because of me.

He stopped. He was missing something. Just two days before she died she gave that happy presentation in the video lounge, bragging about her work. It's not that the invention bothered her. She was proud of it.

It's that someone stole it and she found out.

As soon as he thought it, the pieces fell into place. The sense he'd had that something special had gone wrong that night. The way she blamed herself for things. The way she'd cried to him, "I don't want to hurt anyone else." She would never turn in a friend.

Is that why she'd tried to set the alarm clock? To meet someone? To talk them into giving a copy of this blueprint back?

They'd killed her instead.

The oxygen seemed to drain from the lab. Amirault clawed thin air. The ice shards looked like broken glass on the keyboard. Tell the Navy, he thought. They'll quarantine the base, and the *Queen*, send down fingerprint and DNA investigators. You can get help now. You don't have to do everything yourself. Even if they don't believe you, her work was important enough for them to check.

He saw Evylyn, eternally a twelve-year-old, sitting on a bed looking down at him, legs crossed, one white sock dangling, and she was saying, "You and me, Ami Two." She had always been that twelve-year-old, no matter how they changed, their conversations, their preoccupations. You and me. And then both of them had made bargains with the devil that drove a new kind of secrecy between you and me.

Rick's voice, in the hallway, said, "Okay, let's get in these labs!"

I need a copy, Amirault told himself. Get to the satellite phone upstairs.

There was the sound of a slamming door outside in the hallway.

Her spare disks were in a plastic box beside the laptop, and one was missing.

Whoever had killed her had it.

He could scarcely control his fingers. He inserted the disk in the computer, which began its clunky, wheezing sounds as it copied her work.

Rick cried, muffled, in the hallway, "Window's busted in Gail's lab! Get a mop!"

Amirault grabbed the disk from the computer, shut the machine, whipped a spare lab coat off the table, and rushed to the window. As he shoved the bunched-up coat over the pane, the broken glass, a key turned in the lock. He knocked the glass out and hauled himself up. The door was opening. He saw someone silhouetted, looking back, saying something to someone in the hall.

Amirault gave a final heave and fell out into the drifts. For an instant he couldn't breathe. He was buried. Dizziness washed over him. There was light; it was daytime but just barely. Dawn or dusk or maybe the snow simply distorted the light. There was no sense of direction. It was like tumbling in a wave. He swayed but stood up, lurched away from the window, groped against the building because otherwise he was blind. The snow was waist-high and fat wet flakes slapped into him with a slushy sound like snowballs hitting fabric. He heard a sizzling like drops burning in a frying pan. Amirault's bare skin stuck to the igloolike rime. His ankles were wet. His gums stung.

Amirault passed under a dim square of light, another window. He fought his way around the side of the building, picturing his position as he moved, because he saw no harbor, walkway, people. Nothing but roaring snow.

Amirault fell into the deserted foyer of the building. He shook from cold. The lights flickered and the parkas hanging from hooks had the limp attitude of dead men. He pulled on one of the float-suits. Now anyone seeing him would assume he'd been working outside, trying to help. The shivering would work for him, which was good because it wouldn't go away.

The stairway was deserted. The lights went out but came on

again. In the empty radio room Amirault went for the green re-
ceiver, the satellite line. But he heard no dial tone.

"What are you doing?" a voice behind him said.

Amirault whirled. Kojak was staring at him, eyes traveling down
his body to the puddle of water on the synthetic carpet.

"Calling the *Queen*," Amirault said, thinking quickly, "for
help."

Kojak looked wan and exhausted. He fell into the swivel chair
by the latched window. "We tried it," he said. It was the window
through which they'd looked out at Robyn Cassidy's SOS flags, a
year ago. "We tried it twenty minutes ago but an iceberg took out
the antenna. There's no way to talk to anyone till this blow is over."

Kojak gazed outside, into the storm. The building rattled. There
was a crashing sound, furniture moving, windows breaking, something big fallen on its side. "Ten minutes or ten days. Meanwhile,
we're stuck."

six

Antarctic weather is more violent than anywhere else on earth. Winds sweep across the ice, gather speed and strike the coast at up to two hundred miles an hour. Blizzards materialize in minutes, and rage as long as a month. Yet all that time the sun may be shining ten miles away.

Weather prediction in Antarctica is useless. At best, forecasts apply only a few hours.

By dusk, the wind cups on the Sears Tower had been ripped from their mooring. The weather shack was swept away, with its all-sky cameras and pyrometers and photoelectric metering devices.

The antennas had toppled. The garage door had smashed in. Snow blew inside, with a roar like an express train, as Amirault battled to help lash tarpaulins over the Zodiac boats. He stretched a cord, tied it to the pull-bar behind the snowmobile. Hoarfrost, his own solidified breath, blocked his nostrils and weighed down his eyelids. He kept his face from the wind.

From outside he heard the steady growling of the baby dozer. Haystack drove it to keep a path open to the fuel dump. Elsewhere,

Gail, Cathy, A.Y., and Robyn checked fire-fighting equipment, taped windows, secured loose crates, reinforced the World Trade Center roof.

A hand fell on his shoulder and he turned to see the slitted mask of a balaclava. Rick shouted over the storm to be heard. "Inside!"

Together they battled back toward the Sears Tower, walking backward against the wind and doubled to keep from being blown over. Snow lines advanced across the plowed area outside the garage as someone — a woman, from her size — joined them with a tie-line around her billowing parka. Amirault caught sight of another figure clinging to the side of the building. He fought his way through the storm and helped drag her into the foyer. The sudden cessation of wind was a shock. She pulled off her balaclava. "Thanks," Robyn said.

They all made it back. "Wind's gotta be eighty easy," Haystack gasped, unzipping his parka. The olive oil he used to soften his beard had frozen to a greenish sheen. "I'm worried about the generator building. Roof's weak."

"We might lose power?" Gail looked frightened. "But . . . But we need electricity for heat."

"Doc, we got a spare generator and we moved a dozen fuel barrels to the building," Haystack said. "Don't worry." But he glanced at the red digital wind readout on the wall, and let out a low whistle. "Ninety-two."

They peeled off their hoods and made their way upstairs to the mess. Rick turned the thermostat to 80, but the cold seemed lodged in Amirault's bones. Robyn and Kojak kept their parkas on. Amirault couldn't stop shivering even under his Thermalite liner. But he thought, They'll sleep deeply tonight. I'll break into Rick's office then.

At least, if he couldn't phone out, the storm gave him an opportunity. His chest constricted with urgency. He must do it tonight. Before the storm ended and the *Queen* returned, and the base grew crowded again. Before the winter-overs began their four-month regimen of sweeping, mopping, painting, disinfecting. Eliminating clues.

They fell into chairs at a center table, as if staying together would provide comfort against the storm. The mess seemed eerily empty. The orca mobile by the Plexiglas window rotated by itself, as if a stream of air had gotten in. For a few minutes none of them moved; then A.Y. forced himself to go into the galley. Soon Amirault smelled the spicy odors of simmering meat. His mouth watered. Haystack and Robyn brought pitchers of water, soda, a six-pack of Sierra Pale, and a gallon of apple juice to the table.

Ten minutes later Amirault was wolfing down his second steaming bowl of Dinty Moore stew. He was famished. The meat went down in chunks and burned his throat. He didn't care. The gravy and vegetables were delicious. It was the best meal he'd ever had. He tore off pieces of hot French bread and lathered on butter and washed it down with four cans of sweet, cold Mountain Dew.

He was too tired to talk. Gail had fallen asleep at the end of the table, head back, and snored lightly. Rick poured everyone a round of Dewars. "Keep you warm," he said. Kojak ladeled a third helping of stew for himself, and slurped directly from his bowl.

They all shared a white, drained, red-eyed look.

At least for a moment, full and warm, they felt a sense of relief. But then Robyn jerked her thumb at the picture window and said, "Snow's coming in."

Gail groaned, waking up. "The window's supposed to be sealed."

"I told you to fix it," Rick snapped at Haystack.

The big machinist dropped his soup spoon by his bowl. "You told me about five thousand things," he shot back. "If you hadn't sent everyone off on the *Queen*, maybe someone would have been around here to do them."

Rick flushed and drained his drink. A.Y. shifted closer to Cathy, squeezed her shoulder. Amirault couldn't tell if it was an affectionate or possessive gesture. "How about a duet after dinner? Cool everything down."

Her eyes flickered to Amirault. "We can do it here."

"Music," Kojak retorted. "That oughtta keep the wind out."

Amirault pushed his plate away and sat back, and they all felt the continent outside, its awful indifference. Their layers of protection — clothes, fuel, this building, music — were collapsing around them. The sense of malevolence he'd first experienced in Evylyn's room was back, at this table.

You're going to try to kill me again, Amirault thought.

"If you don't want to listen to music," A.Y. told Kojak, "watch your stupid Rambo movies."

Amirault lowered his head and felt the rush of fury on his face. He didn't want them to see it. He wanted to use it, not squander it.

Kojak changed the subject. "Who took my wrench?"

"Not again," Haystack said.

"My father gave me that wrench," Kojak said. "It was his wrench, and he gave it to me when I was nine. It was in my toolbox at three and it isn't there now."

"I didn't take your wrench," Haystack said.

"I didn't say you did."

"You're looking at me."

"Feeling guilty?" Kojak said.

"Fuck you and the stupid wrench," A.Y. said.

Gail had her memo book out and wrote steadily, glancing from A.Y. to Kojak.

Rick started to say, "Anyone want coffee —" but Cathy interrupted.

"Stop writing!"

Gail blinked out through thick glasses. "Excuse me?"

"You heard me! Can't anyone say anything here without you writing it down? You're driving me crazy!"

Suddenly they were all shouting.

Rick yelled, "What's wrong with everybody!" and Kojak, "I had that wrench since I was a kid!" Haystack: "I *checked* the generator! Screws don't come loose by themselves!" Robyn: "I could have been at Victoria Base by now!"

Rick threw his keys on the table. They smashed into his bowl with the sound of china cracking. "You want skis? Take ours! Go out in *that!*"

They fell silent. The clock turned from 9:50 to 9:51, rolling forward in a pointless progression of time. The wind rose with a ululating sound outside, and in the main note Amirault imagined he heard a smaller, higher keening, like a woman laughing. The harsh overhead light seemed to change their faces, make them tight and shiny with awareness.

Amirault realized the others felt the same way he did, dwarfed and powerless. It was as if the malevolence came from the continent itself, not a person. Antarctica had dozed while they built dormitories, watched movies, drank and danced in their pub, fooled themselves into thinking they were masters here, imagined that the few storms they'd experienced represented the worst things could get. Now the beast had roused itself. They could only hope it would go back to sleep.

"Let's face it." Cathy's words fell flat, in the silence. "There's a Kronsky here."

An electric excitement spread outward in the room. It was the first time anyone besides Amirault had claimed something more than "accidents" were happening. He held his breath. Maybe they would listen. It was clear from the expectant look on most faces that others had been wrestling with the same idea.

"First," Cathy said, touching right index finger to left, beginning the roll call of mishaps, "Evylyn." Rick blurted, "That was an accident!" She waved him away. "Then the generator. Then Kojak's wrench."

"You're making a big deal out of nothing," Rick said.

"Let her talk," A.Y. said.

"It's not just the wrench. Admit it. Other things have disappeared. Hector's medicine. Laticia's earring. Gail's sunglasses. Too many things!"

Rick said, mocking, "Earrings and medical supplies. What's the connection between earrings and medical supplies?"

"That they're gone," A.Y. said.

Yes, yes, yes, yes, Amirault thought. Lieber's Washington slide show came back to him, a vision of the Russian base on fire. He felt it safe to join in now. The others wouldn't be repelled if he did. "With Kronsky, little things went wrong at first," he said.

Rick held his palms out, abandoned sarcasm for reasonableness. "Don't you think things are getting out of hand here?"

"That's the point," Cathy said.

"You're starting to sound like Jack," Rick said.

"Maybe we should have listened to him from the beginning. Maybe if we'd listened, things would be different."

Rick took a long swig of scotch. He seemed nervous. "Listen to yourself. Slow down. You're saying someone pushed Evylyn off the rocks? One of us *killed* her?"

"Well, maybe not that," Kojak said. "But let's search the rooms. I want my wrench."

"Can't hurt," Cathy said.

"Now?" Rick said. "It isn't that easy."

"Why not?"

"Because he doesn't want to piss off Lieber. He's worried about his job," Amirault said.

"Unless he's the one who took the stuff."

Rick told them to shut up.

He rubbed the space between his eyes with two fingers. He looked wan and exhausted. "Sunglasses. A wrench. You're blowing things out of proportion," he said. "How would you like to come back from the *Queen* to find we searched your rooms, desks, closets? Read your diary. Found your dope stash." A joke. Haystack laughed. Rick said, "Besides, your ass won't be on the line when they complain to Lieber. It'll be mine."

"Then you shouldn't have applied for the job," Cathy said.

A light sweat had broken out on Rick's brow. "Don't you feel what's going on here? Panic." He looked from face to face. "People lose things all the time. You can't seriously believe someone loosened the bolts on the generator."

"I check that machine all the time," Haystack said.

"Every bolt?"

Haystack looked uncomfortable. "Well, maybe not . . ."

The lights went out.

There was a scream from the end of the table, and a crash like a pot turning over, and scraping chairs. Amirault started to get up. Everyone was shouting. Something heavy struck him on the shoulder, driving him over.

IT'S YOU!

He started to topple and grabbed air, made contact with someone's shirt, felt thick flannel and held on and pulled his attacker down. Fingers clawed at Amirault's face. He struck out and felt his fist strike something hard. Pain exploded in his knuckles. He and the man he held smashed into a wall together. Glass shattered.

Whoever he was on top of screamed, "Stop!"

A flashlight went on somewhere above him.

Kojak thrashed on the floor below, nose bleeding, and people pulled them apart.

"What are you doing?" Rick demanded.

"He's crazy!" Kojak yelled. "He attacked me!"

Kojak seemed genuinely puzzled.

"See?" Rick said as the men separated, brushed themselves off. Gail gave Kojak a cloth napkin, which he pressed to his nose. "See what happens when we start talking like this? See how quickly things go nuts?"

Cathy switched on a second flashlight and A.Y. brought the black steel Eveready from the kitchen. In the yellow beams, the group stood in a jagged circle. Chairs were overturned. Water pitchers had been knocked over, and plates, and there was a pool of apple juice on the floor. Haystack put down a butter knife. Gail scribbled in her pad.

"See?" Rick said, back in control. "Wanna bet we just lost the roof on the generator shack? We were all here, *everyone* was here."

The others looked chagrined. The wind readout by the barometer had cracked at ninety-four. Cathy said, "Sorry."

"Good. So let's get the spare generator on-line and see what supplies we can pull from the shack."

Amirault was sick with disappointment. A search would have enabled him to look for Evylyn's stolen computer disk. Embarrassed and subdued, they filed downstairs and donned parkas again and tied on safety lines. Haystack started up the Caterpillar. Snow had blown against the tread in three-foot drifts in the last hour.

They needed to get electricity on-line or the buildings would freeze up, the pipes would burst. Woozy from the poison still in his system, and the scotch, Amirault pitched in, followed the Cat like infantry behind a tank, as it bulled its way to the generator building. The roof was gone, all right. Snow already coated the generator, and piled up faster than the dissipating heat could melt it. Snow buried shelves, tools, ski equipment.

They placed clothing, skis, small items that would blow away, into the Caterpillar bucket and retreated to the Sears building, where Amirault poured fuel into the spare generator and Kojak started it up. Lights flickered on. The building had cooled considerably in the short time since they'd left, but the electric sideboard units began crackling and clinking. Heat was coming up.

It was midnight. The storm held steady outside.

"Let's all get some sleep," Rick said. "Haystack, you and I set alarms for five-thirty. To check things. Everyone else might as well sleep late unless we wake you." He added sarcastically, "Or does anyone still feel like searching rooms?"

"Me," Amirault said.

"Maybe my wrench'll show up somewhere," Kojak said. "I guess I got too excited."

Gail seemed to speak for the others. "All I want to do is sleep."

Amirault and Evylyn rode bikes past the wineries in Sonoma, on a fall afternoon. The light was orange. Even grass in California looked blond, long and wavy on the hillsides that were not covered with eucalyptus groves or vineyards. The grapes hung, small and perfect, dark purple. Evylyn was in rapture. "The colors," she said.

"Who's the girl I saw you with at the dance?" she teased, big sister to little brother.

"Robyn Cassidy." Amirault pedaled with his head back, so the church spires and white clouds moved steadily in the opposite direction.

"What didn't make sense that night? You saw it, but you haven't remembered it?"

There was a screeching and Amirault bolted up, and the alarm was ringing. Three-thirty. He shut it off. His muscles ached from the heavy labor earlier.

The faint odor of eucalyptus lingered in the room, died into the ammonia smell of sleep. I've been over that night a thousand times. Did I miss something?

Get to those files now.

He rose groggily and in the weak glow of the clock pulled on jeans and a long-sleeved pullover. His throat was dry. The screwdriver and hammer were under his bed.

The hallways were empty. Reaching Rick's office, Amirault used the screwdriver to remove a strip of aluminum molding running up the doorway. When it was gone he slipped a credit card between the lock and the sideboard. He'd seen it in movies. Hell, he thought. It works.

He slipped into the office, taking the molding with him. He locked the door and laid the aluminum strip against the crack, to block light shining out. Amirault turned on the light.

Hurry, he thought. He counted five file cabinets, two under the desk, three tall ones against the wall. Not to mention the desk drawers and cardboard boxes piled on floor-to-ceiling steel shelves.

He started with the tall cabinets. The top drawer slid open easily, revealing alphabetical files. *Chlorination, Electric, Kitchenware, Plumbing.*

Go slower now, he told himself. Don't skip things. The second drawer held *Health forms, Salaries, Parts estimates, Machinery, Puntas, Fuel bills.*

Shit.

Amirault tried the second cabinet. *Generator building, Weather, Wiring, World Trade Center.*

4:07. An hour left, considering that he'd have to clean up, screw the molding back, and reach his room before Rick and Haystack woke.

Amirault found nothing in the third file cabinet.

The desk cabinets were locked.

He leaned back and peered at the label on the drawer. *Underwater.* He tried the other drawers. They were locked too. *Base,* one read. Then, *Washington.* And *Correspondence.*

Outside, the wind seemed to be dropping, but with the shutters drawn there was no way to see. 4:21. Amirault felt his jaw muscles clenching. He regarded the screwdriver and hammer on the blotter.

Wait till Rick gets to work tomorrow, Amirault said to himself.

It was a bar lock. He wedged the screwdriver between the lock and file cabinet. He hoped a single blow would dislodge the lock and somehow the damage would not be visible. He winced at the hollow sound when the hammer struck, once, twice. The drawer dented, but the lock held.

He smashed the hammer into the screwdriver handle. At the fourth and hardest blow, the lock separated out, half an inch. He pulled the drawer open.

"Whoa," Amirault said, pulling out handcuffs, a dildo, *Hustler* magazines. He held up a leather mask resembling a balaclava, with silver zippers lining the eyeslits and mouth. And a five-by-eight manila envelope marked *Photos*. Amirault hesitated, then looked inside. The first shot showed Rick and a woman Amirault had never seen in a single bed, looking at the camera, copulating doggy style. The woman wasn't particularly good-looking, her stomach hung down, and there was a bottle of wine on a nightstand. Rick looked stringy and washed out in the shot.

Amirault flipped through the photos, woman after woman, his stomach lurching. No wonder the manager didn't want people searching rooms. His gorge rose. He was afraid he'd see Evylyn. But he couldn't stop. With only two photos left he found himself eyeing a slim naked woman who seemed familiar despite the black mask. He flipped to the last shot. Laticia.

Amirault turned the photo over and checked the date. It had been taken last year, when he and Laticia were lovers.

"Figures."

He dropped the envelope, weak with relief. Amirault forced himself to move, but he felt sordid. Rick's sex life was nobody else's business. Amirault wanted to be through with this, to go home.

But he put the envelope in his pocket.

"I don't think we have to worry about you telling anyone I damaged your locks," he said.

He replaced the magazines and sex accoutrements. The mask folded up so only one zippered eye was visible.

Only one drawer left. The lock broke with the first blow. "Personnel," Amirault read out loud.

Pulse hammering, he reached for the first file and discarded it. The man had been on the *Queen* when Evylyn died.

There should be files for all of them except Clyde, the exchange visitor, and Robyn, the uninvited guest.

Rick first. He read silently. Skimmed the history and read the psychological profile with more depth. "Hard worker. Excellent at handling pressure. Devoted husband and family man."

"Some psychiatrist," Amirault said out loud.

He opened Gail's file.

"Hardheaded. Recommended by NASA. Standoffish but not asocial. Envies women."

Cathy: "Does well in group situations. Prone to depression if thwarted in personal or professional life."

He remembered her in her lab, crying.

5:11.

Laticia: "Self-motivated. Slightly self-centered." Slightly? he thought. "Able to make others do what she wants."

Amirault was growing frustrated.

A.Y.: "Brilliant. Athletic. Suffers nightmares about his boyhood in China before his family escaped to Hong Kong. One story: He stands in front of his first-grade class and the children jeer because his father has been arrested."

China would buy military secrets, Amirault thought.

Amirault flashed to his Pentagon briefing, and the three Navy captains eyeing him. "Your work is valuable, Dr. Amirault. Scientists on Antarctic bases don't need top clearance, but it's possible people could try to steal your work."

"Then why let them in?"

He saw them smiling, pitying the poor researcher. Give him a microscope. Give him a seismograph machine. Give him a bunsen burner. Leave politics to us.

5:19.

He opened Hector's file.

"Dr. Carroll has an excellent record. His application for transfer to Antarctica should be given special attention. No hard evidence ever linked him to the U.S.S. *Philadelphia* incident and he's threatened legal action against the Navy if his career suffers now that the investigation is through. Dr. Carroll wishes to end his service in a quiet out-of-the-way place."

Amirault stared at it. "What the hell is this?"

He heard a heavy tread upstairs. Haystack's room was directly above Rick's office.

He remembered nothing about any ship called the U.S.S. *Philadelphia*. Maybe there would be information on it in the library.

He shoved the files back in place, and pushed in the broken locks. "That'll fool them," he said wryly, eyeing the dent marks all over the cabinets. Amirault made sure he had Rick's photographs. He hurried up.

The hallway was empty. Amirault moved lightly to the end of the corridor, peeked out at the mess, jerked back. Haystack was drinking coffee out there.

Next time he looked, Haystack was gone.

Amirault went back, screwed the aluminum molding back in place. He reached the dorm area, and his room, without being seen. He got rid of the tools.

His legs felt shaky. He'd carried it off. It was perfectly all right to go to the library now. Anyone could go to the library. In the hallway, he heard the shower running and hot steam blew into the hall. Rick was singing, off-key, "Ah want you, want you, want you, want you."

Outside, the storm had ended. The sky was dark with approaching winter, but the stars were thick and bright. A warm breeze wafted off the water, sculpting wavy ridges atop drifts on the Dan Ryan Expressway. The snow shone, green, blue, violet. The crystals sparkled in the reflection of arc lights from the garage. He heard lapping water. Normal sounds were back in the world.

The doorway grew closer and he was in the World Trade Center, cold, colder, abandoned ghost building. He could almost hear the music from last week's party. Voices. Laughter. Smells of turkey and whiskey and Evylyn screaming at them, "Nobody cares about us."

And here was the library with its magazines and its Nexus computer, off-line because the phones were out, and its *Reader's Guide to Magazines* over the last five years.

Amirault flipped pages, went back two years. "U.S.S. *Philadelphia*." He pounded the table in triumph. Dozens of articles were listed under the ship's name, the bulk of them written four years ago.

"*Newsweek. U.S. News & World Report. Vanity Fair. Rolling Stone.*"

He found a copy of *Time*, discolored with age, on the shelf.

Reading, Amirault gasped, "I remember this!"

SPIES ARRESTED

FBI agents this week arrested a father/son spy ring in Reston, Virginia, charging the pair with selling military secrets to the People's Republic of China.

Evan Crane, 56, a Pentagon systems analyst, and Jason Crane, 24, seaman first class on the U.S.S. *Philadelphia*, were arrested after a six-month investigation. The FBI charged the pair with receiving $2.5 million over the last six years, paid by a Chinese commercial attaché in Washington.

"What did Hector have to do with this?" Amirault said. He kept reading in a low, awed voice.

Chinese officials denied the charges. They said the diplomat, Wu Kai Nung, has been transferred out of Washington as part of normal job rotation.

China experts here have pointed out that the People's Republic relies heavily on sales of military equipment and technology for foreign exchange and added that the electronic secrets the Cranes were selling would be worth millions to any arms manufacturer.

Amirault rubbed his brow. "Wu. Where did I hear that name? Wu."

Then he remembered. His skin tingled with the sense of urgency. On the radio, he thought. From Victoria Base. They were interviewing him about the treaty. He's there, he's at Victoria, he's there, *they're both there!*

Hector stole her work.

Amirault fell back in the chair. He saw the doctor in the lounge, watching Evylyn's video movie. He saw Hector saying, "What does her work have to do with the Navy?" He saw Hector giving him pills to help him "sleep better," and shots to put him out. And Hector sending Laticia to buy him off with a job offer at Exxon. But more than that, most of all, he remembered the fear he had felt coming from Hector in the lounge, when they watched Evylyn's video.

Amirault squeezed the sides of the table. The room seemed to be rocking. The edges of his vision blurred. He battled to keep himself from jumping to conclusions. All the articles repeated the same news, or followed the trial with no mention of Hector.

The very last piece, dated two years later, was only an inch long in *Time* magazine.

NAVY DROPS INVESTIGATION

Naval investigators today admitted that at least three other seamen have been under investigation for their possible roles in the U.S.S. *Philadelphia* incident, but said the investigations were being dropped after only circumstantial evidence linked two sailors and a doctor to the theft of military secrets on the ship.

None of the three were named. But they have all been reassigned to less sensitive posts, a Navy spokesman said.

It could be a coincidence, Amirault thought. Coincidences happen. I don't want to make a mistake.

It's not a coincidence.

The rage exploded in him. Hector, he thought. *Hector.* He reached his room again without seeing anyone. The antenna should be up in a few hours. I'll call Washington. His room seemed cold. He smelled a faint odor of vanilla, as if Robyn had been there while he was gone. Must be his imagination. He lay on the covers with his jacket on. He took off his clothes after a while and rolled over and stared at the cinder-block wall.

Hector.

In his sleep he was looking for someone, going room to room on base, but no one was there.

Amirault ran through the base, panicked.

"I didn't mean it," he called.

He heard knocking and his eyes opened. He felt a terrible emptiness inside. Haystack stood in the doorway, glaring down at him.

"Someone broke into Rick's office," Haystack said. "And busted into his records."

"Who?"

"Rick wants everyone in the office."

They don't know who it is yet or they'd all be here. He sat up, spotted his jeans on the chair, with Rick's envelope of pictures, jutting from the pocket. He hoped Haystack wouldn't notice it. *Photos*, it said.

He stood up. "Let me brush my teeth," he said. He pushed the envelope deeper into the pocket, realizing he'd been wrong about Rick. The manager wasn't about to protect his reputation if the cost was putting the base in danger. Rick simply hadn't believed there was real danger before. Confronted with a damaged office this morning, he'd changed his mind.

Amirault would go back to the office now, and everyone would stand around and ask each other questions, and get no answers, as usual, and at length he'd call Washington, and later, when things had been set in motion, he'd confess.

"What about the satellite antenna?" he said casually. "Is it fixed?"

"That can wait," Haystack said. "Right now, everybody to the office. We figured out how to catch the person."

Amirault straightened up and tried to hide his fear.

"How?"

Haystack looked grim. "Actually, Robyn Cassidy thought it up. Everyone stays together until then. We'll have the bastard within the hour."

seven

Amirault followed Haystack down the stairwell, toward Rick's office. Their footfalls seemed thunderous in the bare, confined space. Each roll of the mechanic's shoulders made Amirault want to bolt. He thought, They know I did it. They're waiting.

Run.

Run where? There was just the ice-packed harbor outside, and the glacier. The lifeless mountains on Purgatory Road.

"Why would someone bust into the files?" Amirault tried to sound puzzled.

"How the hell do I know? Rick'll kill him. I'll help."

Amirault's throat was raw. "You know it's a guy?"

Haystack spun and studied him. "I didn't say it was a guy."

"You said 'him.'"

Haystack resumed walking. "Yeah, well. Him. Her." They turned onto Rick's corridor and Amirault saw Gail and Kojak outside the doorway, staring into the office. Their faces, turning to him as he approached, showed mixed fascination and fear.

"Can you believe it?" Kojak said. "We coulda been burned in

our beds." Gail had her pad flipped open, but she was too nervous to write. Kojak couldn't stop talking. "Burned to death while we slept."

Amirault stepped past them into the office. "What would anyone want with files?" he said with bravado he did not feel.

Rick said, "What would anyone want with the other stuff he took? An earring. Sunglasses."

Had he been here only three hours ago? The shutters were open. Sun flooded in, creating bright shafts filled with drifting dust motes. The office, cramped normally, was practically airless now; the ceiling seemed lower, the aisle narrower, the prefab walls and honeycomb ceiling offering shelter but not trust. Robyn leaned against the doorframe, arms folded, eyeing Amirault. Haystack crowded him from behind, and Amirault caught a faint gasoline smell. Rick, A.Y., and Cathy crouched at the far end, under the window, examining the damaged cabinets.

Amirault told himself, Leave now. Say you're sick.

Rick said, "All here now," with grim satisfaction. "One of you did this. Who?"

Cathy was peering at the damaged drawers with a magnifying glass. On her knees, one arm extended, she resembled a churchgoer holding out a prayer book.

"Fingerprints," she said, as if lecturing a class, "are moisture. Plain moisture. Little sweat. Little oil."

Amirault grew dizzy.

"Press your finger against many surfaces — glass, steel, aluminum file cabinet — it leaves an impression. Robyn was a genius to suggest fingerprints. They're all over the place here, right by the broken lock."

"Couldn't they be Rick's fingerprints?" Gail said. "It's Rick's office."

"Of course Rick's. But whoever broke in must have left lots of other ones."

Amirault said, "You know how to take fingerprints?"

She looked up. "I don't, yet." Amirault followed her gaze to the dining room tray, cluttered with brown lab bottles and chemicals, on the blotter. They had not been there last night. He saw an open cardboard box of microscope slides.

Amirault's throat was dry. Sliding closer, he looked into the open drawer that had held Rick's sex paraphernalia. He saw only a couple of manila files there now. Rick must have moved things.

Rick's jaw was clenched as he scanned their faces for a tic, averted glance, giveaway. "Whoever did this," he said, trying again, "say so now. It'll be easier for you."

No one spoke.

"You have a problem," Rick said softly. Doctor Rick. Father confessor Rick. "We're not mad at you." Haystack nodded. He was Rick's chorus. "Pressure," Rick said. "It's bad down here. You're mad about something. Tell me. You'll land up with doctors, not police."

"Give my wrench back," Kojak blurted. He reddened when Rick glared at him, "Sorry."

The silence spread outward. Nobody was going to confess. At length Cathy blew out a breath and said, "When Robyn said fingerprints I thought, How *do* police find them? Powders, I guessed. 'Dusting for fingerprints.' Isn't that the expression? A.Y. and I collected all the chemical powders we could find in the labs."

It was just like Cathy, Amirault thought, on the eve of an experiment, any experiment, to grow excited. Practical or theoretical, it was all the same to her. He fought down a bitter laugh. It would be ironic, after her record of unblemished failure this season, if this experiment worked. "We'll test it first," she said. "That way we won't damage the real prints. A.Y.? Gimme a thumbprint, right here."

She picked a glass slide from the box by two fingers.

Outside, from the harbor, Amirault heard the bellow of elephant seals. The storm was really over if the animals had come back. All the violence expended, and the continent returned to indifference. Drifts in new places. New crevasses. New icebergs. Ice in the harbor forming a mosaic of different pieces, different shapes.

He moved closer, repelled, drawn. Cathy said, "Not all powders'll work. Some may absorb the moisture and wreck A.Y.'s print. We need something light enough to settle over the print and outline it, not crush it or absorb it."

A.Y. handed Cathy the slide and she held it to the light and squinted through the magnifying glass. "Perfect," she said, grinning.

Sweat trickled down Amirault's armpits. She laid the slide on the far edge of the blotter, away from the area where he'd placed his hands on the desk.

Choosing the closest lab bottle, she said, "Barium tungstate." It was a pigment in X-ray photography. She picked it up delicately. She looked like a chef on a cooking show, announcing the ingredient to her studio audience. She gently shook the white powder into the soup spoon, and tapped the spoon lightly to let a little powder dust over the side.

Amirault stopped breathing as she held the magnifying glass to the slide.

But she frowned and Amirault breathed again. "Absorbed it. Let's try the zinc laurate next."

A.Y. reached for another slide.

"Damn," she said a moment later. "Potassium manganate."

Amirault heard the combined rise and fall of breathing, and smelled coffee, sweat, after-shave. Everyone watched everyone else, thinking, Was it you?

Get to the Zodiacs, he thought, but then, We brought them into the garage last night. And even if they *were* in the water, Kojak had disassembled the outboards for repair.

And where could he go, anyway? To drive around the harbor?

Victoria Base, he thought. To Hector. To the Navy. The Navy will have ships in that harbor, fifty miles north. Tell them what you found. Show them the copy you made of her work. Once they see the copy, even if they don't believe you, they'll check it out.

"Rubidium carbonate," Cathy said, like a surgeon asking for sutures, her voice slightly harsher as her chemicals ran out.

Amirault wanted to laugh. His options had sunk to fantasies. Even the *Polar Queen*, with its detailed maps and radar, got lost in coastal waters, threading the maze of islands, cliffs, icebergs, fogbanks. Gliding half the time through impenetrable mist.

The logistics, he thought, are multiplying against me. Even if I had a half hour to drag a Zodiac into the water, there's the fuel problem, the orcas and leopard seals, the big waves outside the harbor. The rocks and razor-sharp ice beneath the surface, to rip the bottom out.

I'd try anyway if I could get out of this room.

"Here we go," Cathy breathed. Her tongue dotted the corner of her mouth as she concentrated.

At that moment Amirault understood he was going to be caught. He saw with terrible clarity just how alone he was. He saw the awful solitude that lay ahead. Once he stopped asking questions, once he wasn't distracted by pure momentum, the full impact of Evylyn's loss would hit him. It loomed just out of reach now, but it was visible. It was worse than grief. It was loneliness. Punishment was nothing. He knew just how isolated he would be.

"Lead cyanide."

Roller coaster. Each time a powder failed, Amirault's hopes rose. Each time she reached for another, they plunged.

Cathy bit her lip, a moment later. "Rats. Rats. Rats."

"Keep trying," Gail said. Amirault nodded, thinking, Give up. Quit. Now.

Then he remembered bringing in the skis last night, and the supplies from the generator building.

Could I actually reach Victoria Base on Purgatory Road?

For an instant he entertained himself with a vision of white snow, crisp air, gliding between black, towering mountains. Sliding effortlessly beneath the unreal blue of the calm Antarctic sky.

It was a pleasant scene, even if it did require getting out of this room somehow, and it disappeared when Cathy cursed. "I don't understand," she said. "*One* of them should have worked."

Amirault slid his arm around her. The collective disappointment gave him an opening. "Good try," he soothed. "The theory was right. I bet a different powder would have worked."

"The theory," she said bitterly. "Sure. The theory. My theories are always right. In cancer too."

"They *are* right," Amirault said. "You know they'll work some day. If it was easy, everyone would do it. You'd be bored by it."

"Maybe."

"When you find it, it'll be sweeter after all the problems."

Cathy leaned against him. "You're a good friend."

To the others he suggested, "Let's fix that satellite antenna and call D.C. They'll send professionals down."

He kept the exultation off his face when they nodded, started trickling toward the door. Then A.Y. stopped them with, "If powder doesn't work, maybe some other substance will."

Scientists, Amirault thought. I hate them. They can't leave anything alone. He said, calmly, "We go outside. We get the cable. We get the antenna up. We make the call."

"Makes sense," Rick said.

But Kojak broke in. "Glue? Wait! I know it sounds dumb, but glue! Remember those German guys last year? The insect researchers? They found that dragonfly, whatever it was, in amber. Remember? They said amber preserved things . . . impressions." He looked at Cathy hopefully, and the force of his logic faltered a little. "I mean, fingerprints are impressions." He blushed slightly. "And amber's like glue."

Rick's mouth turned up.

"You want to *glue* fingerprints to the table."

Of all of them, Amirault laughed the loudest. "Glue," Rick said impatiently. "*The antenna,*" Amirault urged. "Let's do it. We could be messing up evidence here, for pros who know what to find."

"I guess so," Kojak said. "He's right," Gail said. A.Y. dropped his hands to his sides. But Cathy stared into the air with a fixed expression.

"Glue?" she said softly. She repeated it, louder. "Glue?"

She rummaged in Rick's top drawer, and came up with a plastic tube of Krazy Glue.

"A.Y.," she said excitedly. "Get a propane torch from the lab."

"What are you *doing?*"

"You'll see."

Glue, Amirault thought. Fucking glue. What can she possibly be thinking about with glue? It was so ridiculous he was terrified. It was one of those idiotic schemes that was going to work. He'd almost used up all his self-control. Get away, now, he thought.

"This is stupid," he said, stretching, yawning. "Call me if you find something. I'm going to work on the antenna."

It didn't work. Rick stepped forward, blocking the exit. For an instant the déjà vu was so strong Amirault was transported. Robyn was on the glacier again. Brian was alive, behind him, and he had another choice, another chance.

"You were the one in the generator building," Rick said.

They all regarded Amirault steadily.

He sighed. "Fine, but we'll have to fix the antenna in the end. We're wasting our time here." Amirault shook his head. "Glue!"

"Buddy system from now on," Rick announced, not taking his eyes off Amirault. "At least until we figure this out. Nobody alone. Everyone in pairs. Work together. Eat together. One goes to the john, the other's in the hallway. Sleep in the same room. Gym. Pub. Everything. Robyn's new here. She'll bunk with me."

Amirault felt a surge of jealousy, as a derisive grunt came from the corner. "Forget it," Robyn said. "You've been staring at my breasts for three days."

That broke the tension. Everyone except Rick laughed. Gail slid between Rick and Robyn, righteous as a temperance activist. "You can sleep in the same room with me." Gail divided the world into victims and oppressors. Nothing existed in between.

"I'll buddy with Jack," Cathy said. "Jack? Okay?"

"No problem."

Rick looked from woman to woman, the flash of hate in his face startling. He hates women, Amirault realized. The photos should have shown me that.

Maybe it wasn't Hector. Maybe I'm wrong. Maybe it was Rick.

They finished team assignments. Haystack with Kojak. A.Y. with Rick.

Cathy pouted. "Don't you guys have faith in me? Another ten minutes, we won't need the buddy system anymore."

Fifty miles to Victoria Base, Amirault thought again. And again a vision of those awesome peaks came to him. Could he really reach it? If the weather holds. If I find the right path. If I don't fall into a crevasse, I could cross-country ski it in three days.

Robyn tried it.

I'd need a half hour to get the equipment together.

Half an hour. I can't even walk out of this room.

Now, as the crowd pushed in again, Cathy said, "A.Y., switch on the torch." The match hissed, the torch shot a sputtering yellow flame which slowly turned blue. Amirault felt the fear start up again. Cathy squeezed a drop of glue into an aluminum ashtray, held the tray with the forceps in her right hand, and rotated the flame around the underside of the tray with her left. The glue bubbled, began evaporating into steam.

The glue disappeared.

"That helped," Haystack said.

But Cathy smiled. "Think," she said. "Krazy Glue. Not Elmer's. It's clear. It sticks to things. Melt it and it turns to vapor. Steam is heavy. As soon as it drifts away from the heat, it turns back to mist and drops."

"So?"

She bent down and touched the toe of her sneaker with an index finger. "So it rains back afterward, in a film. Same as when you boil water in a pot with the cover on. Steam collects inside of the lid. Comes back down. Get it?"

She straightened. "We vaporize the glue over the area we want to check for fingerprints. We hold a pot cover, say, over the steam, so it drifts back where we want. It crystallizes after it falls on the fingerprints, the mist so fine it highlights them . . . revealing patterns."

Rick sighed. "This is the last try. If it doesn't work, we go outside."

"What if you ruin the real prints?" Amirault said.

"We'll test it on a slide first."

"Even if you do get a print, how do you preserve it afterward, to compare it to another one?"

"Scotch tape!" Kojak said. "It's clear. Lay the tape on the hardened glue, the sticky part holds the impression."

Cathy beamed. "Good!"

Amirault inched back, toward the doorway. Once again a terrible inevitability marked events. A.Y. pressed his thumb against a microscope slide. Haystack and Kojak left, buddy system, and returned with the lid of a soup pot. Cathy spotted Amirault edging backward. "Jack, c'mere, will you? Whenever I do a big experiment," she told the others, "Jack brings me luck."

He stood beside her, sweating, looking down at the file cabinet. He had the urge to wipe the top with his sleeve, in front of all of them, smear the evidence away. Cathy rubbed his shoulder hard. "Bring me luck," she said. Amirault had never wished until now for a scientist to fail. "Here goes," she said.

She repeated the melting procedure over the fingerprint as Kojak held the aluminum lid above it.

The glue bubbled up into mist on the underside of the lid. It drifted down over the slide. Amirault wanted a drink.

The glue dampened the cabinet top in a rough circle corresponding to the shape of the lid.

A fine, clear mist coated the slide now. This close, Amirault didn't even need a magnifying glass to see the print emerging. The loops and whorls took shape. Dried to hardness. He looked over a fine, clean fossil of A.Y.'s print.

"Yes!" Cathy cried.

"Those insect guys," Kojak shouted.

And Rick: "Got the fucker!"

Amirault said, "I did it."

They all spun toward him.

"I didn't take the stuff," he said, talking faster. "But I broke into the files. Because of Evylyn. Someone stole her work." They were drawing together, staring. He felt their anger rise. "Listen to me! There was something there about Hector!"

They came closer to him.

"It happened a few years ago. Listen to what I have to say!"

They were about to charge.

Amirault bolted into the packed bodies, fullback style. Hit the line. Use your shoulders. But it was surprise that got him through.

He rammed the gap between Rick and Haystack, charged the door as Cathy yelled, behind him, "No!" Gail's face loomed, he shoved her, she fell away. Kojak hung to his sleeve. Amirault broke the tackle. As he ran he thought, Where am I supposed to go?

He bolted through the mess and kitchen, scattering chairs and pots behind him. He had a vague notion of reaching the ski equipment.

They cornered him downstairs, in the foyer. He hadn't even

realized he'd grabbed a steak knife until, facing them, he glanced down in the direction their eyes were gazing, and saw the bright, long blade in his fist.

He'd never use it. But they stayed back, six feet away.

Amirault gasped, "I . . . broke into the office. I admit that. But I didn't do the other stuff."

"I believe you," Haystack said.

"I mean it," Amirault said. "I wanted to see the files. Hector took Evylyn's research. I can prove it. I can show you. Give me a chance."

They didn't say anything. They didn't move. Amirault wanted to throw the knife away but they'd charge if he did. "I didn't damage the generator building. I can prove it."

Haystack said, "Put that thing away."

Amirault started to put the knife down. But he felt them coiling, readying. He said, "I'll make a deal. Let me talk to Washington. Fix the satellite line, I'll call them, and afterward, even if they don't believe me, I'll do what you want. Okay?"

Rick watched the knife, from the front. "Put it down. Put it on the floor. Jack, put it down. I know you don't want to use it."

"Hector stole her work."

Cathy moaned lightly. Robyn stared. Rick stepped forward and Amirault jerked up the knife. He didn't know what else to do. Rick stopped.

"I'll let you call," Rick soothed. "But you can't walk around like this. Someone will get hurt. You understand that, don't you?"

"If I put it down. I know what'll happen."

"What?"

"The cuffs."

"That's right," Rick said. "I'll put the cuffs on you. But I'll *still let you call.* Isn't that what you want? But I'll do it this way so everyone will be safe."

It occurred to Amirault that Rick was stalling for time. He said, "Where's A.Y.? Why isn't A.Y. here?"

Rick just said, "What would you do if you were me, Jack? You'd do the same thing. Okay? Knife on the floor. On the floor, Jack. Put it on the floor. You'll really make the call."

"No," Amirault said. "I don't trust you. After."

Running footsteps sounded in the corridor, A.Y. pushed to the front, and Amirault's hope died. A.Y. had brought the shotgun. "Damn key didn't work. I had to jiggle it," A.Y. told Rick.

Amirault said, not knowing what else to do, "I'm going to put the skis on. Let me do that. I'll get a knapsack. It's not your problem. I'll just leave. Why would I disable the generator? I was in the building. Why would I hurt myself? For Christ's sake, she was my sister! Why would I want to hurt her?"

Rick asked A.Y., "Is it loaded?"

"Yes."

"It was Hector," Amirault cried. "Hector did it!"

The muzzle of the shotgun came up. Rick's arms were shaking, and he pleaded, "Please. Jack. Please. Put the damn knife down."

The knife clattered to the floor beside the skis, knapsacks, boots. "I wouldn't have used it," Amirault said.

They surged forward instantly. The pressure of the last few days had broken loose. Rick couldn't stop it. Nobody could stop it. They were on him, hitting, screaming. Amirault fell back, kicked out as he fell, felt pain explode in his back and saw Haystack toppling backward, bellowing, holding his stomach. Then Haystack disappeared behind the wall of bodies. Kojak was on top of him. Blows rained down on his shoulders, neck, head. A woman's voice, Cathy's, screamed, "Don't hurt him!"

Amirault rolled over on his stomach and covered himself up.

After a while they stopped hitting him.

Groaning, he rolled back over. The ring of faces looking down at him shared the disgusted expression of human beings who had just seen the ugly side of themselves. Their breath frosted in the foyer. Their fury was expended.

"Get him up," Rick said gently. "Get some bandages and alcohol."

They lifted him, ashamed now. Dimly he heard Rick give instructions. Someone, Gail, went off to look for the stolen materials in Amirault's room. A.Y. and Kojak held him up by the armpits. They headed toward the infirmary, but before they reached it, Rick unlocked the broom closet door. Robyn brought a chair inside and set it down. Haystack hovered close, in case Amirault needed to be subdued again.

"Jack," Rick said as Cathy wiped the blood off his face. "I don't know what else to do with you. There's no way to lock you in the infirmary," he said as they handcuffed him to a pipe.

Gail came back from searching Amirault's room. She opened her hands. Amirault saw an earring. Medicine bottles. Sunglasses.

"They were in his closet," Gail said.

"But I didn't take those. They couldn't have been in my closet." Cathy started crying.

"You put it there. Hector put it there." The pain ballooned out in Amirault's stomach, shoulders, everywhere. Vaguely, he remembered Rick's promise. "Let me call Washington," Amirault whispered. "You said I could."

"Plenty of time to talk to them later, after they come for you in the plane."

Haystack fixed things so he was a little more comfortable, built a plywood platform so Amirault could sit, cuffed to the pipe, and not hold his hand so high. The plastic links chafed. Haystack said he was sorry for that. "I could put foam in there," Haystack said. "But then I'd have to open the cuffs, and you'd get out.

"Antenna's up. We called Washington," he added. "We'll have you out in the morning."

"Let me talk to them."

Haystack pursed his lips and sighed. "Rick said no, you heard him. Want to use the bathroom?" He disappeared and returned with a bucket and a roll of toilet paper. "I'll close the door and wait outside. Call when you're done. I'll bring a wet towel to wash your hand. And Jack. You'd make Kojak happy if you gave back his wrench."

"I didn't take it."

Haystack sighed. "Sure. I'll bring food later. Gail's making chimichangas tonight."

The room was warmer. When he pissed, blood came out. Just before dinner Gail arrived with her memo pad and pen.

"I know you're upset," she said, standing back from the doorway, talking much too slowly, as if to a three-year-old or a mental incompetent. "I know you don't like talking to me. I'll go away if you ask. But it would be a big, big help if you could . . . answer questions. A biiiig help."

"Let me make the call," Amirault said.

She shook her head. "It isn't up to me."

"What questions?"

"Ones that might—"

"Help astronauts. I know." Amirault adjusted his wrist in the cuff. It seemed useless to try to bargain. "Why not? I'm not going anywhere," he said. "Well, I was supposed to go to the movies, but maybe I'll stick around."

"When did you first start stealing things?" she said, poised to write. "The medicine. Earrings. Glasses."

Amirault squeezed his eyes shut and said patiently, "I didn't steal them."

"If you didn't consider it stealing, did you think of it some other way?"

"I didn't take anything."

She wrote quickly, in big loops, in shorthand. She glanced up at him as if considering how far to go with her questions. "They were in your closet. I found them. How else could they have gotten there?"

"Hector."

"Oh," she said softly. But she wrote more than one word. More than just "Hector."

"Let's talk about the generator," she said. She turned red. "Were you trying to . . . you know . . . ?"

"Kill myself?"

"You know . . ."

"I didn't touch the generator," Amirault said wearily.

"Then who . . . Hector again?"

Amirault looked away and heard her say, with more sympathy than he thought possible, "What do you want me to say? That I believe you?"

"That would be nice."

"You want a magazine? Something from the library?"

"Beef or chicken," he said. "Bring me one of those little peanut packages, miss, in foil."

"Huh?"

"Nothing. Keep asking questions. It's okay."

She sucked at her pen. "What were you looking for in Rick's office?"

"The profiles, Gail. You told me about them. Remember? The psychological profiles."

She looked startled, since he'd denied everything else. "But why?" she said.

He told her about the U.S.S. *Philadelphia*. And Hector and the Chinese.

She stared at him.

"Go look yourself," he said.

"I read the file, Jack. No specific accusations were mentioned, and Hector was cleared anyway. Does he have to pay for a phony charge his whole life?"

"Tell them!"

"Nobody's supposed to know about this. I'd lose my job. If I thought you were right I'd do it, but you're guessing."

Nervous, she switched the subject. "Did you and Evylyn have an argument in her room that night? She was yelling at you in the bar. About Brian. Did that make you angry, what she was yelling? She was yelling about him dying, and you being alive."

He looked up at her slowly. "What are you saying?"

She swallowed. "I'm asking if all of this is because you hurt Evylyn that night. You were the last one with her."

"No more questions," Amirault said.

Amirault heard a live radio broadcast from down the hall. The announcer said, with an echoey quality, "I'm standing in a make-shift clinic, at Victoria Base. Doctors from seven countries are taking care of a rash of flu among diplomats here to sign the new Antarctic Minerals Agreement. With me is Dr. Hector Carroll, of the U.S. Navy. Captain, you seem pretty busy here today."

Cathy appeared in the doorway holding dinner. Gail's chimi-

changas, beans and rice, and an uncapped bottle of gold Tecate
Mexican beer. There was a wedge of lime on a plate beside it. And
a mug with an orca on it, full of red salsa dip. "Your fav," she said,
placing the tray on his knees. "Want a folding table?"

"Let me free."

She blinked. She said, "Shut up." After putting the tray on his
knees she sat on the floor and folded her legs in a lotus position.
Amirault said, "A spoon? All I get is a spoon? For Christ's sake,
Cathy, how am I going to eat with a spoon?"

"It's soft. I tried it before I brought it."

After a moment, when he didn't move, she said, "Don't you
want to eat? It's really good."

The chimichanga tasted dry and floury and the beer sour. On
the radio, Hector said lots of people who come to Antarctica get
colds and flus the first two weeks. "You're cooped up together," he
said in his "doctor" voice, "with people from different places. It's
the same principle as flying long distances on an airplane. Same
air circulation system. Same other passengers. You'd get all kinds
of colds."

Amirault tried dessert, a chocolate fudge brownie. He drank all
the beer. When he was finished she came and took the tray off his
lap. She didn't seem afraid of him, like Gail. She lingered, close,
holding the tray.

"I don't know how to say this, Jack, but someday you'll see the
crummy thing the Navy did to you. They shouldn't have sent you
back here this year. Evylyn, too. You were both wrecks. They were
selfish. They didn't care about you — just your work. It's not your
fault what happened."

Amirault spoke carefully, logically. "You know why the Navy
wanted her so badly? She was working on a project, a special
project for them. And she found something, really important. Hector stole it. He's at Victoria Base, passing it, selling it."

Cathy started crying.

The radio announcer was saying, "Dr. Carroll's patient with us
is Wu Kai Nung, a member of the Chinese delegation. Have the
flu, do you?"

Amirault pleaded with her. "Call the Pentagon. Even if you

don't believe me. Tell them I asked you to. Hell, tell them you think I'm lying. Or I'm crazy. I don't care what you say. But *do it for me.* I'll give you the number. It's the Office of Naval Research. I'll tell you what to say."

She shook her head.

"Why?"

On the radio, Wu Kai Nung said, in unaccented English, "Then I ran a fever. Same symptoms as the member from Brazil. Dr. Carroll wants me to try his Western medicine."

"Because," she said, "Rick's been on the phone with a Navy psychiatrist. She told us—she was adamant about this—if you start up, saying things, it's important for us not to play along with it. Talk you down, she said. Actually, I always thought you were supposed to go along. What do *I* know?

"There's no spy here, Jack. Hector didn't kill your sister. There's no secret meeting to sell military secrets at Victoria Base. Okay?"

Amirault said glumly, "Wanna bet?"

There was less noise in the hallway now. It was after supper. Somewhere a CD was playing, something classical, Mozart maybe. He thought he heard the droning of a plane outside, a Twin Otter coming to get him. But planes weren't allowed to land at night.

Footsteps in the hallway, a shadow at the door. Rick looked in at him. Amirault said, "The ape house closed at five. No viewers till tomorrow." He was growing weary of this constant pilgrimage. One by one the others coming to say they were sorry, and then refusing to make the call.

Rick brought in a pillow and blanket. He too was "sorry" for being gruff this year, he said. He hoped Amirault would "get well." He was "shaken" from having to aim the shotgun at him.

"Don't worry. I'm not going to tell anyone about your pictures," Amirault said.

"This isn't about that. Anyway, I found them. I got them out of your pants pocket and burned them."

Amirault repeated his request. Call the Pentagon. He felt like a CD that had jammed.

Rick shook his head. "Is it warm enough for you? Do you need anything before I go to sleep?"

"Make the call," Amirault whispered.

Rick turned away.

"Make the call."

Amirault couldn't sleep. He guessed it was two a.m. His last night in Antarctica. He sat with the blanket and pillow on the floor beside him. His wrist hurt. The pipe vibrated slightly, and sweated; a single warm drop fell on the back of his neck.

It would be funny if Hector really is innocent, he thought. And whoever did it is still walking around on the base.

Which was a bad thought to have at that moment, because he heard shuffling footsteps in the hallway. A shadow grew in the doorway. It stopped. Someone was standing just out of sight, by the door.

Amirault called out, "Are you bigger than a breadbox? Did you live in France in the 1600s? Are you involved, somehow, in the arts?"

It was Robyn.

She entered slowly. He had never noticed the slight inward slant of her feet before. It made her look shy at the moment. Amirault said, "How'd you get into cellblock B?"

"I bribed the guard."

He wondered, if he shouted, would anyone hear? She was standing slightly sideways, and he saw the end of something copper-colored, thin, and reedy jutting from the side of her turtleneck, by her hip. The gray top brought out the blue of her eyes. Her hesitation unnerved him. He said, "Well, here to talk? Or did they give you carnal visitation rights?"

"Did you do it?" she said. "Did you really take those things?"

"No."

"They were in your closet."

Amirault shrugged. His wrist hurt from the handcuffs. He said, "You're the one who told me. Whoever did it would be watching me, too."

"You're saying someone put those things in your closet so it would look like you did it."

Amirault snapped, "Look, either I did it or I didn't. If I didn't, why the hell else would that stuff be there?"

She held up what she'd concealed—a propane torch from the labs. Fear exploded in him. But then she said, glancing toward the pipe, "Plastic handcuffs. Plastic melts."

She didn't move though. She just stood there. She was trying to decide if she should cut him loose or not, trying to decide if it was safe.

"You know," she said, while he begged inside to be freed, "I always put a lot of stock in instinct. Instinct in love." He thought, heart racing, Love? "Instinct in politics. My mother told me a long time ago, instinct is the most logical part of a person, it's facts jumbled up and arranged deep inside you. And it's the part people trust the least."

"Your instinct told you I was a—what was your word?—government drone before."

She laughed. "It did, didn't it? Was it wrong then? Or now?"

"Ask me," Amirault said. "I'm objective about it."

"What will you do if I burn off the cuffs?"

"Call the Pentagon. Like I said."

"Why did you say Hector did it?"

"He stole things from my sister. Secrets," Amirault said. "Military secrets."

"What secrets?"

Amirault considered it. She said, "That's the deal."

"I tell you and you let me go."

"Right."

"And you tell the press."

"Who knows?" she said. "If it's bad enough, maybe it'll shake things up at Victoria. All that bullshit they're talking about international cooperation. Meanwhile, if you're right, people are already getting killed over this place."

"That wouldn't stop anything."

She shrugged. "Worth a try."

Amirault tested the cuffs. They hurt his wrist. "Nope," he said. "I can't do it."

"You're kidding."

He slumped in the chair. "I made a promise to the Navy. Evylyn did too."

She looked astounded. "What did the Navy ever do for you?"

"They got me here. And that's not the point anyway."

"You're kidding me, right? Last chance."

Amirault grinned. "I'll give you a nickel if you let me go."

She lowered the torch and with an expressionless backward glance walked out. Her footsteps receded down the hall. He sat, wide awake, in the harsh light of the closet. He heard wind outside. He heard the building creak. He heard footsteps coming back, and she stood in the doorway again.

"I hate you," she said. "I don't understand you. I can never figure out what you're going to do."

"I knew you'd take the nickel."

She smelled of vanilla standing beside him. "Watch out. The plastic's hot," she said. He heard the torch sizzling. White gobs of plastic fell on the wooden platform, congealed.

When Amirault stood up, she said, "You knew I was bluffing. Didn't you?"

He looked at her a long time.

Then he said, "Yes."

The radio room was empty. The number for the Office of Naval Research was in the Rolodex. The red phone issued a calm soothing dial tone when he picked it up. Robyn stood behind him, listening, but he knew he'd be able to tell the officers on the other end enough, without spelling it out, for them to grow alarmed.

"Hello," a recorded tape on the other end said. There was only a two-hour time difference between Ellsworth and Washington at this time of year. "This is the Office of Naval Research. We are closed." Shit! "We are open from eight a.m. until five p.m. Monday to Friday, and closed Saturday and Sunday. Please call back. But if you wish to leave a message, do so, in a clear voice, at the end of the long tone."

"I don't believe this."

Hanging up, Amirault called Washington information. There was static on the line now. He called the Pentagon switchboard and asked for the Office of Naval Intelligence. An operator answered. Whom did he wish to speak to? Amirault didn't have any particular name.

"Can you tell me what this is in reference to?"

There was more static on the line. Amirault hoped another storm wasn't moving in. What the hell do I tell an operator, he thought, in the middle of the night? He told her he was calling from Antarctica. He said he was on a U.S. research base.

"I can't hear you."

He said it again.

"In Alaska?" she said.

"Not Alaska. Antarctica."

"You're *in* Antarctica?" she said. "Now?"

Yes, he said, he was a scientist employed by the Navy, and was calling to report the theft of naval work.

"Freddy, is this you?" the operator said.

Amirault said he wasn't Freddy.

"Antarctica, huh? It's Freddy, I know it. I told you not to do this anymore."

The line went dead and came on again. He convinced her to pass him on to an officer. A lieutenant came on the line. Amirault said, "This is going to sound crazy. But listen. Please. Check the call. You have equipment to do that, don't you? You'll see it's really coming from Antarctica. My name is Amirault."

He told the man that Evylyn's work had been stolen, that she had been killed. The officer listened; the static grew worse. The officer asked who was handling the inquiry. When Amirault said nobody, they thought it was an accident, the voice grew wary, and the man said, "I see."

"Check it out," Amirault said, trying to keep his voice steady. He gave the man his Social Security number. "Check who I am with the National Science Foundation. Check what she was working on. You can do it with a phone call." He gave the number of Lieber's office. But he was losing the man's interest. He heard him yawn. He realized that even if the lieutenant called Lieber, Lieber would provide a vastly different version of things.

Jack Amirault? Poor guy. He cracked up. They've got him re-

strained down there. Went nuts last year, you know. We told you it was a bad idea to bring him back this year, but the Navy insisted.

It was one thing for Rick to make the call to Washington. Amirault saw he'd been fooling himself. Without the NSF behind him, his pleas might have no weight at all.

"Hector Carroll," he persisted. "Wu Kai Nung. U.S.S. *Philadelphia.* They're both on Victoria —"

The line went dead.

"I still don't know what she was working on," Robyn said when it became clear the line would stay dead. "Will they do anything? That didn't sound so good."

"They'll call Lieber, and Rick. And Lieber and Rick'll tell them I'm off the wall."

Amirault left the radio room. She kept up. "Where are you going?"

He reached the kitchen and began rifling closets for provisions. Dehydrated soup. Granola bars. Dehydrated lamb stew. "You'll get a kick out of this," he said. "Purgatory Road."

She froze. "You're going to try that?"

"You tried it." Amirault gathered Power Bars. A mess kit. Nine meals, he thought. Keep it light. Twelve meals. Allow for one extra day.

She gripped his sleeve. Her face, close up, looked white and frightened. "You can't do that. You haven't practiced."

"I know how to ski."

"You don't have the maps!"

Amirault broke away and she kept up the barrage of arguments. They hurried down the stairwell. "Even I wouldn't go without the maps," she said. "There are a million canyons, wrong turns, it's crazy. It's only fifty miles if you do a straight line. The maps show food drops. *You need the maps!*"

"Which are on the *Queen.*"

"That's right!" In the foyer, Amirault selected equipment they'd brought in last night from the ski shack. A knapsack. Goggles. A balaclava. Polypropylene underwear with zip-up rear flap for the bathroom. Hollofil socks. Fur gloves and liner gloves. The clothes would need knee space and extra give in the arms and shoulders. A lightweight stove. Pint bottle of compressed gas. Headlamp. Mukluks of reindeer hide. Toilet paper.

"Jack!"

He thought, I need to stay dry, that's the most important thing. Can't sweat too much. I need to stay warm. He added a down sleeping bag and ensolite foam ground pad and bivouac sack. A Kelty tent, high enough to sit up in, with vents on the side for air circulation, and two front doors. Vapor barrier boots and super gaiters to cover his feet. If a storm arrives while I'm out there, in the open, he thought, I'm dead.

He memorized where he put supplies. Right outside pocket: face mask, extra gloves. Left: sunblock, wire, waterproof matches. Inside pocket: compass, granola and Power Bars.

No second chance if you forget something.

Rope. Ice ax. The weight was increasing. There was nothing he could do about it. He decided to load the stuff on one of the base's wooden sleds.

"I'll scream. I'll wake them up," Robyn Cassidy said.

Amirault went back to packing. She said, "I studied the route for two years. Even without maps, you have a better chance with me. You shouldn't be doing this, but if you're going, I am too."

It was what Brian had said.

He stared at her. The choice had been so clear then, and it was clear now too. He was thinking that if he showed up at Victoria Base with the disk showing Evylyn's discovery, they'd have to investigate. They'd have to. It was a weight lifting from him.

He could not have stopped Brian, and he wasn't going to stop her. He said, over his shoulder, "Hurry up."

It took fifteen minutes; then they judged they were ready. They carried seventy pounds between them. Amirault said, "We'll tie ourselves together when we get on the ice."

Outside, it was almost dawn; there was a mild breeze off the harbor. The snow looked lavender and peaceful in the moonlight, and underfoot had a slightly slushy quality. They took off silently toward the black mountains. Déjà vu, passing the antenna and approaching the moraine by the end of the glacier. When they reached the generator building, Amirault opened the door and skied in.

He stood there a moment, the roof off and snow burying the generator in an eight-foot-long mound, sparkling white. The shelves were covered with snow. Robyn, beside him, said, "Why are we stopping here?"

Amirault said, "Sorry," and, hard as he could, shoved her. It was so unexpected she went down on her skis. He had already turned. Outside, he slammed the door shut and locked it. Her scream was muffled. "You can't do this!"

He answered, "They'll come looking for you when they get up. Light the stove. They'll see the smoke."

Ahead, beneath the bright sickle moon, was the jagged top of the high chain of mountains. The wind coming down off the plateau was colder. Already, in just a hundred yards, the consistency of the snow had grown slightly more granular, and the long glacier was dusted by wavelike sastrugi. Amirault picked up his pace.

He felt freed, and determined, and utterly ignorant of what was going to happen. The glacier was different tonight, folded up in places, from turbulence and ruptures in the ice during the storm.

He felt himself being swallowed in insignificance the closer he got to the mountains. He skied carefully, slowly, watching the surface for crevasses. The air in his lungs was cold and fine. It seemed to spread through his body, invigorating every cell.

An hour later he stood beneath the closest of the mountains. The moon was lower in the sky now, and there was the faintest coral glow to the south, as the sun would soon begin its circular journey through the Antarctic sky. The constellations were bright up there. Hercules. Diana. The Southern Cross. When he turned northwest, he faced a long gauntlet of white, hemmed in by mountains. Amirault didn't look back. He tested the straps on his knapsack. He felt the breath going in and out of him. He headed up Purgatory Road.

eight

The wind died. The world was silent. Amirault eased into a rhythm. Pole forward. Glide. Pole forward. Slide. Dwarfed, he skied north, running a gauntlet of ice and rock. He was hemmed in between four-thousand-foot mountain ranges, the basement rock glazed blue, midsections scoured by wind, peaks white and indifferent as cumulus clouds.

Pole. Kick. It amazed him to see that the same storm that had battered Ellsworth had deposited only half an inch of powder here. It made skiing excellent. The sky, at dawn, went from Prussian blue to coral, and flamed into molten red as the sun's tip broke above a saddle in the mountains.

He checked behind him. Nobody there. For the moment, freed from the base, Amirault basked in a sense of well-being. His muscles felt good. His mind was clear. The only sound was the *shoosh* of his skis.

Moving, he pictured aerial photos he'd seen of Purgatory Road. Within ten miles, like a river hitting islands, the glacier would divide into narrower ice streams, canyons, valleys. He scanned the passing ranges with professional interest. The rock to his left looked smoother, soft and rounded, wind-eroded sandstone with bare patches banded in flame and rust. The peaks to the right were more jagged and violent — granite, Amirault noted, sparkling with silvery mica in the sharper hollows, towers, ridges, plateaus.

Run one of the fossil team's laser coring devices into the glacier, he thought, and you could get a drill bit down there. Would oil burst out?

Amirault's eyes swept the glacier, watching for crevasses or depressions that might hide a drop. He listened for the creaking of weakening ice, but heard only the steady scrape of his own skis.

"They'll wreck this place," Robyn had said.

He pictured the minerals meeting forty-seven miles north. Men and women in business suits bent over long tables, looking over maps. We'll give you Purgatory Road if you give us the coastline. Our explorers claimed Purgatory Road before yours. Let's trade: minerals rights for loan forgiveness. Mineral revenues for us and we'll bankroll your refineries, and ships, and vote to open the Ross Sea to your whaling fleet.

Amirault had surprised himself. This was the cynical way Robyn thought. But he pictured the inevitable fleet of tracked vehicles lumbering up this valley. He heard their engines growling and saw the pall their exhaust would make in the sky. He saw the disassembling of pipes and drills and coring devices on the snow. Maybe it would happen this year. Maybe not for ten years. At the moment, Purgatory Road was a wilderness, but it was about to become a frontier.

Robyn, get out of my head.

But then his bad mood evaporated as a light show started. Ahead, the air shimmered with diamond dust, drifting ice crystals. The crystals coalesced into a mirage of pillars, cylinders like glass pipes of a church organ, a thousand feet tall, midway between earth and sky. The pipes shattered. Pieces fell across the sun and turned the lower sky violet. Then a sudden shaft of platinum shot up, into the sun, and smaller orbs, refractions, appeared in the northeast quadrant. Three suns shone down on Antarctica.

He gasped at the beauty of it. He was barely aware he was

moving. He told Robyn in his mind, I couldn't take you with me, not after last year.

But Amirault remembered how beautiful she had looked, standing beside him in the radio room. He remembered the slight slant of her eyes, and the lovely white curve of her neck. Amirault followed the slope of her shoulders down and grew hard thinking about her. Her collarbone would be prominent, because she was small and slim. Her breasts would be small, with purple aureoles. The lines of her rib cage would point to her flat belly, and there would be a slight sinewiness to her muscles from all the working out.

He actually smelled vanilla for an instant.

Then Amirault felt the surface give way. The cracking sound was sharp and sudden, and the sickening feeling of falling had already begun. The mountains tipped sideways. He clawed air, windmilling, and his poles fell and his gloves hit the lip of the crevasse. There was nothing to hold on to. Amirault looked down and saw the flash of blue ice.

Forty-seven miles north, at Victoria Base, Captain Hector Carroll stood bundled and alone in the lee of a Navy runabout, terrified over the abrupt summons he'd received ten minutes ago. "Drop whatever you're doing and proceed to the icebreaker *Polar Sea*." No explanation. Just a stern voice on the wireless. "Forthwith!"

They know about me, Hector thought.

The *Polar Sea* was anchored in deep water half a mile from the *Polar Queen*. Between them, the runabout threaded a maze of ships: double-hulled, ice-strengthened vessels, military, research, corporate models flying flags of Germany, the Ukraine, Brazil, Russia, Norway, and a dozen other countries. The air filled with the buzz and drone of outboards, and small patches of gray-brown haze — exhaust — made the air shimmer so the ice cliffs and mountains inland looked like a mirage.

They're going to arrest me again.

Beyond the gray-orange penguin shit that splattered the volcanic rubble lining the shore, the base itself, a quarter-mile away — which had consisted of four Quonset huts and an antenna two weeks ago — was now a town of one- and two-story huts, observation towers, a dining hall, an auditorium for movies and press briefings.

Thin threadlike lines, safety ropes, crisscrossed the rubbly peninsula like a cat's cradle at this distance, strung between buildings on bamboo poles. They looked useless and ridiculous on a sunny day. But if a storm came up, anyone caught outside would be able to feel their way inside on the lines.

Amirault must have found out.

Hector heard a droning and looked up. A Chilean Air Force Hercules transport angled in after crossing the Drake Passage, heading for the ice runway above Victoria Base. Ice coated its wings. There must be a storm out there.

His dread increased as the runabout rounded the prow of the British icebreaker *Hero*, a wall of red, and ahead loomed the *Polar Sea*. In the last fifty yards he noticed an odd effect in the water, a greenish-orange column of light, pulsating, its edges expanding and contracting as it streamed across the bow. Krill swarm. Soon hungry penguins and seals would converge on the spot.

A grim-faced ensign saluted as Hector came aboard. "Captain's expecting you. Follow me."

They picked their way around the bollards, coiled sea lines, and hatch doors on the foredeck. Hector spotted a news cameraman in a float-suit in the aloft conn, filming the base with a long-distance lens. He followed the ensign up a stairway to the pilothouse, a long, comfortable room bathed in red from instruments. A twenty-foot window looked out on the bay. No one was at the big wheel, but a knot of officers stood around a chart table.

"That's an island, not an iceberg," one was saying. "Can't you tell the difference?"

"Wait here," the ensign said, and whispered something to the speaker, a short, powerful-looking man, who straightened and strode toward Hector. Military posture. Slight bowlegged walk of an athlete. Grim intelligence in the gray, scrutinizing eyes.

The captain said, without introducing himself, "Dr. Jack Amirault. He's a patient of yours. Right?"

"Yes."

"There's been trouble at Ellsworth."

Hector's legs went weak. But he realized nobody had accused him of anything yet. Instead, the captain was telling a story. *Concentrate.* A message had come from the State Department. Amirault had "cracked up," the captain said, and "stolen things." He'd "sabotaged a generator." Pulled a knife on the base manager, and it was even possible he might be responsible for a death on base that had previously been considered an accident.

"His sister," Hector said.

The captain's brows rose. "His *sister?*" There was a clanging noise somewhere inside the ship. That the captain hadn't known about Evylyn improved Hector's mood. The captain hadn't been told much. "Amirault was caught. But he broke out and stole skis and fled up Purgatory Road. He may be trying to reach here. He's raving about spies," the captain said.

Hector's mood plunged again. He shook his head for the captain's benefit. It was all right to show worry. He was supposed to be shocked by what he heard.

"What spies?"

"I don't know. The man's gone crazy."

Better, Hector thought, still worried. He tried to reconstruct what had happened at Ellsworth. Rick must have called Lieber, and Lieber the State Department. Nobody believed Amirault. Either they hadn't passed on his accusations or the State Department had discounted them. In the end, this captain had only been told that Amirault had cracked up.

But Amirault was still trying to get here. If he did manage to do that, Hector would be brought back to the U.S. in the brig.

It would all start again.

And Amirault was resourceful.

Hector asked, "How can I help?"

"He pulled a knife on his superior," the captain said, still appalled.

"Well, he's under pressure."

The captain looked astounded that Hector would make an excuse for Amirault. "Liberals," the captain said, disgusted. "We've been ordered to mount a rescue operation."

Hector said, "I want to go."

"You will. But right now, we need an idea of how he might react when we reach him. You've treated him."

Hector considered. "He's troubled," he said reluctantly, as if not wanting to give a negative impression of Amirault. As if forced by duty to say something he'd rather not. "And insubordinate. Last year he disobeyed orders and went up on the glacier to rescue Robyn Cassidy. You must have heard about this."

"He was *that* guy?"

"Yes. And as a result, another scientist, a friend of his, was killed in a fall. Amirault never got over it. He blames himself for it. He's capable of violence. I never thought he should have been allowed to come back."

In the harbor, a ship's bell rang. The Koreans were holding a cocktail party on their research ship this afternoon. The captain's frown deepened. He was pondering strategy. "The Brits have to be told. Their base. Their operations." He sighed. "The State Department really wants things here to go smoothly. There are at least five helicopters on the ships here, and the New Zealanders brought dogs and sleds. But the problem is weather. There's already been a bad storm up there, and it's apparently coming back. Everything's grounded, at least tonight."

"But what about Jack?" Hector protested, knowing his concern would make no difference.

"I don't like it either. But you'll be with the first team to go out. Maybe you can calm him."

"I'll try," Hector said. "But we might want to be armed when we look for him. I'll pray for him. Poor guy."

Amirault had been lucky. Incredibly lucky.

He picked himself up, fighting fatigue. He was standing in a slit trench three and a half feet deep. Loose snow, clumps that had fallen with him, parts of the collapsed ice bridge, lay on his boots and dotted his clothes. He'd come out of his ski bindings when he'd hit bottom, but his left ankle ached slightly and his right knee hurt where his ski had hit it. His shoulder smarted where he had struck the shelf of ice. He remembered the sickening moment of collapse.

Amirault hauled himself from the crevasse, fastened his skis on, and adjusted his pack.

He started north again.

Half an hour later he'd relaxed a little, but he would never regain the carefree attitude he'd had an hour earlier. Only a year ago he'd skied for pure pleasure on the glacier. Amirault thought back to those daily dawn trips — exercise sessions — with Brian, Rick, Haystack, Gail. Friends, then.

The world before Robyn. The hikes with Laticia or Evylyn. The picnics on Elephant Island. The whale-watching rides in the Zodiac. "You will find," Lieber had told him in their interview, "that with the right attitude, you will make friends on Ellsworth that will last your whole life."

Amirault's gut ached.

"Pretty up here," Brian's voice said, beside him. "I remember those whales too. Remember the time we saw the mother and calf in the harbor? We got too close, going after them in the Zodiac. Remember the baby coming up and bumping the boat?"

Amirault smiled. I thought it was going to dump us.

He knew Brian wasn't really talking, it was just in his head, but the sense of presence grew so strong he actually looked around. The feeling seemed to come from his left, from a spot a couple feet off, where Brian's face would have been had he been there. Amirault played with it. It was harmless. "You there, Brian?" he said. His self-amused laughter echoed across the valley. "I'm talking to myself now. If you're there, give me a signal."

There was no signal. Amirault shrugged. "Then, if you're there, *don't* give me a signal."

Nothing happened.

"I knew you were there," he said.

He was not religious. He had never been religious. He flashed back to the house in Louisiana, when his parents had been alive. A clear night, starry, and he and Evylyn sleeping on cots on the back porch. "Camping out," his mother had said. And the smell of bougainvillea, and watching, through the mesh screen, the yellow moon suspended above the thick, bent willows. The humid salt smell off the flats. The distant, comforting bells of the shrimpers' boats coming as regularly in the dark as the hooting of swamp owls.

Amirault saw his mother's oval face as he knelt between the cots. The nightly ritual. Read a book. Get tucked in. Say the prayer. "Now I lay me down to sleep." Sometimes the two of them trying to outshout each other at it. Sometimes taking turns. Or groaning, I'm too tired. Can't we skip it tonight?

Amirault poled, his shoulder muscles aching with the effort and repetition. He rose and fell over a light-chop sastrugi. He saw another building now. A church. His aunt, slim-hipped, long gray hair — lustrous and youthful — was leading him by the hand into the family church in Sonoma, for "counseling."

What a laugh! Every Wednesday and Friday, at three, after school. Adults, he remembered telling Evylyn. They don't do anything when it counts, when they can save people. And afterward they have a million ways of trying to explain why. Now they need us to go along with it. Otherwise they can't fool themselves and think they did the right thing. It's funny, we're just kids, but look how much they need us.

The noon sun limped weakly, a small orb in the western quadrant of the sky, barely able to keep itself in view above the mountains. This time of year, it never reached 45 degrees high.

Call me Kyle, Amirault remembered the pastor saying. He remembered the man's round, fleshy face, hair brushed back, reading glasses, green sweaters. The second-story alcove office looking out on his uncle's vineyards, filled with hanging wire sculptures the pastor had made. An elephant. A girl holding an umbrella. A fishing rod. A piano.

Want one, Jackie?

No thanks.

"Your mom and dad are in heaven," the man had said, twisting wires with pliers, making gifts for hospitals, old people, the man who'd had a heart attack, the parents who'd lost a child. Making a policeman directing traffic. A dog. A cow.

"We don't always know why God does things, Jackie. But faith makes you strong in the end, even if you don't understand why."

"What's faith?"

"Believing in something bigger than you."

"Like my parents coming back?"

"No. Like believing in heaven. And forgiveness of those men you keep talking about."

"Jesus came back," Amirault said.

"That was different."

"You mean he was better than my parents?" Amirault said. "I don't believe anything you say."

Brian spoke up again, the voice in Amirault's head, but it seemed to emanate from a spot five feet off the ground. "Have you figured it out yet, Jack? That I don't blame you."

That is what you'd say. But you're not here, Amirault thought.

"Then why are you talking to me?"

Ha ha.

"And why are you thinking about forgiveness so much? And who cares if I'm really here or not? That's not the point, is it? Listen, Ami. Is there any way you could have stopped yourself, last year, from going after Robyn?"

No.

"And is there any way you could have stopped me from coming along?"

I don't want to have this conversation.

"Then stop it. Go ahead. It's all in your head anyway, isn't it? You're making it up, isn't that what you believe? That I'm not here?"

Amirault had no reply. His heel ached. Blister, he thought.

"Don't forget me, pal, I'd hate if you forgot me. But don't be an asshole about it. Don't stop living, and turn into a coward, and blame it on me." Brian relented a little. "I mean, give me a little voyeuristic pleasure. There's not a lot else to do around here."

Meaning what?

Brian imitated him, mocking. "I'm talking about Robyn. Who the hell else do you think I mean?"

She's my business.

Brian went on relentlessly. "Sure, sure. You're too scared to do anything about it. You make excuses. You're afraid of losing some-one else you love."

Amirault grew furious. Who are you, fucking Sigmund Freud? Geraldo Rivera?

Brian thought that was funny. "Yeah. That's me. Dead guy with a talk show. Who's the sponsor? Morticians? You're very funny. You're a funny guy. You're a chickenshit funny guy. You knew Laticia was wrong for you so you started up with her. You know Robyn is major, so you stay away and blame it on me. By the way, there's a crevasse coming up."

Halting, Amirault saw it. But he hadn't seen it until Brian mentioned it. The slight shadow across the valley and the roll of the land had made it invisible. Amirault looked down into a ninety-foot drop. The jagged maw crossed the length of the valley.

Amirault told himself, I saw it myself. Brian didn't warn me.

Brian's voice faded into amusement. "Whatever you say."

Amirault skied right, staying back a few feet from the lip of the crevasse. A few minutes later he found an ice bridge, fifteen feet thick, five feet long.

Don't look down, he thought, crossing the ice bridge. He looked down. Sunlight rippled like water on pillars of turquoise ice below. A frigid stream of air blew up, into his face. Reaching the other side, he noticed his right hand on the pole trembling. He reached down and sucked at snow as he started moving again. A thin trickle of liquid cooled his throat and made the edges of his teeth ache.

"You're talking to yourself, Jack," he said out loud, and the echo drifted across the valley, rolled up against the ice and rock, came back to him. "You haven't even gone half the distance, and already you're talking to yourself," the echo said.

The easy part was over. The glacier was starting to divide. Amirault checked the sun, guessing it was one o'clock.

Ahead he saw a nunatak, a black peak jutting above the ice, looping like a breaching whale. Beyond that, the glacier split right and left, flowing around a third range that jutted into the ice like a ship. Which way? Amirault considered his options.

He wished he had a map.

Amirault checked his compass. Neither way went exactly north, toward Victoria Base, and besides, readings became inaccurate this close to the South Pole. The earth's magnetic field affected the compass.

I'll go left, Amirault thought. That valley is wider. Twenty minutes later the canyon walls began narrowing. The sky shrank to an unreal blue slit overhead, framed by basalty black. The canyon began curving back on itself, looping south, toward Ellsworth Base. It was impossible to tell if the detour was temporary. Amirault kept going but was relieved when the canyon swerved back the other way.

Amirault skied around a curve and cursed. He was in a box canyon.

He'd wasted two hours, and would need another two to get back.

And he'd wasted good weather.

Amirault forced himself to sit down in the lee of the mountain, out of the breeze. Don't hurry. Haste is the enemy. With measured movements he unpacked the Primus stove and used his first two matches lighting it. The white gas hissed and steamed. He took twenty more minutes melting snow, then added a pack of dehydrated beef broth to the bubbling water, and a Power Bar. The gloppy mix wasn't too terrible, and it gave him energy. He'd not realized how tired he'd grown.

His left cheek was sunburned, where he'd been in the sun; the right was dry and hard, with prefrostbite. He smeared on sunblock.

Refreshed, he headed back.

The wind grew worse. The sky went dull at the far end of the valley, and the sun dissipated to a low glow at the bottom of the cloud deck. A flutter of large flakes began, and stopped, but the sky promised more soon. Skiing harder, Amirault smelled ozone. In the thicker air his waxless skis sounded louder, the swooshing noise tailing off and bouncing back behind him as if another person followed ten feet behind.

The valley widened again. He skied through warm and cold patches. Ahead, the wind sent up a smoky white haze of loose granules, and drift floated toward him in slithering tendrils.

From the distance came a muffled boom, like a dynamite blast. A snowfield contracting, falling into itself.

Amirault reached the junction where he'd turned the wrong

way. The day was over. The sun was a quarter way over the mountains. He'd brought food for four days, and even with good weather today, traveling the easier section, he'd scarcely gone a fifth of the way to Victoria Base.

He looked for a place to spend the night. A cave, maybe. The glacier seemed slanted here, he noticed, the snow higher on the starboard side. Which meant the mountains on the opposite side provided protection.

Skiing close to the range, he scanned the sandstone cliffs for holes, caves, alcoves. The basement ice was yellow here, from debris swept along by the glacier. Bits of boulder and rock scraped the bottoms of his skis. And he smelled sulfur and saw steam venting from the rock. Amirault skirted the ruptured, rough ice at the edge of the glacier, spotted something softer poking from the ice. He bent to examine it and froze.

It was a balaclava.

Amirault reached for it, but it was half stuck in the ice. The fabric had faded a long time ago.

It's Brian's, he thought. It couldn't be Brian's. The glacier couldn't have moved so far in just a year. It was someone else's, some explorer who'd passed here years ago. It was absolutely impossible that it was Brian's balaclava. Unless it wasn't impossible.

Amirault took off his gloves and ran his fingers over the rough wool. It was real wool, not synthetic. He told himself balaclavas had stayed the same for a hundred years. It was not Brian's balaclava. Definitely not. Amirault was growing angry at himself.

Fifteen feet up from the balaclava, Amirault noticed a dark alcove in the rock. It looked like shelter.

If I hadn't stopped to look at this, I wouldn't have seen it.

Shit.

Amirault took off the skis and used the ice ax to help himself up the rubble. The alcove wasn't exactly a cave — it was too shallow — but it was protected from the wind, and he could wedge his sleeping bag in the hollow, and there was a flat place for the Primus stove, and if it started to snow, which seemed likely, the alcove was slightly raised off the floor of the valley, which would give him some protection when the snow began to drift.

He was halfway up when he heard it, the soft scraping swoosh of skis again. But he wasn't skiing anymore.

Amirault turned slowly and peered into the gloom. He blinked. The terror started in his belly and moved into his throat and he thought, It can't be. He died. He fell. I saw it. He couldn't live up here.

Dim and shrouded, the figure slid across the glacier, toward him. Pole and kick. Pole and glide. The half light and emptiness made it seem even more solitary. It wasn't a mirage. Amirault sat on the rock and waited.

Coming closer, the figure took on color. Blue parka and hood. Orange knapsack.

The figure stopped directly beneath him. Eight feet away.

The voice floated up to him. Angry. A feminine throatiness carried by the wind.

"Who the hell are you to lock me in there?" Robyn Cassidy said.

nine

The wind died. The sky clouded over. Large wet flakes fell, thick and silent, as on a storybook Christmas Eve. From the sandstone alcove, Amirault and Robyn gazed out on the dark glacier, rapidly piling up with undisturbed snow.

The only sound was the hiss of white gas burning.

"Rick was furious when he found out," she said.

He'd spent half an hour trying to calm her. After a while she'd just ranted herself out. Finally she'd said, "I guess I understand why you left me there, but I make my own decisions." Now the glow from the Primus stove heightened her features. She seemed more vibrant in the outdoors, unconstrained and alive. The temperature had risen temporarily, and she sprawled, one boot out, leg over knee, inverted V shape, head propped in palm, elbow on sleeping bag and ground sheet. Overhanging rock shielded them from the storm.

"He wanted to lock me up but Lieber ordered him not to." She grinned, remembering. "I'm screaming. We're all screaming. I say, 'You're going to do what? I'll sue you! Wait till CBS finds out you tried to kill me last year!' Rick's going on about destroying property, and I'm yelling, 'Property? Fuck property! You tried to kill me!' "

She tossed her head. "Bureaucrats. You have to threaten them personally. So finally Lieber says, 'Promise you'll behave?' Stern, but watching his ass. Worrying about TV coverage. I say, 'Yeh, I'll behave. I promise.' Everybody goes back to work.

"Then I leave."

Dehydrated chicken stew bubbled with melted snow in the pot. Amirault's mouth watered. His tent was snug against the rock wall. An errant flake sizzled as it drifted into the stove.

"You nut," she said, but she seemed excited now. "You shouldn't have come here."

He tasted the stew. "So why'd you show up?"

"I told you. Because even if I don't have maps, I studied them. I'll have a better idea which way to go."

Their gloves brushed when she took the spoon from him. She licked the spoon. "You went the wrong way before. I saw your tracks," she said. They added clothes, an extra pullover hat, glove liners, from the pack. "Besides" — she grinned — "Purgatory Road is my project. I'm the one who gets the glory. Not you. I started the whole thing."

"Duck à l'orange," Amirault said, pouring the stew into tins. They ate greedily, gasping at the heat. Dessert was Kit Kat bars she'd taken from the mess. Amirault melted snow for Earl Grey tea. They each drank three sugarless cups of the strong brew.

So much snow fell that the valley floor seemed to be rising. Snowtide.

"My father," Robyn said quietly, after a while, "was one of those nuclear soldiers. The last batch. You know who they were? Soldiers marched into the Nevada desert, in the late 1950s, so the Army could see the effect of nuclear blasts on troops."

The lines in her face grew longer. The familiar note of protest came into her voice, but sadness tinged it.

"I didn't know this when I was a kid. All I knew was he got tired sometimes. He looked older than other daddies. When his hair fell out, it didn't do it the same way as my friends' fathers'. Their hairlines" — she touched a gloved finger to her cropped hair, and

Amirault had the urge to take his gloves off and run his fingers through it—"receded. My father's fell out in clumps. We were eating breakfast one time, sitting at the table, and this ball of hair dropped in his corn flakes. It was the most humiliated I ever saw him. He stood up. He didn't say anything. He walked out of the room and went to work."

"Sounds awful."

Amirault stood and stamped to keep warm. The temperature dropping again. He wished he could give her a better memory. He loved the way her nose curved up, and the rosebud shape of her lips. He loved the way they glistened in the half light from the sputtering stove.

"My father said that on the morning of the blast, his platoon was so close that when it went off he shielded his eyes and saw the bones in his hand, through the skin, clear and black, like an X ray. It was fun, he said. All his friends, the guys who would come to the house sometimes, sign petitions, hire lawyers—sick guys, dying, all of them—they thought they were part of history at first."

Amirault poured more tea. His muscles ached after a day of poling. There was no storm, no glacier. There was only Robyn and her sick father at a breakfast table. Amirault filled in details. Sun coming through a window. An all-news radio show. A cat on the windowsill, beside ripening tomatoes. Flowers—geraniums—in a pot.

"Ten, twelve years later the pains in his bones started. Elbows. Knees. Psychosomatic," she said bitterly. "That's what the Veterans Administration said. My dad was an architect. A few more years went by. It got tough for him to draw. He stopped working. Bone cancer."

The forces of gravity seemed to be working on her face. He saw how she'd look when she was seventy years old.

"The doctors started cutting parts off him." She touched her sleeve. "Right arm, from the elbow down. They thought they got it all. Up to the shoulder next." She shuddered.

"How old were you?"

"Six to eleven. When I understood what was going on I used to sit with him at night, after chemo. He couldn't eat. He threw up.

My mom gave him injections to make him feel better. He'd roll up his pajama legs, and squeeze his thigh. She'd hold the needle like this." She gripped an imaginary hypodermic with four fingers, and pushed the invisible plunger with her thumb.

Amirault reached across the gap between them and took her gloved hand. It was limp.

"Drones," she said. "Army, Veterans Administration, Social Security. Coming to the house. Trying to get him to sign things. Statements that he'd participated voluntarily. Then, when he wouldn't sign, they offered deals. A scholarship to college for me, if he'd agree not to sue. He told me, Fight them."

She wiped her right eye with her sleeve.

"He said, Pick something you care about, there are plenty of things, and fight them. Don't just have a job and spend your life ignoring them, letting them get away with things."

She sipped her tea. "I thought you were one of them. But you're not like you." She smiled. "I mean, you're not who you're supposed to be." She rapped her knuckles lightly against her head. "I'm babbling."

"I like it."

"Well, I don't like it."

The snow fell, thicker. It cut the alcove off from anything outside. She rummaged in her pack, pulled her tent out. Like Amirault's, it was a two-person model with a doorway and waterproof top sheet. They lay in their sleeping bags, in their tents, with the flaps open. The silence extended outward.

"I never met anyone like you," she said.

"Wind currents above the peaks are treacherous. Don't put your copter in danger. I needn't remind you of the American DC-9 that crashed last year into Mount Erebus on a rescue mission."

The briefing room at Victoria Base was small, sparse, warm, standing room only, its four rows of seats packed with pilots, newsmen, doctors, Greenpeace crew.

"One bright note," said the British naval commander at the podium. "I am struck, even as we prepare for this mission, by the way your effort epitomizes the spirit of the new Antarctic. In this room are helicopter pilots from nine countries, and even our friends from Greenpeace. The New Zealanders have their dog-sleds. The French and Germans will start north, from Ellsworth Base. This joint effort symbolizes our cooperation."

Hector Carroll, in the first row, rubbed his forehead, stared at the blowup photos and maps of Purgatory Road hanging behind the speaker. The Antarctic Peninsula resembled a great dark tenta-cle in one, fat at the bottom, tapering and thinner at the top, where it broke into a small archipelago that dotted the Bellingshausen Sea. Peaks and ridges marred the interior. To Hector, there seemed no clear straight path from Ellsworth Base to Victoria. It was a maze of passages in there. Despite the narrowness of the peninsula, the helicopters would be unable to crisscross it in any kind of regular search pattern. They would be forced to fly in and out of the canyons.

"If winds get rough, come home immediately," the commander said.

The satellite photos, gridded blowups, made Hector think of a real estate developer's chart, divided into rectangles with numbers on the side.

"Be ready to take off when the sun comes up. We don't know if they are traveling separately or together. If you spot them, radio back first. If the terrain is rough, don't attempt landing. We'll drop supplies and use dogs to reach them.

"Finally, you will have to be armed. The Americans have warned us that Dr. Amirault is dangerous. He may have killed someone at Ellsworth Base. He may hurt Robyn Cassidy. Don't hesitate to protect yourselves. Or her. Amirault's doctor, Hector Carroll," the speaker said, "will join the first party, to try to talk him down."

Hector squeezed his eyes shut.

"Any questions? Good luck."

Hector moved toward the door with the others, thinking, Maybe they won't find him. Or the weather will turn bad again or he'll hurt himself.

I have to keep him from talking if we do find him.

"Dr. Carroll?"

He turned. The commander stood just inside the door, beckoning him over as the others filed out. What now? Hector thought.

Then he saw Clyde at the commander's side — that round, boy face, stupid in its eagerness — and he knew this was going to be bad and Clyde was babbling something about Evylyn; all the way here on the ship he'd never shut up. Clyde wanted to help, the commander said, and Clyde was saying, "I'll be going with you."

"You?"

The commander said with maddening politeness, "Two of you might have a more calming effect on him. Clyde's a friend of his too, and we do need a British presence."

"But Amirault is dangerous."

The commander smiled. "You're going, aren't you?"

"I'm his doctor."

"You two will make a good team," the commander said. "By the way, Dr. Carroll, you do know how to use firearms?"

Clyde was practically clutching the commander's sleeve. "You don't know Dr. Amirault. If you did, you'd know what they say can't be true. Hector, you have to feel that way too. You know Jack would never hurt anyone."

"Anyone's capable of anything if they're put under enough pressure," Hector said.

Amirault told her things he didn't tell other people. Unimportant things he hadn't thought about in years. He told her about lying around in the vineyards in Sonoma, on warm evenings, drinking wine his buddies had pilfered from their parents' vineyards. The time last summer, after Brian, when he'd been hiking in California and sat on a rock by a lake, listening to a woman's voice come through the woods, singing *Aida*, for two hours.

Little things. She seemed fascinated when he told her what it felt like on the boat, when he heard rock under the sea. "Like it talks to me," he said. Whispered through the earphones. Granite had a hoarse whisper, like someone with the flu. Sandstone was higher. A woman. Mother earth. Uranium, with its wavery tone, made him think of a little kid crying.

They'd talked about Antarctic explorers, shrimping, movies, raphael spaghetti sauce, Labrador retrievers, Bob Shacochis books, the baseball strike. He didn't care what they talked about, as long as they kept talking. He didn't want to go to sleep.

"I lived with him for two years," she said a while later. He felt a stab of jealousy, remembering the blocky, bearded man who'd put his arm around her on television, when she'd announced she would walk up Purgatory Road.

"He'd go out in those little Zodiac boats, on the open ocean, and get in front of whaling ships. The Norwegians shot a harpoon at him once. He was jailed in Tokyo. He was fierce, and sexy. He lived on the beach, in Texas. We'd spend weeks in that shack. His politics were right. He hated the right people."

"That's a biggie," Amirault said.

She smiled. "He would have hated you, would have said you're one of the puppets. The people who allow themselves to be used."

Amirault said, "Whaddaya mean? I get fifteen bucks an hour."

She looked at him fondly. "He slept with every woman he met, but if I found out, he'd swear that was the last time. The lies you tell yourself. And when he got mad, or did cocaine, which he liked a lot, he broke things. A telephone. A TV. A car window. Then he tried to cut himself when I said I would leave him. That's when I knew."

"I would think so," Amirault said.

She fell silent. He knew she never talked about this. Then she said, "Even so, when I left, it almost killed me. That was three years ago. I haven't been with anyone since then." Amirault must have looked surprised, because she laughed. "I see the tabloids too. You shake someone's hand, they write you're pregnant."

"Or married to a space alien."

"I went back home, to Washington. I'd lie on the floor for hours. I didn't eat. I did things, crazy things, I can't believe I did them. One night I drove back to Texas, I mean, a thousand miles, and I get there and just sit outside his house, in the car, watching the light go on or off. This is so sick. It was a disease. I was crazy about him, even when I hated him. I'm an extreme person. I only know one way to do things. All I had to do was get out of the car and walk to the door. It would open. He'd start crying. He always started crying after he broke things. We'd make love. It would be wonderful. It would be the best thing in the world, even better than last time. We'd have coffee in the morning, and read all the papers and make love again. And after a month he'd look distracted. It had happened so many times. So I didn't go in."

Amirault pictured her in a car, crying. Staring at a little house in the rain. He had not thought of her as vulnerable before. It surprised him, and shamed him.

"People have perverted ideas of what's hard in life," she said. "They think it's hard to go to Antarctica. They think it's easy not to walk to a door. It killed me. I told myself, Never, you will never feel this way about someone again. You will not do it. You will stop it if it starts. But it won't start, because you don't feel like that twice in life. That's the good thing about dying. Real people only die once."

Amirault said, "You didn't go in."

"But I didn't leave, either. Like a junkie, I'm sworn off the drug, but I'm staring at it. Who will be stronger? Finally, I was sitting in the car, I'd been there two days, McDonald's wrappers on the floor, and a Dunkin' Donuts box, and Snapple, real health food, you know? It was raining, and the shade pulled back and his face was there, suddenly, looking at me. He'd known the whole time. He looked like a boy at that window, scared and hopeful, like he's going to get punished when his parents get home. But maybe he won't get punished. Maybe a miracle will happen. Maybe he'll get away with the bad thing he did." She shook her head, remembering. "He looked like a kid."

Amirault thought, I love you.

"I don't know how much time went by. Does this sound stupid? I drove home. Each time I looked in the rearview mirror I expected to see his face. I didn't stop all the way, except for gas. I got home and it was morning. I made a big breakfast, really huge. Eggs and bacon and toast and jelly. Coffee. Lots of coffee. Sweet buns. And then I went to sleep. All that coffee and *still* I slept for two days."

Amirault's heart beat hard, and steady, and it seemed to fill his whole body.

"But you were on TV with him."

She said quickly, "That was business."

The snow fell harder. The valley was filling up. Amirault looked up, out of his tent, only instead of sky there were millions of heavy white flakes falling. Snow blew in, on his face, melted on his eyelids and in his nostrils, ran down the crevices in his skin. He looked back. She was watching his mouth.

Amirault started to get up. Her face froze instantly, her body stiffened and the old cool exterior was in place.

"I'm going to sleep," she said.

Robyn half sat up in her bag, in her tent. She unzipped her parka and pulled her turtleneck over her head. Her waffle-iron long johns were lemon-yellow and soft and clung so tight to her body that he felt a wave of weakness come over him. She zipped her sleeping bag up again.

"Good night," Robyn Cassidy said, turning away from him. "We have a long way to go tomorrow."

"I don't know about this," Hector Carroll said. He took the M-16 from the lieutenant. They stood on the aft deck of the *Polar Sea*, and the weapon was heavy, and tended to jerk to the right when he fired. The lieutenant watched him load.

"Hold it to your shoulder. No, tighter, sir, that's the way, sir, because you don't want to blow yourself backward. Very slowly, sir, when I say so, pull the trigger. There's a recoil. Ready? Pull."

The blast seemed deafening. The stock drove painfully into Hector's shoulder. There was a flash of light from the muzzle, and the bullets went out into the harbor.

In despair, Hector thought, How did things ever get to this point?

"It's funny," he told the lieutenant. "I'm in the Navy, and I hate guns."

"Well, sir. Lots of guys join for job training. Ask me, bring back the draft."

Hector had a vision of Amirault in a parka, in the snow, throwing his arms out. In the vision Amirault was blown backward as the bullets shredded the fabric protecting his chest. It made it hard for Hector to breathe.

"Is this really necessary?" Hector said. "It seems extreme to me."

"Captain's orders. All noncombatants who go out have to know weapons. I understand the guy's gone a little bonkers out there. Anyway, probably you'll never have to use it. One more time, sir. Ready?"

"I've never even been in a fistfight," Hector said.

Amirault woke hours later. It was still night. He looked out of the tent. Her flap was open and she gazed back at him. The earth was silent. The snow had stopped. It was warmer. He unzipped his bag. She seemed to pull back. He crossed the four feet of rock between them.

"What are you doing?" she said.

As he reached for her bag her hand touched his; the feeling was electric. He stopped, but she entwined her fingers with his. Unzipping her sleeping bag together was the most erotic act of undressing he had ever known. He climbed in with her, and drew his own bag, like a blanket, over them. It was warm in her bag; he felt the heat through their long johns. The wool interior, the clothes, the confined space, accentuated all the female odors.

She was much smaller without her parka, thin and wiry but supple. His penis was so hard he slipped it out of the flap of his long johns.

She reached down, her sleeping bag was partially unzipped now, and her hand was warm and it circled his penis. He kissed her, little kisses at first, on her mouth, neck, face. She kissed his ear, his forehead, his lips. She sucked his tongue into her mouth. She groaned, her nails dug into the top of his shoulders. He reached down and slipped her top over her head, and he kissed her breasts. "Bite them," she said.

He bit them. She gasped and threw her arms around his neck and said, "Harder." He bit harder. Her hands were under his waffle-iron tops, running along his biceps, squeezing his nipples, pulling at his chest hair. He bit hard and she raked her nails down the middle of his chest and tangled her fingers in his pubic hair.

He slid her bottom off, lifted the top of the sleeping bag, gazed

in wonder at her pale body outlined against the darker fabric beneath. Every one of Amirault's nerves seemed excruciatingly alive.
He felt the air on his back moving, and the bottom of the bag was
sopping from her juices.

When he pushed inside, she said, "Jack," and her legs came up
and her body slammed against him, reverberated, she was clawing,
biting. He wanted to come this second. He never wanted to come.
He wanted to stay like this forever, in delight, poised at the edge of
orgasm. She said, "Now, now, come in me, *in me.*" He let go. All
the fluid pumping out of him, gallons of it, it seemed, blood,
semen, sweat, water, his tissues dissolving and erupting. "Jack," she
said. It echoed off the rock. A chorus of Robyns out there, crying
his name.

The valley was silent.

Amirault lay on top of her. His lips, crushed against her chest,
tasted sweat. He brought his fingers up, her juice on them, and
rubbed them across his mouth and she caught them and sucked at
them. His groin was itching again.

She laughed. "Already?"

This time it went slower.

He was so happy. There was a vanilla smell in the sleeping bag,
and it was warm at the moment, and there was a salty taste in his
mouth. The snow, which had stopped, had begun to fall steadily
again.

Her head was on his shoulder. She was already falling asleep.

In the morning he heard the helicopter. The quick, mechanical
chopping from the south.

"They're looking for us," she said.

They had curled around each other in the bag. In the daylight,
her eyes were softer. The snow had stopped, and an uncommon
warmth was in the air. The sky was an odd grainy blue gray,
somehow farther away and closer at the same time, and there was
an unsettling quality to the light, dull and lifeless, which filled
Amirault with disquiet although he did not know why. The sun
was a dim glow behind the cloud deck. Amirault had the odd
feeling, looking at the glacier, that a tide had risen during the

night. The storm had dumped a foot and a half of snow, so the valley floor was closer.

They watched the sky hopefully. But the helicopter sound faded. "The faster they spot us, the faster we get up there," he said. "And find Hector."

But she thrust her head against his chest and rubbed back and forth against him, slow and fierce. Her veneer of disinterested irony, he knew, had always hidden something, and he was overjoyed at the passion beneath.

She bit his nipple. She said, "I couldn't stop thinking of you. During the year."

"Me too."

"I dreamed about you."

"We better get moving," he said. They made love instead. Slow at first. Amirault threw the sleeping bag off and took her from behind. She reached around, under his thighs, caressed his balls, groaning, head on her arms, wonderful ass thrusting at him, against him. She was small inside, her muscles tight. He wanted to see her face. He turned her over. Her hips bucked and her legs strained against his back. Her hands, gripping his hair, were light and trembling. When she came, she said, "Oh, oh."

They dressed quickly, aware suddenly of the damp cold. Amirault would smell the sex all day. It was on his skin, bag, waffleirons. Famished, they drank two portions of chicken broth and ate two candy bars apiece.

The helicopter sound came again, an echo. They weren't sure from which direction. It faded. Amirault said happily, "We better make double time today, or we'll run out of food before we're even halfway to Victoria."

But she answered, "I don't think we'll be doing that." Surprised, he saw she was looking beyond him, over his shoulder, up the valley. The air there had gone milky white. It seemed to flow toward them, very quickly, absorbing rock as it came.

He'd read about this. Of all the weather the continent threw at explorers — blizzards, winds, storms — this produced the most dread.

The glacier was disappearing, and the mountains. The sky was being swallowed up. Amirault had a sense of the whole universe disappearing. They would be engulfed in minutes.

"Better rope up." Already his voice sounded different, small, lost, disembodied, in the last bit of clear air before the effect hit.

Robyn looked combative.

"Whiteout," she said. "Forget the helicopters now."

ten

It was a French-made Lama helicopter, with a one-man crew and two passengers, a medical cot, oxygen and first-aid supplies in back. The pilot fought the control stick in rough wind, righted the shuddering craft, and banked it past a snow-covered outcrop into a narrow mountain pass.

Behind him, Hector and Clyde sat strapped into leather seats. Their parkas were zipped despite the roaring heater.

Hector battled sickening vertigo as the copter swept over an eight-thousand-foot ridge and the earth plunged away. He squeezed his eyes shut and pressed into his seat. Sweat popped out under his armpits. The copter shot so swiftly into the glacial valley he feared they were out of control.

"Why can't we find them?" Clyde cried.

The chopper stabilized. Outside the bubble window, they scanned the glacier stretching north in a magnificent curve, buckled in places, striated, deep blue in the middle and stained charcoal at the edges, where the ice picked up dust from passing rock. Hector gripped his seat at a tearing noise, envisioning gears breaking.

"Can't you go lower?" Clyde shouted.

Hector hated flying. He thought it was a miracle they hadn't crashed. He'd seen the victims of too many copter crashes in the Gulf War. He didn't trust aircraft with only one engine. The chopper seemed puny against all this rock and turbulence.

Clyde must have a stomach of iron, he thought, remembering their instructions. "You're a spotter craft," the British-search coordinator had said at Victoria Base. "If you see Dr. Amirault, or Robyn Cassidy, don't land. Wait for assistance. We want soldiers to deal with him, and your copter's not designed to carry a prisoner."

Now the pilot turned to Hector and shouted over the engine and babble of foreign voices — other pilots, in their earphones — "Twenty more minutes. We're low on fuel!"

They tacked across the glacier as Hector monitored reports from other search craft. The Germans reported nothing. So did the Lynx, Bell, Sikorsky helicopters. And the Chilean Twin Otter plane, a dark dot in the sky to the south.

"I don't understand why no one's spotted tracks," Clyde said, pressing his nose to the Plexiglas. His palm left smudges on it.

"It snowed last night." Hector was hoarse from shouting over the engine.

"One valley looks like another."

"Maybe they fell in."

Clyde regarded him with a frightened look, and the copter pitched as if a giant hand had shaken it. The earth tilted. Hector clawed air.

But Clyde pointed as they righted. Far ahead, midglacier, Hector spotted two tiny forms.

"It's them!" Clyde cried.

The silhouette of the fuselage raced over the snow. The forms grew closer. Hector squinted, shielded his eyes.

"Damn. It's bloody rocks," Clyde said, announcing the obvious as usual. A note of familiar appeal returned to his voice. "You don't think they got hurt, do you?" He clutched Hector's parka. "Do you think they're all right?"

Hector glanced back at the cot, backpacks filled with food rations, ropes, syringes, extra propane/butane fuel. There was a carbine bolted to the floor, and a box of shells. The pilot wore a sidearm. Amirault would have a knife, Rick had said. Could he have other weapons?

Rick would have reported it if he had.

"Ten minutes," the pilot said.

They flew over an enormous ice chasm. Below, indigo blue faded into deep gloom. Hector gaped down at a series of concentric crevasses, jagged parentheses, narrow at the top but Hector saw wider, scoop-shaped walls stretching down. So many crevasses marred the surface here, it seemed only a thin membrane of ice, glaze, ready to shatter at the slightest weight. The real planet lay far below.

"Bottomlessssssss," Clyde said, the word torn from him as the copter began to spin. The pilot said, "Bloody hell!" and pushed the convergence stick forward, for altitude. The chopper swung violently, like a toy on a string.

"Crosswinds here," the pilot announced. "Too dangerous. We're going back."

"Five more minutes," Clyde begged.

But Victoria Base was calling all search teams back. As they climbed higher Hector felt relief at the cushion of air separating them from the glacier. The sky grew closer, the peaks sank to eye level. They passed over a thick, milky cloud blanketing the surface.

"Whiteout," Clyde breathed. "I'd hate to be in that."

Hector soothed Clyde as they headed back to base. "Maybe Jack's ahead of us. Maybe they made good progress. We'll go out again later. There's still twenty miles to go."

There was no wind in the whiteout, only dreary mist. Amirault knew he was moving but had no sense of it. Pole and glide. His ski tips dipped into the murkiness and reappeared. The space around him glowed; it lacked beginning or end. He toppled over, disoriented. When he hit solid ground, it was a surprise.

"You okay?" Her voice floated, disembodied, everywhere.

"Yes."

Amirault stood, nauseous. He associated this kind of disorientation with blackness, with night. Light was supposed to provide clarity, not obscure it. His mind told him he was standing, but the world lacked depth. He'd known he'd lose vision in a whiteout, but had been unprepared to sacrifice space, distance, contrast. He felt ten feet tall one minute and upside down the next. He felt his muscles working, but emotion told him he stood still.

"Your turn," Robyn's voice said from the gloom, not even coming from the direction of the rope. "Nineteen ninety-two. Best memory."

"Halloween."

Her laugh seemed to come from overhead, from the sky, if there even was a sky anymore. "Go on."

"In San Francisco. Four of us. Brian. Evylyn. Laticia. Me."

"Old girlfriends," she said, teasing, invisible.

"They block off Castro Street. No cars allowed. About a million people are dressed up. Evylyn wore a Bali monkey mask. Brian and I had Chinese masks, half leopard, half man. Laticia had . . . I don't know how to describe this — springs coming out of her eyes, like Slinkies, bouncing, with plastic eyeballs at the end. Half the people on the streetcars were in costume. *Star Trek*, mummies, ghosts." He laughed. "And bands playing, music echoing off buildings, signs on shops saying, 'Won't Open Till Three A.M.' "

"You're making this up," her voice said, coming from left and right at the same time.

"The gays were out. Wigs four feet tall. Stiletto heels and phony plastic breasts as big as cantaloupes."

Her laugh sounded flat in the milky gloom. "Maybe you and I could have Halloween in San Francisco."

It thrilled him to picture her in his future. He reeled her in by the red rope. They kissed through mouth slits in their balaclavas.

"You taste like fuzz."

"There's ice on your face."

"That's not my face," Amirault said like a spook in a movie. "It's not? Uh oh. Then whose face is it?"

"Maybe we should wait for this to clear."

"No," Amirault said. "We had good visibility yesterday and the valley goes straight before we have to make a choice. Besides, we're eating more than I anticipated. Stay to the left all the time. That's what you said."

"Left of what? I don't see anything."

His thigh and shoulder muscles ached from yesterday. The sled seemed lighter, the glacier was running downhill. He tried to slow himself. Speed was dangerous without visibility.

"I hear a helicopter," he said. "*Hey!*"

"It's fading."

The slope grew slicker. Amirault didn't have to pole anymore. But he was not used to skiing with a sled behind him, and the weight plus the disorientation made him clumsy.

Then they broke from the whiteout into bright gray, and a cold so profound it struck him like a blow.

"That's better," Amirault said, blinking in the glare. They were descending at a brisk pace, in a cup-shaped valley. The black, snow-dusted ranges soared above them, close, immense, barren, clean. Wind gusted in his face; the temperature dropped so steeply his breath began to pop.

Amirault felt a slight sandpapery abrasion in his eyes, the first symptom of snowblindness. He stopped and put on glare-proof goggles. The glacier went a soothing rose color.

But they'd lost more time, slowed by the whiteout. They stopped talking, concentrated on skiing. His feet grew cold and a sweat spot itched in the small of his back.

After a while it started to snow again, hard and icy. They put on extra glove liners. They were making good progress, but his energy was dropping. The bridge of his nose grew raw. He felt his lips cracking. His breath made a sound like ice snapping as it floated away from him. Despite the extra layer, the flesh at the ends of his fingers began to tingle, and go numb, and he was hungry.

"They'll arrest you when you get there," she said.

"Probably."

"Rick must have radioed ahead if a copter was out here. Told them what he thinks you did."

"Optimist."

"You have no proof about Hector," Robyn said.

Amirault touched his heart. "I have conviction."

By nightfall Amirault estimated they'd gone fifteen miles, which, if true, would put them halfway to Victoria. As they pitched their tent in the snow, Robyn said, "You'll say Hector did it. Hector says no. The doctor against the mental patient. Who do they believe?"

Amirault used the thin, sharp reamer on his Swiss Army knife to refasten a loose screw on the stove. He fished foil packs from the knapsack. "Tonight," he said, "spring rolls to start. Then fried dumplings and scallion pancakes. Hot and spicy soup. Moo shu pork and eggplant with garlic. String beans and tofu. And lichee nuts for dessert."

He stirred the last pack of dehydrated chicken into melted water.

"I'm serious," she said.

"Okay. Not lichee nuts. Hot apple pie."

Amirault tasted the soup. "Look, Hector was scared of me. I know what I felt. And I know what I found. *And* I have a copy of her disk. When they see what she discovered, even if they don't believe me, they'll investigate. But the point isn't whether they believe me. And anyway, since when did bad odds stop you?"

"Worrying about me is one thing," she said glumly. "Worrying about you is another. Fifty-fifty on the soup, mister. Nothing extra for me."

Amirault handed her the steaming tin. "You cut me loose back at Ellsworth. Why are you having these problems now?"

"That was so you could use the satellite phone, not go up Purgatory Road."

They zipped their sleeping bags together. Amirault said when he climbed in with her, "You want the upper bunk or the lower?"

She giggled. "Lower."

Amirault woke in a soggy mess. The inside of the tent had become an ice cave from condensing breath, and pools of water dripped off the glaze onto the sleeping bag. More frost coated the inside of the bag, which smelled like a locker room. The cloth rack above spilled water on his head. The tent shook in the wind, and he was hungry.

The words of Lieber's safety drill came back to him. "You must stay dry in Antarctica. If you get wet, you freeze."

He made an extra-big breakfast, sensing how tired they were. It gave some energy, but further depleted rations. Everything I do kills people, he thought. The sky was gray and ugly, the clouds thick, too low for search planes.

Within a mile they went the wrong way, found themselves in a box canyon, and lost time retracing their tracks.

His toes were losing sensation. He told himself, Don't lift the skis. Glide. But they had to remove the skis to climb rotten ice blocking a canyon, and another time to hike up a saddle in the mountains. The wind was worse atop ridges.

By afternoon, as they headed directly into the wind, his lungs were on fire, the wind constricted his breathing passages. He gasped but no air came in. He felt the beginning of suffocation panic. "Turn the other way. Breathe into your glove," she said.

Robyn doubled over coughing. He felt her head.

"Hot," he said, alarmed. "We better pitch the tent."

"We have another two hours of light."

"You're getting sick, Robyn. I could make tea. There should be aspirin in the medical kit."

She started to protest but broke off, hacking. Green phlegm fell on the snow.

Amirault surveyed the valley. They were in an enormous glacial cup, rimmed by high mountains on three sides and a lower saddle of wind-carved sandstone to the north, on Purgatory Road. As he watched, snow shot into the air in an inverted mushroom shape below the saddle. There was a roar like a freight train and an instant later, massive wind hit them so hard they held each other until it passed.

"What the hell was *that?*" she said.

"Some kind of microburst. It's double wind shear. The wind rushes down, hits the earth, and washes up again. That's what makes the mushroom shape."

She pointed at the side of the mountain. "Is that a cave?" she said.

Using ice axes, they climbed up crumbling basement ice toward a dark oval opening in the basalt cliffs. As they reached it there was another roar and another snow geyser shot into the air. "The mountains here must form a kind of wind chute," Amirault said.

"And we have to climb through that tomorrow?"

But her eyes were red and feverish. Amirault fought off welling panic.

He pulled himself onto the ledge. He was relieved to see there really was a cave, with a good-size opening. They stooped to enter and Robyn gasped.

Amirault found himself staring at mummified seals. Half a dozen carcasses, brown-gray, shrunken, like rags with heads on the dark rock, where they'd starved or frozen to death. Blackened teeth showed crooked in muzzles collapsed in on themselves.

"How'd they get here?" She sneezed.

"Must have been an ocean here once."

Now there was just a glaze of ice stalactites on the ceiling.

When he touched his boot to the nearest mummy, the rib cage snapped, loud, brittle, sharp.

Amirault shook off a vision of himself and Robyn, two hundred years from now, mummies in perfectly preserved parkas in the cave. Discovered by oil workers or miners or tourists traveling the peninsula.

The cave turned out to be large, sixty feet long with a dogleg curve to the back into an hourglass-shaped vault, which was slightly warmer because the wind was cut off. Ice glazed the wall in patches. In back, a pair of waist-high outcrops jutted up, the black-green rock like rotten velvet. The ceiling was craggy with ice stalactites but the floor was lava-smooth and sloped enough, except for a few loose rocks, so they'd be able to find a comfortable spot for sleeping bags. The first outcrop, the size of a small kitchen table, rose on one side like the Rock of Gibraltar, but went flat on the end where Amirault unpacked and set the stove.

Robyn, exhausted, lay on her padded ground sheet five feet off, against the other outcrop, which was twin-humped like a saddle. Amirault rummaged in the pack and handed her an aspirin.

He suggested she roll out her sleeping bag. "I thought you're supposed to drink fluids, not lie in them," she said.

"I'll be better tomorrow," she said from the bag, but her voice was hoarse. Amirault unzipped his bag and laid it over her like a blanket.

"What will you sleep in?"

"I am a P-fifteen model android, madam. And do not need, as you humans call it, sleep."

She smiled wanly. The light faded. He needed the Swiss Army knife reamer again to fix the stove, and soon the only illumination came from the small flame. He melted snow and gave her a double ration. She drank four cups of tea.

There was a blast of wind outside, and Amirault envisioned the mushroom-shaped snow cloud erupting off the glacier floor. The sweat spot at his back was freezing.

He gave her more aspirin to bring the fever down. "Isn't this where you came into the picture?" she said. Already the inside of her sleeping bag was getting moist. Soon it would be soaked. He wished there were a way to keep her dry. As for himself, he paced to keep warm, and stamped his feet, but the temperature dropped so much his joints began aching and his knuckles wouldn't move.

He gave up and zipped the bags together and got in. He held her close. After she fell asleep, her chest made quick, frightening rattling noises. Amirault lay awake listening to her.

She was too sick to move the next day. Her fever was worse and they stayed in the cave. He gave her double rations again, his own food, the last of the food. He kept the stove on, turned it up, placed it near her so it might warm her even a fraction. But her breathing grew worse, and the sweat coating her palms and forehead had an oily sourness. Her breath, over the last couple of days, had assumed a natural human rankness, and now became slightly sulfurous as well, and an ammonia odor like bat guano filled the cave.

Robyn, tossing in feverish sleep, said, "Not now, Hector. Do it later."

The next morning when the light began to go gray Amirault found himself staring at the seal mummies. Stay here and you'll end up like us, they seemed to say.

The fuel ran out and so did the fire. He rummaged in his knapsack for an extra canister, and as he contemplated leaving by himself, he placed on the rock table, by the cold stove, his lighter, the Swiss Army knife, a roll of hard candies he had not known he had but which he could melt in the tea for sugar. The manufactured items looked unreal to him.

"I had a dream about you," she said, waking.

"What?"

She tried to smile. Her voice sounded a little stronger. "X-rated. I must be getting better."

She closed her eyes and one waffle-iron-covered arm draped over her forehead. Wisps of hair were plastered to her skin.

Gingerly, Amirault unscrewed the empty canister from the stove and took a full one from his pack, inserted the top into the stove's copper input tube and twisted hard, and the tube punctured the pressurized canister, which he screwed into the stove. He lit it. Now he could make tea.

He went outside, blinking at the gray glare, the lightly falling flakes, the snow funnel roaring in the valley. As he scooped snow for tea he thought, I should try to get to Victoria Base alone. It'll be a couple of days before she can travel, and if the weather turns bad while we're waiting, we'll have to stay here longer than that.

Robert Falcon Scott, the famed British explorer of the Antarctic, he knew, had died in a tent, waiting for a storm to stop, only eleven miles from a food cache.

He turned at a scraping sound to find her standing outside the cave, parka on, utterly white. She leaned against the rock with one gloved hand.

"I know what you're thinking," she said. "Go."

But Amirault cocked his head, not trusting what his senses told him. "Helicopter."

She moved out of the entrance. Together, they scanned the cloud deck to the north.

"They might not see us on the rocks," she said. "We ought to get on the snow."

The drumming grew louder. They scrambled down the footholds they'd cut in the ice. Amirault slipped, fell on his back, slid the last twenty feet to the valley floor. Unhurt, he stood, watched Robyn lumber toward him, pointing.

"There."

At first he saw only a red blinking light, far off, then white lights too, then a speck, moving in and out of the mist at the bottom of the clouds. Amirault and Robyn began jumping, screaming, "We're here!" The craft veered toward them. Amirault made out the glass-bubble cockpit. No aft cabin, probably just a spotter craft.

Robyn doubled over, coughing.

The copter swooped lower, only a hundred feet off the ground, colors visible now, red hull beneath the bubble, and French tricolor on the side.

Robyn stood still, both arms up, as if surrendering.

"What are you doing?"

"Signaling," she said without lowering her arms. "It means, Pick us up. I learned this stuff before I left."

The copter hovered; its noise rolled across the glacier, struck the cliffs and came back, magnifying itself.

"JACK!"

The name came from a loudspeaker under the fuselage. Amirault's smile died. "It's Hector," he said.

"Oh God."

"IT'S HECTOR, JACK. CAN YOU HEAR ME?"

Robyn had both arms up diagonally, in a Y shape, like a cheerleader. "Means yes," she said.

"ARE YOU ALL RIGHT?"

Amirault watched Robyn lie down on the snow, on her back. She stretched her arms straight out. Now Amirault made out Hector in the bubble, a hundred feet up, over the helmeted pilot's shoulder, small, gesturing at the pilot, who seemed to be explaining Robyn's signals to him.

"YOU NEED A DOCTOR?"

Yes.

"YOU ARE INJURED?"

No.

"SICK?"

Yes.

"BOTH OF YOU?"

No.

"DO YOU HAVE FOOD? FUEL?"

No.

Amirault was grateful for the copter, but sensed the doctor was acting. Pretending concern. The copter, drifting lightly, moved slowly south in the wind. Every few seconds the pilot made adjustments.

Amirault saw Hector and the pilot arguing. Hector made quick jabbing motions toward the ground. He seemed to want the pilot to land.

"WE'RE NOT ALLOWED TO LAND. WE CAN DROP FOOD AND MEDICINE. ANTIBIOTICS. DO YOU UNDERSTAND?"

Yes.

"YOU HAVE FEVER?"

Yes.

"PAIN?"

Yes.

"WHERE?"

Robyn touched her elbows, knees, forehead.

"STOMACH?"

No.

"TAKE THE VIBRAMYCIN. STAY WARM. GET IN YOUR SLEEPING BAG. ONE PILL EVERY FOUR HOURS. TRY TO EAT. WE TRIED TO RADIO FOR HELP BUT THERE MUST BE A STORM BETWEEN US AND THE BASE. WE'LL COME BACK WITH HELP. YOU ARE ONLY ELEVEN MILES FROM VICTORIA BASE. DO YOU HEAR ME?"

Yes.

"WHEN WE COME BACK, YOU AND I CAN TALK, JACK. EVERYTHING IS GOING TO BE ALL RIGHT."

But Amirault, watching the casual drift of the chopper, realized in horror that the pilot had stopped making adjustments, thinking they were safe, and the copter was almost in the wind chute.

"Get away from there!" he shouted.

He grabbed Robyn. "Tell them! Get them away from there!"

"JACK, WHAT ARE YOU DOING?"

Robyn said, "I don't know how."

"LEAVE HER ALONE, JACK."

Robyn crouched and extended both arms out, like a pistol shooter, pointing toward the safe side of the valley. But she said, "This just means, Land over there."

"I TOLD YOU. WE CAN'T LAND," the loudspeaker said.

Amirault said, "Son of a bitch. Clyde's in there." Clyde was gesturing too.

"If we make an E in the snow, that means emergency," Robyn said.

Amirault quickly began outlining it with his boot.

"ARE YOU TRYING TO TELL US SOMETHING?"

The copter door opened and Clyde tossed something small and red out. It fell to the ice and sent up a small spray of snow particles. Amirault ran toward the chopper, heedless of the untested surface. He waved his arms frantically. "Get away from there!"

Too late. Amirault heard another sound, deeper, the swelling roar he'd been listening to for two days, like a geyser gathering strength. An invisible hand seemed to strike the copter sideways. It pitched left. Amirault had a glimpse of Hector thrown against his seat, arms flying, and the pilot fighting the collective-pitch lever. The chopper veered toward the rocks, forced down as the snow below billowed up in an inverted mushroom. The mountain rushed at the copter. The engines screamed as the pilot tried to pull out. But the skids hit an outcrop, the copter tilted vertically, the main rotor smashed into rock, broke off, and the whole machine was tumbling, rolling, and crumpling, and a rush of liquid gushed out, fuel as the pilot jettisoned it, trying to prevent an explosion.

The copter slammed into a ledge.

For a half-second it seemed to jut from the rock.

Then, with a groan of tortured metal, it rolled over twice, bouncing, hit basement ice, and slid thirty feet to a shuddering halt.

The wind funnel had stopped. Snow drifted to earth.

The quiet was immense.

Amirault smelled gasoline, and burned rubber from the torn skids.

He ran toward the shattered helicopter, seeing movement behind the broken windscreen. He was astounded anyone in there was alive. The people in the rear seats struggled to get out.

The engine might blow.

Then it seemed that an optical illusion was happening. The copter was moving again. Settling into the snow, with a groan. Three inches. Five inches.

The undercarriage was disappearing into the glacier.

There's a crevasse under it, Amirault thought.

The snow gave way beneath him and he plunged down, hit bottom after a foot, dragged his boot out, and heedless of the quaking surface, kept running. Hector had extricated himself from his seat, but seemed caught, half in and half out of the shattered windscreen, bending back into the cockpit, as if attending to the pilot.

Amirault reached the chopper and kicked out shards of razor-sharp Plexiglas and pushed into the cramped space beside Hector. The doctor was staring in shock at the pilot, who, through a mass of steam and smoke and torn electrical wiring, leaned sideways across his control stick, goggles down over his mouth, eyes wide, right hand in death still clutching the wider part of the Plexiglas shard that was embedded in his neck. The other hand dangled near an empty holster.

Amirault smelled the tart odor of gasoline and a sweeter blood aroma. Blood streamed down the right side of Hector's dazed face from a cut in his forehead, already congealing. Amirault said, "Get out of here! It's going to fall."

He took in the scene at a glance. A section of console had been ripped from its mooring and lay outside, against black rock. Clyde was tearing at his seat belt control, which seemed stuck. He looked terrified but unharmed. Amirault spotted a shotgun bolted to the floor but the copter was settling again, a heart-stopping lurch downward, and he fought off Clyde's tearing fingers to work at the seat belt switch. It was stuck. The fuselage groaned. Amirault said again, "Hector, get out of here!"

The doctor slid sideways out of Amirault's field of vision. Clyde moaned and Amirault heard liquid bubbling, fuel spilling. He forced himself to work gently at Clyde's seat belt lock. There was a metallic snapping, loud and sharp, the belt loosened and Clyde threw it off, and together, Amirault and Clyde scrambled backward into the snow as the chopper dropped six more inches.

Amirault heard the surface straining to hold the weight. He shouted, "Back!" And they picked up Robyn on the way back and all four of them were running from the wreck.

The ice was vibrating now. Amirault pulled Robyn toward the

rocks. The chopper gave a final lurch, and there was a crack and the rotor caught the edge of the opening crevasse, the whole machine dangling, twisting for a fraction of a second. There was a high-pitched scraping, rotors against ice. The chopper disappeared. After some moments, they heard a crash from far below.

A rumble echoed back up at them. An explosion shook the whole valley. A ball of smoke rolled from the crevasse and spread slowly, with a smell of burning gasoline, diminishing, as the chopper burned.

Small avalanches slid down the drifts along the northern ridges.

In the vast silence none of them spoke or moved, stunned by the destruction. "It's like the chopper was never here at all," Clyde said, voice trembling. "Thanks, Jack."

His face was white. He looked from Amirault to Hector. He said, "Hector? What are you doing?"

Hector stood a few feet off, blood coloring the right half of his face. Amirault stared down at his hand and the silvery gleam of metal in it. Hector had taken the pilot's sidearm.

"Come over here, Clyde," Hector said in a hoarse whisper. "He's dangerous."

"What do you mean? He saved us. He pulled me out. What are you doing?"

"Orders," Hector said.

It started snowing harder. Flakes fell, huge and soft, melting into small drops on the barrel of the gun.

Hector seemed to become aware of the valley, mountains, the isolation. He was far enough from Amirault to look around. The blood was drying, or freezing, on his face.

Hector's voice went soft, dangerous. "No one knows we're here," he said. "We never got through on the radio."

Robyn moved close and Amirault put his arm around her as Hector pressed his free hand to the gash on the right side of his forehead. He swayed. Amirault hoped he was going to fall.

The vast empty space around them swallowed Hector's slurred words. "I've been wanting to talk to you. We really . . . really need to talk."

eleven

The snow turned gray, Amirault thought in wonder. Then he realized it was ash drifting down from the crashed helicopter, in the falling snow. Bits of burned fiberglass, paper, wiring, clothing.

His throat had gone dry as sandpaper. He had to open his mouth to breathe.

Hector aimed the gun at his chest, from five feet away. Ash and snow dusted the doctor's shoulders and the top of his head.

"I'd love to talk, Hector," Amirault said.

Clyde stood anxiously beside the doctor. "Your forehead, Hector." The doctor's mouth was slack, and his parka had ripped so padding wadded out of a sleeve in a cauliflower shape.

Hector's speech was slurred. "Would you mind getting the rucksack, Clyde? We'll need it."

"What if that thing goes off by accident?" Clyde said.

"I won't shoot by accident."

"That's a comfort," Amirault said.

Clyde scrambled off. He seemed to have decided cooperation would lessen trouble.

When he was out of earshot Hector said, "Was that a cave we saw you come from? Let's get out of this storm."

"You going to do it up there, Hector?"

Robyn had gone still, her breaths coming in short, quick bursts. The crash and the gun seemed to have robbed her of any freedom of movement. At the moment she was no threat to Hector, and no help to Amirault.

"I'm not going to do anything." Sweat was turning to frost on Hector's yellow-white face.

"All three of us? How will you explain it when they come?"

Hector flicked the gun at the rocks, and Amirault looked up at the dark opening. It seemed ominous, much too private, even though no one else was here.

"You're being ridiculous." Hector jerked the gun irritably. "Move."

Clyde ran back with the knapsack. He's the key, Amirault thought. Hector pays no attention to him. Except he won't believe anything I say. "Sandwiches, medicine, bandages, extra fuel," Clyde said too brightly. Clyde was near enough to Hector to touch the gun and Amirault felt the short hairs on the back of his neck rise. Grab it, he thought. But Clyde just said, "Hector, I don't think this is necessary." No reply. Clyde's voice rose a notch. "He pulled us out." Hector blinked as if clearing his vision. "For Christ's sake, Hector," Clyde said. "Jack won't hurt us."

"Then he has nothing to worry about."

Clyde made an imploring gesture, palms out. If he couldn't calm Hector, he'd try to soothe Amirault. "They said you were dangerous, Jack. I know you're not. But they told us to take precautions. That's why we weren't supposed to land. He's only doing what he thinks is right."

"Good old Hector," Amirault said.

Hector nodded. "The gun's for our protection. Clyde's and mine."

"Clyde's, eh?" Amirault set the edges of his teeth together. "Clyde, you think I'm dangerous?" He took a step forward. Hector fired at the ground without hesitation. Clyde cried out as a woman might have. Whatever impact the bullet made in the snow at Amirault's feet was obscured by blowing flakes.

Clyde said, "For God's sake, let's get out of this!"

Amirault lifted his shoulders in a gesture that accepted defeat for the moment. They trudged up the crudely cut ice steps, which were more slippery now. Amirault glanced back, encouraged that Hector was limping. Slip, he urged silently. Hector didn't.

As they entered the cave, Clyde rushed forward with pleasure, seeing the seal mummies. His moods changed like a boy's. "Look! Five of them! Incredible!"

The rear of the cave was gloomier but warmer, and Clyde pulled a fluorescent pocket light from the pack and flicked it on. Hector leaned against the saddle-shaped outcrop. More blood marred his face; his mouth was set in a grimace. He seemed to need his concentration to fight pain.

Amirault helped Robyn into her sleeping bag, zipped her in, and she leaned across his lap, against the larger outcrop. "I'm all right now," she said. They watched Hector slide to the ground against the other outcrop, six feet away. Only Clyde was standing, and Hector told him to tie Amirault's ankles together with the climbing rope. "Not too tight." And to bring the ice ax over, and the medical kit.

Amirault said, "The wreckage in the crevasse will be visible from the air. And the ice will be black from smoke. Come out of this alone, Hector, they'll figure it out."

"I told you." Patiently. "I'm not going to hurt you."

"Yeh. I see that." Clyde sprinkled alcohol on a bandage, cleaned Hector's head, and wrapped it. Hector said, "We'll stay here until the storm ends. Then go outside and wait for the choppers. Robyn, your symptoms. What are they?"

The question, coming from a man aiming a gun, seemed to Amirault the height of absurdity. "Fever. Shakes," Robyn said, baffled too. Then Amirault saw what Hector was doing, acting as if he had done nothing wrong.

He knows I don't have proof.

It gave Amirault hope. He won't kill us. He doesn't know I have a copy of Evylyn's work. I'll wait it out, he thought, and make my accusations when the choppers come.

But then Hector said, "Why are you heading for Victoria Base, Jack?"

"To watch the Forty-niners on big-screen TV."

The doctor sighed. Clyde was carrying snow in for broth, to the stove on the far side of the outcrop. "I've been a bad doctor to you," Hector said. "I was selfish. Un-Christian. I was worried about myself. I was afraid."

There was the hiss of the stove starting up and Amirault heard the rustle of a foil packet and a ripping noise as Clyde opened it, behind him. He supposed the gun would sound very loud in here.

"You found out about the ship," Hector said. "I knew you would."

At that, Amirault knew Hector wasn't going to let them go. I need at least thirty seconds to free myself. Five to reach him. It's too much.

Clyde said, with more curiosity than alarm, "Ship?" He was too far from Hector to help.

Hector slid down an inch. Even slight movement made him grimace. "Four years ago," he said, "I was accused of stealing secrets. Navy secrets." His eyes glazed and a spot of red welled from his right nostril.

Clyde gasped. "You?"

Hector seemed in no rush. "I had a family. Two a.m., on a July night, the doorbell rang. I thought, Somebody had an accident. That's what you think at that hour. But it was Navy investigators. They cuffed me in front of Annie. What's this about? I'm saying. What did I do?"

Clyde said, as if confirming it to himself, "They arrested you."

The doctor's voice went so low Amirault had to strain to hear. He had a feeling Hector wasn't acting, at least about the arrest. "They interrogated me. For days. How often did you meet him? they asked. Where do you keep the money?"

"Where *did* you keep it?" Amirault asked. No point in denying things now.

The gun pointed midway between Amirault and Robyn. At neither and both at the same time. Bitterly, Hector said, "There wasn't any money."

"They made a mistake," Clyde said happily.

"Yeh, when they let him go," Amirault said.

"It took two years to prove it," Hector said. "Annie left me. You know, from a cell, when you look out, the wire mesh divides grass, trees, sky, into little pieces. Your memory of outside is more real than what you see."

"Why are you telling us this?" Robyn said.

Amirault heard bubbling water behind him. "At first," Hector said, ignoring her, "I thought the charges would be cleared up quickly. And even when they finally realized it was a mistake, they didn't admit it. Not enough evidence, they said. I had a good lawyer. I agreed to a deal. They dropped all charges and kept me in the service. I wouldn't sue or go to the press. I asked for a transfer as far away as I could get."

"To Antarctica."

"That's right."

"Wu Kai Nung. He's at Victoria Base," Amirault said.

Hector just said, "I went to a picnic and my life fell apart."

"What a nightmare," Clyde said.

"You believe him?" Amirault said. It didn't make a difference now if he pushed. "Then why were you scared of me, Hector?"

"*Because I was afraid it would start again!*" Hector brushed a glove to his forehead. His right nostril had begun oozing blood. "Don't you see? Another accusation. They'd come after me again. I wanted to shut you up. To stop you. Nobody hurt Evylyn but I was terrified someone might start to believe you. I can't go through that again. I'm due to retire."

Amirault said, "And the stuff they found in my room? Who put it there?"

"You."

Amirault guffawed. He looked at Robyn but she wasn't smiling. Amirault said, "Give me a break."

"Jack," Hector said, tried to get up, and fell back. "I'm telling you this, I'm admitting this because I want to help you. *Nobody murdered Evylyn.* Nobody tried to kill you. If another chopper had found you, if you'd been hurt when they apprehended you, I wouldn't have forgiven myself. You sensed I was afraid of you. You were right but for the wrong reason. I was afraid to talk about this before. Now look what's happened."

"He's lying," Amirault told Robyn.

"You think so? Look at me. Can't you feel I'm telling the truth? You felt my fear and you were right. What do you feel now? You don't feel I'm lying. I know it. You can't."

Amirault wasn't sure what he felt. The fear wasn't in Hector anymore. It was Amirault who was afraid. Hector said, "You've been down here long enough to know what can happen to people, what the isolation can do. Imagining things. You, last year. You were sure Brian was climbing back up that crevasse, and he wasn't, but you didn't believe that at first. The pressure is enormous. You were having problems even before your sister died. *You* stole those things. *You* hid them in your closet. It's a cry for help. I should have realized it but I was worried about myself. Forgive me."

Clyde had started stirring the broth again. Robyn said, "And the generator building?"

Hector wiped blood away. "Nobody locked him in the generator building. The door was open. Carbon monoxide, Jack. It screws your senses up."

"I didn't steal anything," Amirault said.

Clyde walked around the front of the outcrop, half blocking Hector's view. "Oh, Jack," he said. "We loved her. We both loved her. I miss her. I think about her every day."

"He's lying!"

"You keep saying that. Show us. Show *them*," Hector said, nodding at Robyn, at Clyde. "They're your friends. They'd believe you. Even if you think I harmed her, you know *they* didn't."

Amirault struggled to get up but the ropes prevented it. "It's not true!"

"I have no intention of hurting you," Hector said again. "Or anyone. This," he said, raising the gun, dropping it back to his lap, "is self-defense. I told you. We wait till the storm ends. The copters come. You can tell them your story. If it means problems for me, I'm ready now. I should have been ready before."

Amirault felt grief welling.

"Her death was an accident," Hector said. "Think about it. When I get excited over things, I look back later and it seems like a dream. Does it seem like that to you? Even a little? No one is going to hurt you. Clyde, is that food ready?"

"Minute or two."

"You're saying I imagined it?" Amirault said.

"Oh God, Jack," Robyn said.

"Don't you see what he's doing? He's pretending he didn't do it!"

"Ready now," Clyde said.

From outside came the howl of wind.

Amirault searched his memory frantically. "But the diplomat, the Chinese, at Victoria Base. You still haven't answered that."

Hector's lips compressed into a thin white line, whether from anger or pain Amirault didn't know. "That's what they used to say in Washington," he said. *"You still haven't answered!* But I just hadn't told them what they wanted to hear."

Hector shook his head. "Coincidence, Jack. Crazy, unfortunate coincidence. That's right. It's possible and it happened. Babies are born with two heads. People get hit by lightning. But that coincidence meant they'd come after me for sure. *Coincidence.*"

Amirault's eyes narrowed as Hector picked up the gun, and looking deliberately into Amirault's face, held the stock up and ejected the ammunition magazine into his hand. Hector threw the magazine across the cave. It clattered against the wall and fell. Hector laid the gun at his feet, kicked it away, far from him. He looked disgusted with himself.

"I don't need it anymore," he said.

Amirault whispered, "Coincidence?"

"I sure didn't want him there," Hector said.

There was nothing to say after that. Amirault reached down, still locked onto Hector's face, and untied his ankles. Nobody stopped him. He stood up. Hector regarded him without fear. Amirault walked across the cave, picked up the cartridge, looked back. Nobody had moved. Clyde stood by the stove. Robyn lay in her sleeping bag. Hector leaned against the outcrop.

Amirault examined the magazine. There were bullets in there, all right.

Amirault came back across the cave and knelt beside Hector. He picked up the gun. They all watched him. He slid the magazine into the stock and stood up.

"You don't look good," Amirault told Hector.

"I feel worse."

Amirault laid the gun back on the ground. It felt silly holding it.

"Can I help?" he said.

Hector laughed. "Turn back the clock."

Robyn's expression was wide, dark and earnest. "That's it? That can't be it." Amirault saw a brightness in her eyes go out.

"Well, there's still the small matter of getting home," Clyde said, glancing toward the mouth of the cave. But the tension was out of them.

Amirault sank to his knees. He refused to believe what had happened. "If it isn't you," he told Hector, "it's someone else."

"You know it's no one else."

"But I didn't steal those things," Amirault said again, to Robyn. "At least I don't remember stealing them." She blew on her broth. Her condensing breath mixed with the steam. She didn't look at him.

"Sure, Jack. There's an explanation," Clyde agreed, having trouble meeting Amirault's eyes too.

"Tell me what's happening at Victoria Base," Robyn said at length.

"You are a glutton for punishment," Hector forced out.

"The meeting," Clyde said, glad for the diversion, "is going tops."

"Tops," Robyn repeated in a defeated tone. "I take it that means the new treaty has passed."

"They expect to sign tomorrow or the next day," Hector said. "At least that's the scuttlebutt. The diplomats seem to have finished dividing the spoils."

"And who gets Ellsworth Base?" Amirault asked, trying to think.

"We do. That's the rumor," Clyde said, meaning the British. "Or there may be some sharing arrangement on the peninsula. I mean, weather's best here. Minerals will come out first here. Chile. Argentina. All three claimants dividing it up. I imagine the U.S.'ll get a piece."

"Very nice of you," Hector said. He was gray.

"Plenty to go around," Clyde said. "I mean, with all the resources, bloody Third Worlders won't be able to hold anything over our heads anymore. That's the ticket! Independence! Enough of this blackmail every time they don't like something we do! Oil! Gas! Molybdenum! Titanium!"

Amirault looked up sharply, caught Clyde's eyes as Clyde realized his mistake, but Amirault was too surprised, too slow to react in time. As he started to rise the Brit threw his broth and Amirault, turning to shield his face, felt the hot mix strike the back of his parka and burn his neck.

Hector shouted, "Jack!" and Amirault was up, but Clyde was closer to the gun.

Clyde held the gun on Amirault. They eyed each other over the astounded faces of the others.

"I'm the only one who found molybdenum," Amirault said. "And I haven't told anyone except the Navy."

Clyde's face had transformed itself. It didn't look so youthful anymore. The nervousness had been replaced with a deliberate economy of movement, an intense quiet. His eyes had gone blunt.

"My mum used to say," he said, in a harsher voice than Amirault had ever heard from him, "there's no such thing as a slip of the tongue. Only wanting to say something, and fooling yourself into thinking you said it by accident."

Robyn had half risen from her sleeping bag. One hand was poised midway to her mouth. "It was you?" She looked baffled. "It can't be you."

"That's right. It can't be me." Clyde's self-mocking laugh echoed. "Not Clyde. Not eager-to-please Clyde. The lovesick patsy. Feels good to talk normal. Sit down," he told Amirault.

Amirault didn't move. "Kill one or kill four," Clyde shrugged. "All the same to me."

Everything seemed to be happening in slow motion. Clyde squatted on the soles of his feet like a native in a jungle, reached with his free hand to sip broth from Amirault's tin, never taking his eyes off them. The wind keened outside.

"The really hilarious part," Clyde said, "is that it was you they were interested in, not your sister. I was there to watch you. You have quite a reputation. Your own people may not respect you, but believe me, you strike fear into the opposition."

"Opposition?"

"Oil, Jack. Molybdenum. And who's going to get them." Clyde finished the broth. Amirault remembered all those letters from oil companies, offering jobs. He flashed to Evylyn, in his dream, saying, *What happened that night that you don't remember?*

"You were in my room," Amirault said slowly, seeing it. "You told me you were looking for her, but you were in there with the door closed."

Clyde said, "Rifling your reports."

"And Rick said he was listening at your door," Amirault said, his blood setting the surface of his back tingling. "He heard you and Evylyn laughing." Clyde nodded like a teacher urging on a pupil. "Thirty minutes later she shows up at the party. Whatever upset her must have happened with you."

"Frankly, Jack, I thought you might have figured things out before this. Then again," he said, "I did fool everyone, didn't I? But I am a scientist. Or started out to be one." He seemed to relax a bit. He had a little time now. There was no rush now. He was savoring it. "I've wanted to tell this story. The way they woo you. Study your tests in school. Parents. The way they sound you out through someone you respect. A teacher. And then the second man talks to you. The way they appeal to your vanity. The way they pay."

"An oil company."

"The Foreign Office," Clyde said, grinning. "Or rather, the British Antarctic Survey. I've never been exactly sure which one they were."

"The *British* Foreign Office?" Hector said. "You're a . . ."

"Spy?" Clyde laughed. "I think of myself as a researcher." But he liked the word. "James Bond and all that. Three years ago. At Cambridge. I was going to be a climatologist. The man who took me to lunch — Pike, his name was — was young, eager. Smart. He's at Victoria Base now. He's a member of our delegation. 'Why me?' I said. 'Because,' he said when we finally got around to things, weeks later, after the probing and testing and silly walks and questions. 'Because these days we recruit people with specialties. Because your psychological profile is just what we want.' "

"Psychotic," Robyn said.

Clyde smiled. " 'And because there are going to be some tricky negotiations over Antarctica, and we need information. Countries are supposed to share research, but nobody does.' "

"See?" Robyn told Amirault.

Clyde shrugged. "You Americans live so much in the present. You're only starting to imagine what things will be like when your resources run out." He nodded. "But I didn't do it because of politics." He whispered, "I thought it would be fun. And at first I don't think they dreamed of spying on a close friend. They wanted to know about the Japanese."

Amirault looked around for a weapon. The rocks lay too far away. The ice ax leaned against the wrong outcrop. The Swiss Army knife, open to the reamer, lay by the stove on the closer outcrop, but how could he even pick it up? And anyway, it would be like coming at an armed man with a safety pin.

"Whitehall," Clyde said, following Amirault's gaze, "believed the Japanese had found oil, a sea of it, but were sitting on the information. My ozone job — they made sure I was the one who got it — would take me to different bases. Hopefully I'd learn what the Japanese had found." His brows rose. "I turned out to be good at it. I found it rather stimulating."

"Jolly good," Amirault said.

"And easy," Clyde said, leaning against the rock. "There's no security on bases. Such an odd twilight zone here, a combination of secrecy and openness. All of you burying reports, waiting for the new treaty to be signed."

"And afterward they'll 'discover' oil in their territories," Robyn said, disgusted.

"Or molybdenum," Clyde said. He seemed to be thinking about something. "After Japan I spent three months on the Argentine base. Then Russia. Less friendly countries. It's funny," he said. "Gail studies isolation. She thinks being far from home is isolation. Deception is isolation. That's what it is."

"Let me give you the phone number of a psychologist I know," Amirault said.

Clyde's smile grew crooked. "At each base I'd find a girl, pretend to fall in love, follow her around. The Argentine, Moira, was so ugly. But nobody questions a jealous lover. You go where you want."

Amirault felt sick. "My sister."

"You start to hate the people you deceive. It's too easy to manipulate them. You wonder, How far can I go and still fool them? You push it. It's a science. And London was afraid of you, Jack. You were all the other seismologists talked about, on other bases. You find things they don't! They were sure the American Navy was hiding your findings."

Which is true, Amirault thought. "You're the Kronsky," Amirault said over the hissing of pressurized gas in the stove.

His heart quickened. Pressurized gas?

Clyde said, "When I go back to London, I'll be well-off. I'll never have to come to this lifeless place again. I've brought them more information than they ever dreamed of. But if they find out about Evylyn, things will turn out rather differently, I'm afraid."

"And as for you," Clyde said, "you're not that smart. You wouldn't give up! But we were never a match. I was always smarter than you."

Pressurized gas can explode.

"But what happened to Evylyn," Amirault said, "if you were there for me?"

This time Clyde seemed embarrassed. He let out a long stream of air. "I said you push things. I found out by accident. I pieced together what she was trying to discover. And then she got excited one day, I realized she'd done it. If I could get a copy! It took weeks until I saw her key her code into her computer."

"The Nobel Prize for theft," Amirault said.

"I made a copy when she was out in the Zodiac the night of the party. I brought it to my room. Later she was there. We were . . . having fun. She was drunk." Clyde frowned. He went nasal, mocking her. " 'I want to play a game.' I had to go out for a while, to send up a balloon. While I was gone she must have started going through my things, looking for Nintendo." He looked disgusted. "Going through my fucking things. Looking for a fucking game."

"I can see what you mean about being smart," Amirault said.

"When I came back she had it in the computer. She was staring at it. She attacked me. Fighting, clawing. I was sure everyone else could hear. If you hadn't been at the party, it would have ended then."

Clyde began to pace in agitation. "I gave the disk back," he said. "I pleaded with her. 'Evylyn, please, they'll put me in jail. It'll ruin my life.'"

Amirault remembered her crying, in the hallway, *I don't want to hurt anyone else.* He said to Clyde, "She wouldn't turn you in."

"But she was going to. I could tell. She was torn up, but in the end, she would tell. She said she had to think about it. She stormed out. I was terrified. And then at the party, she started yelling. You took her to her room. All I could think was, What is she saying?"

Amirault pictured it. Clyde watching Cathy go off with A.Y., leaving Evylyn alone in the room. Clyde waiting until the party ended, opening her door, waking her, starting the conversation again, begging her to come outside where they could talk privately. Clyde taking her on the rocks.

"The funny thing is," Clyde said, "I was thinking about pushing her in, but I didn't think I'd really do it. It was this picture in my head. I kept saying, *'What did you tell your brother?'* And then we're *on* the rocks, and she's in the water. I don't remember pushing her. That part's mixed up."

Hector slumped. He rolled toward Amirault, onto one shoulder. Blood flowed from his nose, and his eyes were shut. Amirault started toward him but Clyde said, "Stay put."

"No worries about him now," Clyde said, touching his boot to Hector.

To explode the gas, I need a fire.

Clyde wanted to finish now. "I watched you. You were figuring things out. I don't actually remember locking you in the generator building. I remember loosening the bolts. But Gail was coming. I had to open the door again too soon."

Robyn had begun to tremble.

"Do you know," Clyde said, "why so much British literature elevates spies? Fleming. Kipling. Because we're a little nation. We know the value of information." Clyde giggled. "I have another vision. You. Lying in this cave. I don't think I'll really do it. Except it seems that's the way things always start."

Hector's eyes opened but Clyde didn't see it.

Clyde told Amirault, "Get up."

Amirault hesitated and Clyde said, "I thought about your excellent warnings before. You're right. If I shoot, they may find your bodies. A small chance, but possible."

"The point of that argument was to make Hector give up."

Clyde waved the gun slightly, sliding away from Hector. "Strip," he said. "You heard me. How long will you last without clothes in this cave? Evylyn lived less than three minutes in the water. Parka off, please."

Robyn was shaking.

"Temperature must be close to zero now, and dropping. Twenty minutes, half an hour. Then I put your clothes back on, drag you out, snow'll cover you. Storms'll pile up for the next six months, and nobody will be here a long time after I leave. How long do you think those mummies have lain undiscovered?"

"Someone will find us sooner or later," Amirault said.

"Later, I should think. If at all," Clyde said. "And there won't be a mark on you. Hector died of injuries from the crash. I started back for help. You and Robyn froze to death. Who's going to question that?"

Hector's mouth moved, but it was impossible for Amirault to make out what he was saying.

"I'm not going to strip," Robyn said.

Amirault turned to her. Her face was blazing. He'd mistaken her trembling for fear. "Sick, perverted bastard," she hissed. She took a half-step toward Clyde. "Delusions of grandeur. James fucking Bond," she said. "Now I've heard everything. I'm not taking off my clothes." Amirault reached for her and she shook him off.

"Guns. Men and guns. You feel big with that gun?" she said. "You touch him, hurt him, I'll kill you." Amirault, astounded, realized she meant him. "*You hear me?* I'll kill you."

"Too bad you weren't on base instead of Evylyn." Clyde grinned. "One . . ." he counted.

She said, "I'll find a way and—"

"Two . . ." The gun listed toward Amirault.

Robyn reached for her zipper. Amirault pulled his sweater and turtleneck over his head. Then his boots. Pants. Long johns. The cold hit him like a blow. Robyn kicked the sleeping bag away from her feet.

"Hypothermia," Clyde said as Hector closed his eyes at his approach, "was my favorite lecture. Do you know campers can die of hypothermia when the temperature outside is only fifty degrees?"

Naked, Amirault and Robyn wrapped their arms around each other.

"You know what you look like? Photos of Jews going to the gas chamber," Clyde said.

"I'll kill you," Robyn said.

Clyde said, philosophically, "We're nothing without our protective layers, are we? Clothes. Fuel."

Amirault felt any heat inside retreating deep into his body, away from the surface. Quick stabbing pains started up in his joints. His forehead throbbed. The pain spreading from his bare feet burned like dry ice.

"Blue becomes you," Clyde remarked.

Hector's eyes fluttered open again. Amirault thought, Grab the ax.

Clyde sighed. "It's making me cold just looking at you. Tell me what you're feeling. It'll help pass the few minutes you have left. Where does it hurt most? I would think feet. Spirit of research, Jack . . ."

Amirault kissed Robyn. He whispered, "When I move grab the fuel canister. The knife. Puncture it. You—"

Clyde barked, "Stop talking!"

Then Hector moved.

The doctor's arms snaked out, wrapped Clyde's ankles, and Clyde said, "What—" reeling. His hands jerked into the air and he fired. The shot sounded thunderous. Amirault was already moving but his legs weren't working properly; his coordination was off. And Hector lacked the strength to pull Clyde down. As Amirault closed, Clyde swung the gun down and fired. Hector grunted, let go. Amirault plowed into Clyde, driving him back as he grabbed unsuccessfully for Clyde's gun hand.

They crashed backward over the outcrop, onto the rock. The

gun went off by Amirault's ear. Amirault was weakened now, he had trouble holding on. Something heavy smashed into his shoulder, and hit him again. Clenching his teeth against the pain, he brought his knee up, heard a grunt and Clyde's mouth opened but no sound came out. The ground was hard, too cold. Amirault couldn't stand it. He'd lost too much strength. Clyde straddled him. The gun swung down.

Clyde screeched and arched backwards.

The gun clattered to the ground.

What happened? Amirault thought, rolling painfully on his hip, half frozen, dazed, rising. Over Clyde's shoulder he saw Robyn by the outcrop. Clyde groped behind him with one hand. He turned slowly, like a doll atop a music box. A great gush of blood erupted from his mouth. Amirault saw the ice ax protruding from his parka.

So cold. Amirault picked the gun off the rock. He had to will his fingers to wrap the stock.

Clyde reached back and with a heave pulled the ax from his back. Robyn, transfixed, made no move to get away. Clyde stumbled toward her, raised the ax. Amirault's fingers wouldn't work. He could not fire.

Amirault pulled the trigger, twice. The impact drove Clyde back. He looked down. His parka had been shredded by the bullets. A great ocher stain spread across the left side of his chest.

"Bloody scientists," Clyde said.

Clyde's knees buckled and he crashed to the ground.

Amirault heard someone's teeth chattering.

Then Robyn said, in a little voice, "I'm shot."

He turned. The cold was awful. He had the dry heaves. He was shaking. Where she held her right arm, blood seeped through the fingers. He could barely speak. "C-Christ, Robyn, oh g-g-ggg . . ." Clyde had slumped, away from them, legs tangled in a limp-doll attitude. Amirault knew his own body would stop functioning if he didn't get warm.

We have to get dressed, he tried to say. No words came out.

Amirault pulled her clothes to her, shoved them in her arms. She didn't move. He tried to dress himself but he was shaking so badly it was hard to pull on long johns, sweater, turtleneck. The clothes didn't help. The cold was in his bones now. The central source of heat inside him had gone out.

He helped her get clothes on but her skin had gone brittle, parchmentlike. A dark bruised patch covered her cheekbone. The blood was slick and shiny on her hand. He had to get her warm. He couldn't even go for the medical kit yet.

Hector's chest rose and fell fitfully. The front of his parka seemed covered by blood.

He's going to die. They're both going to die if they don't get help. Amirault fell over, he was losing muscle coordination. He didn't know a human being could be so cold.

Burn something.

He stripped Clyde and piled the clothes and one sleeping bag, the sled, knapsack, Clyde's boots and socks by the outcrop. He punctured the extra fuel canister and soaked the clothes. He lit them and a great whoosh of flame went up. Smoke billowed everywhere; he began coughing but he needed warmth. He burned the extra gloves. The sled crackled. He smelled chemicals burning. He covered Robyn with the other sleeping bag.

Heat, blessed heat. But it seemed to last only minutes.

Amirault gave Robyn a shot of morphine, directly into her shoulder. He was afraid the needle would break he was shaking so hard. He got a bandage on and taped it and hoped he'd done things right. He shot up Hector.

Don't die.

At length some feeling came back into his body. As his muscles thawed, pain shot up his legs. He made coffee. He made her drink. He tried to get coffee into Hector, but the doctor would not swallow.

"Robyn?"

She lay shaking. The fire had gone out and tendrils of blue-gray smoke twisted up, saturating the cave with a burned fabric/rubber smell.

There was ice on her lashes, frozen sweat. Between the shock, wound, and morphine, she was barely conscious. He said, "Can you hear me?" She didn't acknowledge him. He said, "Hector'll

die if we wait." He was thinking there were no good choices anymore. Only bad risks.

"I have to go," he said, terrified he was doing the wrong thing.
"I'll try for Victoria Base. Hector said it was only eleven miles. I
can do it in hours if I have luck."

Luck, he thought? Since when did I have luck? He wished she'd
look at him. The hardest thing he'd ever done was to tear himself
away. He suited up, still shivering. He thought, I'm stronger than
this place. I won't let them die.

Robyn had turned to him. Her lips moved. A lazy, semicon-
scious look glazed her eyes. The cave was filled with carnage; the
corpse, the sound of labored breathing.

Through the blood smell Amirault caught the faintest whiff of
vanilla.

Robyn squeezed his hand with two fingers. It had taken a tremendous effort.

Her lips moved. "Your sister . . ." she forced out.

"Yes?"

"I won't tell them . . . what she worked on . . . Don't leave
me . . . don't go."

twelve

Amirault found a protected spot in the rocks and waited for the regular downdraft in the wind chute to begin. Every minute was precious but he couldn't start climbing until the wind had come through. Ten minutes later the draft swept down, almost knocking him over despite the protection, exploding past in a shower of snow and rocks.

He began climbing. He used the ice ax to cut footholds. It was stained brown and left flakes of dried blood in the ice. He had to hurry. Soon more wind would come.

Amirault reached the top of the saddle, and below, to the north, stretched the glacier in its immensity. Snow fell less thickly on this side of the range. He estimated his visibility at a mile. The surface looked flat and white and skiable, but he knew he could never tell about crevasses.

He glanced back one more time at the valley. There was no sign that a chopper had ever been here, but in the snow under the cave, he'd planted Robyn's ski poles, with the red pot on top. He'd also dragged Clyde's body out and laid it on the rocks so a chopper crew might see it. Let the dead Englishman be good for something.

If the snow didn't stop, though, he knew no one would come, and drifts would cover the poles, pot, body. Amirault descended slowly, slipping on ice patches. When he reached the glacier, he donned skis and took off. He hated Antarctica. He cursed it. He couldn't believe he had ever wanted to come here. It was a dead place. It killed anything living. There was no color here. No green, red, no moist hues. Snow but no moisture. And only the coldest blue. It was a corpse of an island, with the alabaster beauty of the dead.

Amirault skied beneath the soaring snow-covered ranges, faster than he should, but the motion warmed him. He had taken no supplies, nothing to slow him or weigh him down, nothing Robyn or Hector might use.

Eleven miles. I should be able to make eleven miles in a few hours. He saw Robyn in her sleeping bag. He saw her eyes rolling up. He couldn't believe she'd offered to keep the story quiet. *She'd do that for me.*

"This area looks brittle," Brian said, appearing beside him. "Watch for crevasses."

You're not here, Brian. You're dead. I'm not spending time with the dead anymore.

Brian disappeared. Amirault skied harder. The surface angled upward, making progress slow. The snow stopped, but the sky was lead.

After a few hours he thought, What if it isn't eleven miles? I should have gone eleven miles by now. It's getting darker.

He grew terrified. What if he was skiing off on a tangent again? Maybe he should turn around, get back to the cave, feed them, stay with them, give them medicine. He saw Robyn needing another shot.

Amirault fought off the doubt and skied harder. He tried to ignore his tormented muscles. But his knee ached. He was thirsty. His shoulder throbbed where Clyde had hit it with the gun. I should have taken the stove, he thought. But then they couldn't melt water. I should have taken one sandwich.

No. One sandwich could mean the edge for her.

Amirault tried to suck snow but it made his teeth ache. The glow in the lower cloud deck, the sun, touched the highest mountaintop. In twenty minutes it would be night.

And then it was dark, but he kept going, slower. His skis scraped rock and, squinting, he saw he was too close to the mountain. He veered back toward the middle of the valley. He was losing strength; he hadn't eaten since yesterday. He must have hit something, because he fell. When he reached to put his ski back on, he saw the tip had broken. He could not ski anymore.

The temperature dropped. Amirault began walking. Without the skis beneath him, he sank into snow up to his knees. The ends of his fingers went numb. The sweat spots under his arms were burning. At a junction of two valleys, he remembered Robyn's words: Stay to the left.

In the end, he figured, we'll all be together. Evylyn and Brian and Robyn and me. Or maybe tomorrow, if the sun rose and copters went out, the pilots would spot the red pot. And they'd land. And maybe Robyn and even Hector might still be alive.

He struggled forward in the drifts. The sky cleared and the moon came out, as if to permit him some last moments of visibility. It was as quiet as death. He wasn't sure anymore what was moving, his legs or the surface beneath him. The snow rose like waves in an ocean. Swelling and undulating with unreal slowness. A pale tide.

His feet were wet. His knees were wet. The cold was seeping back up into his body.

But then even the cold diminished and the drifts looked peaceful. A little sleep. A nap on a feather mattress. A huge pillow. Just lie down a minute. Close your eyes.

Amirault sat down, lay on his back and looked up. You could see more stars in Antarctica than anywhere else on the planet. Stars you wouldn't see at home. Orion. Hercules. As he watched, a small twinkling red dot moved slowly across the sky, a satellite, maybe even carrying messages from Ellsworth Base to Washington. He imagined the words drifting toward space, reduced to electrical impulses. Rick's voice in that airless void up there. Saying Jack is gone. Robyn is gone.

Amirault watched his breath condense and rise away from him.

He made himself stand up. What the hell, he thought. Two hundred more steps.

Then a hundred.

Then another fifty. And fifty. And fifty after that.

Twenty more, he thought, stumbling forward, for Robyn.

He smelled salt.

He saw stars near the ground now, straight ahead, not even in the sky anymore.

Hallucinations, he thought. Terrific.

Amirault blinked.

Electric lights?

thirteen

Lord Anthony Harvey, chief negotiator in the Antarctic for the British Foreign Office, ex–Vice-Admiral in the Royal Navy, decorated hero of the Falklands, respected peer in the House of Lords, and majority stockholder in the North Sea Refinery Corporation, stood filled with exultation and curiosity in an overheated Quonset hut beside Victoria Base's ice runway, watching a fleet of seven helicopters returning from a rescue mission they'd embarked on one hour ago.

The copters, closing fast, presented a beautiful sight. The night was clear and starry. The red and green running lights created a jewellike panorama, and the choppers directed powerful search-lights at the ground as they flew. The scene reminded Lord Harvey of his nine-year-old son's favorite video, *Close Encounters of the Third Kind*, when flying saucers visit Earth.

Lord Harvey was tall, silver-haired, square-jawed, and he had the lean build of a long-distance runner, even at the age of fifty. His exhilaration stemmed from the fact that three hours ago, in the negotiations hall, delegates from twenty-six countries had finally agreed on the new map of Antarctica, to be officially approved tomorrow morning, less than twelve hours away. After months of squabbling, the lines had been drawn.

Lord Harvey regarded this as a personal victory. He had pushed Whitehall for years to prepare for this day, study the continent, pinpoint which areas would produce the best profit.

As he never tired of telling his bored wife, Club members, hunting friends, and dinner partners, "Antarctica could fuel British growth for a hundred years. Territory! If we're ever to be great again, we need territory!"

"The choppers should be touching down in five minutes, Lord Harvey," his number two man said. "This Amirault chap will be in the medical one."

Lord Harvey's zeal was boundless as he pictured the new Antarctica. Britain to get fifteen percent of the peninsula and its offshore oil areas, outright. To share revenues with Chile and Argentina from another ten percent. To receive undersea rights, enormous eventual oil and gas revenues, in the Ross and Bellingshausen Seas. To be guaranteed a lucrative refinery contract in Punta Arenas.

"Within twenty years, Mr. Pike," Lord Harvey told his number two, "we will operate the richest mines in the world right here."

Lord Harvey experienced a mild anxiety, however, over this Amirault, who was probably looking back from a porthole in the lead Huey, landing now. Night flights were normally banned at Victoria Base, but when the bedraggled American had stumbled into the canteen an hour and a half ago, with his story of leaving two half-dead people eleven miles away, the rescue mission had been organized quickly. It included a contingent of hated media photographers. The whole thing would be on TV tonight all over the world.

The key for Lord Harvey at the moment was to keep everything calm. His precious treaty still had to undergo ratification in Parliament, and the government, at the moment, hung on by a narrow margin. The opposition party was against the treaty. Lord Harvey feared that between the bad economy and recent Lord Barrier love nest scandal, it was remotely possible the PM might sacrifice the treaty for some political gain back home.

"Never count on a treaty until it is ratified," Lord Harvey's father, Lord Nigel Harvey, had taught him years ago.

Now, Mr. Pike said, "We have put Dr. Amirault under arrest, at the request of the Americans. He'll be handed to them but he's asked to speak to you first. Actually, he's . . . um . . . threatened . . ."

"Just say it!"

"His exact words, Lord Harvey, were, 'I'll blow your precious negotiations to hell.'"

"Such passion! I'm curious."

"Here he comes."

Amirault was easy to spot. He was the only one in handcuffs. The powerful-looking figure stomped off the ice runway beside the first of two manned stretchers. "He admitted shooting one of our rescuers," Mr. Pike said. "A London boy. A friend of his. He attacked his base manager. I'm not sure you should risk meeting him."

"Tshah! The man is in handcuffs."

"The woman has also been shot. She's unconscious. And the American doctor is in critical shape."

"Tell me more about our chap."

Clarence Pike went paler than usual. "He studied ozone damage, Lord Harvey. He was lying in the snow, naked."

Lord Harvey squeezed his brow. "Let's get this over with."

The door opened and Amirault walked in, guarded by two privates. Despite his captivity, a blazing intensity marked his weather-beaten face.

"You're Lord Harvey?" Amirault demanded.

"I am."

"Do you have identification?"

"You're being impertinent!" Clarence Pike said.

Amirault sat down without invitation. "I said the head guy. Are you Lord Harvey?" He seemed coiled, angry. "Let me see proof."

Lord Harvey condescended, against Pike's protests, to show his driver's license. But then he said, "It's late and I'm tired. If you're going to ask me to protect you from your own people, I'm afraid that's out of the question."

"No. I'm here to negotiate," Amirault said.

Lord Harvey's brows rose.

"Oh?"

"I represent a party who can't be here, but has great passion, great interest in this meeting."

"Who might that be?"

"My sister."

"And why can't she be here?"

"We'll get to that. First let me explain what you get in this deal," Amirault said, looking ridiculous, trying to bargain. The cuffs jangled slightly when he raised them. For an instant Lord Harvey feared the American would rush him, but Amirault was just making points. "First, you keep a discovery your people stole from Ellsworth Station."

"What discovery is that, Dr. Amirault?"

Amirault's smile widened. "You don't know? I wonder if you know. A new kind of torpedo which will revolutionize undersea warfare. You get the guidance system — well, not entirely, since the U.S. Navy will share it. Let's just say British and American companies will profit equally from this. Except in your case, the money will come from stolen property."

Lord Harvey was starting to enjoy this. It would make an excellent story at the Club.

"Stolen and turned over to a member of your delegation," Amirault said. "To a man by the name of Pike, I believe."

Lord Harvey frowned. "Pike?"

"Well, that's the name I heard. So did Robyn Cassidy. And Dr. Carroll. Three witnesses. Shall we continue this in private?" Amirault asked. "Or do you want to hear the rest in front of all these people?"

"Perhaps," Lord Harvey said after a moment's hesitation, "it would be better to clear the room. Private, watch Dr. Amirault for a minute. And you," he said to Mr. Pike, "step outside with me for a moment, please."

When Lord Harvey returned some time later, he looked a lot less amiable. A flush suffused his face. "Second," Amirault continued, counting on his fingers, as if he had never paused. "You avoid enormous international embarrassment. No one finds out about your spy. No one finds out he murdered someone. We all tell the lie together. Clyde went a little round the bend, see? He couldn't take it down here."

"Are you finished?"

Amirault leaned forward. "You get a lot from this deal, Lord Harvey. You get a new torpedo. You keep everyone's respect. We keep this secret. Relations with Washington stay tip-top, just tip-top. And whoever sent Clyde down from London, coupla heads roll, and nobody knows but us.

"On the other hand, if the truth comes out, you might lose your precious treaty. Once the accusations start to fly, my bet, the vote will be delayed. There'll be an uproar in London. And even if the treaty goes through after that, what concessions do you think you'll have to make? Or would you rather take a chance?"

Amirault shrugged. "Hell, what do I know about politics? I'm just a stupid scientist. I look for rocks. I'm probably all wrong about this. Probably a big press conference on TV won't change anything. Maybe Japan and Chile and Argentina, hell, good old U.S.A. too, all the countries you spied on down here, stole things from, tricked in negotiations, publicly humiliated, murdered a scientist, maybe they won't make any protest at all. Not to mention the opposition back home. What do you think?"

Lord Harvey was having trouble breathing.

"What does your sister have to do with this?" he said, trying to think.

"She's the one Clyde murdered."

Lord Harvey was silent a long time. Then: "And my part of this deal?"

Amirault told him. Lord Harvey burst out, "That's blackmail!"

A slow smile spread over Amirault's face. "Yes, that's exactly what it is."

"And it's totally against the interests of your own government. They want this treaty!"

"My sister and my government," Amirault said in a flat voice of finality, "never saw eye to eye on this. And here's the beauty. If you go along with what I want, you lose nothing. You get another chance up the line. You lose nothing in the long run."

"How do I know you'd keep your side of the bargain?"

Amirault grinned. "Trust," he said.

"What's in this for you?"

"I'm doing what my sister would have wanted."

Lord Harvey remained silent a long time. He gazed out the window at the ice runway. Beyond the parked copters, flags of forty-two nations flapped on hastily erected poles ringing the prefab town. Smoke rose from the kitchen Quonset huts. The cooks were preparing a celebratory lunch to follow the signing in the morning.

"I'm sorry. Your disclosures won't change anything," Lord Harvey said.

Amirault nodded. "Then," he said, "I think there are some journalists outside. They shouted questions when I got out of the helicopter, but I didn't answer then."

Lord Harvey said slowly, "I have no knowledge of anything you are talking about. But if you don't mind, I'll call the Foreign Secretary. It's not my decision to make. Sit here, Dr. Amirault." Lord Harvey sighed. "For the moment, at least, you have no choice."

Two weeks later Amirault strolled onto the deck of the U.S. icebreaker *Polar Sea* as it passed out of the Drake Passage and entered Argentina's Strait of Magellan, on its way home to Wilmington, North Carolina, first port in the United States. Robyn Cassidy held Amirault's arm.

The *Polar Sea* was equipped with medical facilities rivaling any found in finer hospitals of North America. Robyn had been recovering on the ship.

"So beautiful," she said, eyeing the craggy gray cliffs they passed. The passage was a deepwater channel flanked by vertical cliffs of granite. Fir forests sprouted from clefts in the rock, and lined the top, which was snowless. "It's green. So green. I feel like I haven't seen green in a long time."

A lone Weddell seal played across the ship's bow and dived. Ahead, by a bend in the channel, was a small fishing village beneath the cliffs, and hearth smoke, and a wooden fishing boat with Argentineans in yellow slickers waving on deck. A chilly drizzle made the railing and deck of the *Polar Sea* slick. Behind them, fifty feet up, Amirault made out the face of the Argentinean pilot who'd come aboard by law as they negotiated the channel. "Rain," Amirault said in wonder, holding his palm out to the drizzle. "Water."

Robyn squeezed his arm. The color was back in her face, and her clothes emitted a faint medicinal hospital odor. "All those huts dismantled now. All those angry diplomats gone home now. Victoria Base back to normal. I love that picture. Show it to me again."

He unfolded a ragged clipping from the *New York Times*, showing British soldiers hauling down the flags at Victoria Base.

SURPRISE ENDING TO
ANTARCTIC NEGOTIATIONS

In a surprise move, Great Britain reversed its stand on the proposed Antarctic treaty today, cited "environmental concerns," and vetoed the proposal at the last minute, astounding participants and observers at the conference. The move ended any chance that the continent's status will change for at least five years, when it comes up for international review again.

"Great Britain continues to support harnessing the resources of the great Antarctic," chief negotiator Lord Anthony Harvey announced. "But only in a responsible manner. We cannot in good conscience support this new treaty unless more environmental safeguards are built in."

The announcement came as a complete turnabout. The British had been proponents of the proposed accord, which would have allowed mining and drilling in Antarctica for the first time.

Environmental groups welcomed the move but were baffled by it. Britain apparently changed its stance after Lord Harvey met with an American scientist, Dr. Jack Amirault, whose walk up Purgatory Road made world headlines last week. Speculation abounds that Dr. Amirault told the British something that changed their minds.

The subject of their meeting remains secret. Informed sources say Lord Harvey was furious over his new instructions, and plans to resign when the furor dies down. Lord Harvey had no comment.

Dr. Amirault also had no comment. Nor did the American environmentalist Robyn Cassidy, or U.S. Navy doctor Hector Carroll, third survivor of the trip. Dr. Carroll is in the intensive care unit on the U.S. icebreaker *Polar Sea.*

A U.S. State Department spokesman said, "As you know, any change of the current Antarctic treaty has to be unanimous. We worked for five years to convince New Zealand to finally approve the new accord. It's incomprehensible that Great Britain did this at the last minute. They never mentioned any environmental concerns to us."

"In five years everything starts again," Robyn said.

Amirault squeezed her shoulder. "You never know what can happen in five years to screw them up." He winked. "You'll think of something."

The colors, so vivid, seemed to grow richer. Amirault saw a flash of red in the sky, a flock of tanagers, winging above the cliffs. Heading north, to the United States, for the warm months, for summer. And there were shades to the world: olive, walnut, pear, gypsum, carmine.

Robyn said, "What if Lord Harvey had said no? What would you have done?"

He grinned. "Gone to the press. But that would have embarrassed Lieber and the National Science Foundation, and put our whole program down here in jeopardy in Congress. And despite what those assholes think of me, I like what we do here. Anyway, it's five, six months till Halloween in San Francisco." He put his arm around her. "What should we do until then?"

"Cross-country skiing?"

They burst out laughing.

Robyn sighed. "What will you tell Lieber when he hauls you in and demands to know what you talked about?"

Amirault said, "The same thing I tell the Navy and the State Department. That we talked about Clyde, how he cracked up, how he died. Who the hell knows why the British changed their minds?"

"They won't believe that."

"I know. But what can they do if we stick to the story?"

Amirault leaned down to kiss her; a long kiss. He felt her arms come around him, and her leather gloves on the back of his neck.

When they pulled apart she said, "A friend of mine has a cabin in Oregon, very private, in the Willamette Forest, near the ocean. Wines. Salmon. He offered it for my recuperation."

"You'll need private medical attention," Amirault said, grinning. "Private doctor."

"My thought too."

"Stay in bed," Amirault said. He put his ear to her heart. Even through the float-suit he imagined he heard her heartbeat, fast and strong again. He felt her heat coming through her clothing.

"What do you hear?" Robyn asked him. "Oil or gas?"

"Lava."

"What are you doing here?" a voice demanded. Turning, they saw the chief nurse storming from the hatch onto the deck, holding down her wind-whipped dress. She was a usually good-natured Bostonian with a Back Bay accent and a face full of freckles. "I told you it was too soon to go outside! You'll have a relapse!"

"But it's so beautiful," Robyn said.

"And cold," said the nurse, who was finishing her first tour of duty here. "You! Inside! No argument! Don't you know it's fifty degrees out here? You're weak. And what's so funny, I'd like to know?"

They were laughing. Amirault said as they went inside, "Yeh. It's freezing out here."